GHOSTS
OF THE
WEST

ALEC MARSH

ACCENT

The right of Alec Marsh to be identified as the Author of
the Work has been asserted by him in accordance with the
Copyright, Designs and Patents Act 1988.

First published in Great Britain in 2021 by
HEADLINE ACCENT
An imprint of HEADLINE PUBLISHING GROUP

1

Cataloguing in Publication Data is available from the British Library

ISBN 978 1 7861 5806 2

Typeset in 11/13.5pt Bembo Std by Jouve (UK), Milton Keynes

Printed and bound in Great Britain by Clays Ltd, Elcograf S.p.A.

Headline's policy is to use papers that are natural, renewable and recyclable
products and made from wood grown in well-managed forests and other
controlled sources. The logging and manufacturing processes are expected
to conform to the environmental regulations of the country of origin.

HEADLINE PUBLISHING GROUP
An Hachette UK Company
Carmelite House
50 Victoria Embankment
London EC4Y 0DZ

www.headline.co.uk
www.hachette.co.uk

For Ashley

Chapter One

September 1937
Gravesend, Kent

Sir Percival Harris stood on the platform beneath a broad black umbrella. The water streamed off it, making him resemble a dreary sculpture in an elaborate fountain. Despite his sodden appearance, his pink, cold-looking face grinned from ear to ear. As the train jerked to a halt – throwing Ernest Drabble off balance in the carriage – Harris splashed forward and yanked open the door.

'Bloody good to see you, Ernest. Have I got something to show you!'

Drabble pulled the coat flaps of his tweed greatcoat over him and stepped out into the deluge. He shook the proffered hand; Harris's glove was soaked through.

'Christ alive, Harris. You'll catch the death –'

'Trust me, it's worth it.'

Before he said another word, Harris was on the move, seemingly oblivious of the standing water as he splashed through the puddles. 'Come on, Drabble,' he trilled. 'Not a moment to lose . . . the light is fading fast!'

The station clock showed a quarter after five. In the background, a seagull cried out, cutting through the din of the passengers, engines, and chatter. Fittingly, Drabble caught a tickle of salt in the air amid the sweet smell of coal smoke. Harris hurried them out, past the waiting taxis and omnibuses, and into the high street, where he wove through the shoppers and children returning home from school. The rain ran down the awnings over shop windows and raincoats glistened under a glaucous sky.

Harris was too preoccupied to talk. He focused on navigating the human traffic, glancing back every now and then to ensure Drabble was keeping up. Drabble understood that his old friend would be incapable of discussing the matter in hand until they had arrived at it – physically and mentally: Harris could not do two things at once. Especially when he was on a quest.

'Come on, Drabble!' He dashed across a road towards a church, evading a swerving taxicab. Drabble dodged out after him, his impatience getting the better of him.

'Are you going to tell me what this is about?'

Harris turned back, glaring indignantly from behind fogged-up spectacles.

'Surely *you* of all people know why you're here?' He gestured towards the building behind him – a dark brick Georgian church, its square steeple topped with a spire.

'You're joking . . .'

Harris smiled. 'Want me to introduce you?'

Harris heaved open the tall oak door, and peered inside.

'All right.' He pulled off his hat and gestured for Drabble to follow.

The interior of the church was gloomy, with the dim afternoon light seeping in grudgingly through small, high windows. Rows of pews culminated in steps leading to a marble-topped altar housed in a Romanesque apse supported by natty neoclassical pillars. On the left, a stately organ clung to a wall that was otherwise covered in memorial tablets and brass inscriptions. So far, so Georgian.

2

Harris strode up the aisle like an occupying Prussian, his soles leaving wet footprints on the tiles.

Drabble knew *she* wouldn't be in here. She couldn't be, not unless they'd built the ruddy church *on top* of her. That, of course, was possible. And now he came to think of it – all too possible when you considered what the Georgians were capable of.

'Harris –' he called out. 'Are you telling me, they've found the grave?'

Harris spun around and squinted ferociously towards the door.

'*Shhhhhh!* Come on. Leave your bloody bag there. We don't have long.'

Passing the altar, Harris ducked down through a small door. Within was a spiral staircase, clearly of some antiquity, judging by the hollowed stone steps. It struck Drabble as odd, until he realised that they might well predate the newer Georgian structure above. 'Shut the door behind you,' Drabble heard Harris say, as he stomped down the steps.

They arrived in a chamber lit scarcely by slithers of glass: broad stone pillars supported a low ceiling over an undulating floor of marble. Here and there a stone inscription marked out a burial.

Harris bent down and scratched with a matchbox, lighting a lamp.

'Come on,' he repeated. 'Get your coat off.'

In the far corner, Drabble saw that a stone slab had been prised off, leaving a dark hole through which poked the top of a ladder. He stripped off his wet overcoat, his trepidation mounting. Was she really in there?

'Tell me you've got permission to be rooting around here.'

Harris held up the lamp, and grinned. 'Of course I have, old man. But we mustn't dally.'

Harris climbed awkwardly down the ladder, taking the light

with him. Drabble cursed, and followed. Sometimes there was nothing to be done but to indulge Harris.

Drabble's feet connected with soft earth at the foot of the ladder. It smelled pungently of soil and damp. He bent down under the low ceiling and immediately saw an exposed skeleton bathed in the yellow light of the lantern. Harris was gazing down at it, mesmerised.

'There she is,' he beamed, his sodden hair matted to his forehead and the light glinting from his dirty lenses. 'There she is!'

Drabble stared down at the skeleton in disbelief. Of course, it was the first thing he had thought of when Harris had telephoned him in Cambridge that morning, telling him to '*drop everything immediately*' because of a historically important find in Gravesend. She was said to have been buried here, but no one had ever found the grave. And even now, confronted by this diminutive skeleton, he could not believe that this was . . .

He turned to Harris.

'Who says it's her?'

'The rector.'

'And how does he know?'

'He told me it's a secret that's been passed down from one rector to the next for generations.'

Drabble viewed the exposed bones sceptically. 'I suppose it's not every vicar who can boast having a full-blown Iroquois princess – not to mention the first of her people to convert to Christianity – in his undercroft.'

'I should say –' Harris smiled and bobbed his head towards the ceiling. 'I'm told her name is actually inscribed on the marble slab up there – but it's so faded and written in impossibly squiggly seventeenth-century copperplate it could ruddy well say Dick Whittington for all I know.'

'Except he's in St Michael Paternoster.'

Harris did not appear to hear Drabble's comment. He nodded towards the remains.

'What do you think?'

'What do I think?' Drabble repeated the question, a new light dawning on him, albeit belatedly. He scolded himself. 'Is that why you asked me here ... to confirm that this is her? I'm a historian, not a ruddy archaeologist.'

Harris grinned boyishly.

Drabble reviewed the skeleton, his mind working quickly.

First things first, if this was Pocahontas, daughter of the chief who had ruled much of the region of Virginia where the first English colonists had settled in the early 1600s, then the skeleton would obviously need to be that of a woman. The cranium, turned slightly to its left, was small and delicate. Drabble could tell from the angle of the mandible that this was likely to be a female. But it was not conclusive.

'Here –' Drabble pointed towards the middle of the skeleton and Harris moved the lamp closer. Drabble was looking for a small fan-shaped opening in the rear of the pelvis. 'There –' he pressed his thumb into the space in the bone. 'That's the greater sciatic notch.'

'And?'

'It's good news, Harris –' He wiped his finger on his handkerchief and saw Harris's mouth break into a smile. 'This is the skeleton of a woman.'

Harris's smile subsided into disappointment. 'Ah ...'

'Here, shine the light on the skull there –' Drabble moved out of the light and peered closely at the cranium. Despite its great antiquity, he could see the zigzagging sutures, the fusion lines between the bones of the head, which indicated this to be a young adult, one whose skeleton was not yet fully formed. This was consistent with Pocahontas's death at the reported age of twenty-one. All this he explained.

'Much more than that – I can ascertain that this woman was of medium height for the era, indicating she must have had a good diet and perhaps been high-status. Her teeth are in good shape, which shows she was not blighted by an excess of sugar – that suggests the woman lived before sugar became commonplace, which is fine as far is it goes: if you were rich in the early 1600s there was enough of it about . . .'

'She mightn't have had a sweet tooth?'

'Quite possibly . . .'

'None of which categorically contradicts what the rector says –' Harris's eyes glistened with calculation – 'or the swirly writing inscribed on the slab. Excellent!'

Harris set down the lantern and began scribbling in his notebook. Drabble's heart sank.

'One more question, Professor – do you think anything is *missing*?'

'What?'

Harris lowered his voice conspiratorially. 'Someone broke in to the church last night. They lifted the slab and got in here and did God knows what to the remains. You'll read all about it in tonight's newspaper.'

'I see . . .' So, as well as being asked to confirm the remains, he was now being required to ascertain if anything had been taken.

'Well, what do you think?' asked Harris.

Drabble exhaled irritably and motioned for Harris to pick up the lamp. It was possible that she would have been buried with her wedding ring, so he located her left hand and blew the dust away. He took out his pen and began prodding the dense layers of silt and dirt, formed by centuries of rot and decay – and Lord knows what else. No ring was present, and the bones in the left wrist had come adrift from the remains of the hand. The right hand, meanwhile, had also fallen apart. This wasn't archaeology so much as guesswork.

'It's just possible that the neck has been shifted – but whether it was last night or last century, I couldn't be sure.'

6

Harris looked up from his notebook, an eyebrow cocked. 'A necklace or pendant?'

'Impossible to say.'

'Care to speculate?'

'I'll leave that to you.'

'All right. What about the wrist?'

'The burial has been disturbed is all I'll say.' Drabble frowned at him. 'And you're not to quote me by name. You understand?'

'You have my word.'

'I've had *that* before.'

Harris coughed in such a way as to communicate the closure of that topic of conversation. 'How *recently* would you say that the burial has been disturbed? Yesterday or decades ago?'

'You'd need an archaeologist for that.'

Harris growled, 'Come off it, Ernest. Some of those marks in the dust look pretty fresh to me.'

'So what do you need me for?'

It was Drabble's turn to smile mischievously.

'I'll say this: if someone *did* go to the trouble of finding this grave – which, don't forget, archaeologists failed to locate back in 1923 when they excavated here – and they broke in at the dead of night to achieve it, then you must wonder what they wanted.'

Harris's eyes lit up. 'Well *exactly*, old man –'

'Either something was here and has been taken, or they will have been gravely disappointed, so to speak.' Drabble looked down at the skeleton, at its slightly mangled spine and sternum and that dislocated left wrist. 'If she was laid to rest with a bracelet or necklace then this could well be consistent with robbery. Plus, those marks in the dust *do* look pretty recent.'

Harris looked up eagerly from his notes.

'Fresh?'

'Don't quote me.'

'Heaven forbid.'

A breeze sent the flame in the lamp flickering over and they heard a rising creak — like the door at the top of the stairs opening. Hadn't Drabble latched it? Harris seized the lamp.

'Come on, we'd better not outstay our welcome.' He crawled over to the ladder, and looked back, smirking. 'This place gives me the crypts!'

At the station they bought a copy of the second edition of Harris's paper, the *London Evening Express*, and boarded the next train for the capital.

Harris slammed the first-class compartment door shut, and plumped down opposite Drabble, who was stowing his Gladstone bag. He pulled out his pipe.

'Grave robbery in Gravesend!' he declared with relish. Plumes of smoke ballooned from his pipe as he began to jot down his story with the stub of a pencil. 'But what did they steal? A necklace or pendant; a bracelet of some description? Both, perhaps?'

'Aztec gold?' suggested Drabble with a lift of an eyebrow, as he glanced about for a radiator or heater. The carriage was cold and damp.

'It's a mystery –' Harris referred back to his notes and then leafed back and forth, scribbling down shorthand notes from an earlier conversation into quotes for his story. All the while smoke poured from his pipe and dispersed from his mouth. It was a wonder he could see what he was writing. He grinned over at Drabble through the mist, pipe gritted between his teeth.

'You staying at the club?'

'Where else?'

'Bloody marvellous. We can have a right old binge!'

Unfolding the *Evening Express*, Drabble was able to read Harris's first story on the case – just five short paragraphs, detailing the fact that the remains had reportedly been found – *Pocahontas's grave 'discovered' in Kent'* – and *'likely disturbed'* but nothing more:

The alarm was raised by the churchwarden, Mrs Wyndham, shortly after seven a.m. this morning, according to the Kent County Constabulary. 'It's a violation,' she told this paper's correspondent.

Drabble looked up from the paper. 'Did she really say "violation"?'

'With the usual prompting.'

'How did they get in?'

'Broke a window in the vestry. Didn't take anything, mind.'

'Just after Pocahontas?'

Harris nodded and returned to his notebook. Drabble read on:

Speaking on behalf of the American people, the United States ambassador welcomed news of the discovery of the resting place of Pocahontas, and expressed concern over the break-in. The official spokesman confirmed the ambassador would be visiting directly in the coming days to see the burial for himself, and to pay his respects.

Drabble looked over at Harris.

'You spoke to the rector, didn't you?'

It took a moment for the question to register before Harris looked up.

'What?'

'The rector. Did you speak to him?'

'Oh, yes.' Harris's face lit up. 'And strangely enough, he was rather irritated. But not about the break-in, rather about the fuss . . . the *attention*. If I didn't know better I'd have said he was annoyed that Mrs Wyndham raised the alarm at all.'

'It stands to reason. You said yourself the grave was a secret they've guarded for generations. Presumably he would rather she hadn't told the police.'

'Good point.'

'Don't forget, he has been happy to contribute to the fiction that the precise location was lost, so it must have been galling for him to have to own up to the fact that he and his forebears have been lying to all and sundry for centuries. Bearing false witness and all that.'

At Waterloo station, they took a cab to the Granville club.

Once there they headed straight for the Long Bar and were but paces from the first drink of the day, when a voice hailed Harris.

'Sir Percival, *sir*?'

Harris turned back to confront the speaker, a look of repressed rage informing his features. He really did have an enormous thirst on.

'Message from the office for you, sir,' the porter said timidly. 'You're to call the moment you arrive. Most insistent, the gentleman was.'

Harris nodded, the *gentleman* would be. And Harris was a Dutchman if whoever had telephoned from the office was a gentleman.

'Thank you, John.'

They went straight to the bar.

'What a day,' declared Harris as he raised the tankard to his lips. He leaned his head back, tilted the near-full vessel to his mouth, and held it there at forty-five degrees for ten seconds, fifteen at most.

'Right –' He slammed down the tankard and exhaled like a man who has just sired a deity. 'Order up another brace, Professor. I'll be right back.'

Drabble watched his old friend hurry towards the lobby, where there was a row of telephone booths, and smiled. Harris never changed. Well, not much, and never for the better.

Drabble caught the eye of Le Goff, the barman, and ordered a second round. He was just beginning to enjoy a moment of peace when Harris erupted back into his presence, roaring.

10

'Holy smokes!' He clapped Drabble on the shoulder and seized up his pint. 'I'll tell you this for nothing, old man. *This* is right up your street ...'

Before Drabble could discover the cause of Harris's excitement he had to wait for him to drink. He watched the man's Adam's apple bob up and down as he gulped. Finally, Harris came up for air. 'Somebody's just burgled the British Museum!' he gasped. The pint went back to his mouth as the information sank in.

'The British Museum?' Drabble repeated, his mind filling with terrifying prospects of endangered national treasures large and small – items the value of which could not be calculated in simple financial terms. 'What's been taken?'

Harris stood his tankard on the bar and stifled a belch.

'A pipe belonging to *Sitting bloody Bull*! Now, get your hat ...'

Chapter Two

The taxi pulled up outside the proud iron railings of the British Museum and Drabble and Harris hurried in through the gate. A policeman stood under the streetlamp, swathed in an oiled greatcoat. The rain had relented but the poor sod looked like he was there for the duration. He touched the rim of his helmet.

They crossed the forecourt, bounded up the darkened steps, and were admitted by a flustered-looking clerk, who reviewed them savagely.

'And you are?' he sniffed imperiously. Harris's reply was met with a shout towards the darkened cavernous interior. 'McMillan ... show these gentlemen of the press to the Americas room.'

They were led through the museum: Drabble glimpsed the Rosetta Stone in the gloom, he saw winged, human-headed Assyrian lions and the faces of forgotten gods. They passed rooms full of coins and urns and pottery, zigzagging through doorways, corridors, centuries, and continents. There was plenty here to attract a burglar.

The door in front of them opened into a brightly lit room: Harris strode in ahead. Drabble saw a totem pole and a two dug-out canoes ...

'Ah ... the *Evening Express*!' The voice came from a fleshy face that bore a lascivious expression. 'Early as always.' The man spoke breathlessly, and smiled as he spotted Drabble, showing teeth that wanted a dentist's care. 'You've just missed the *Standard*, and *The Times* were here earlier.' The man's ginger hair was unwashed and he was dressed in an exhausted grey suit. His complexion leaned towards yellow.

'Inspector Stephenson.' Harris bowed his head with ironic courtesy, and introduced Drabble.

'*Professor* Drabble,' replied Stephenson with emphasis. Judging by his tone, he held academics in higher esteem than journalists.

The policeman led them across the room past several display cases filled with American Indian artefacts: there were several paddles, their blades painted with deities, and a totem pole carved with animals and strange faces. The inspector paused before a display case from which the pane of protective glass had been removed. Any shards had been cleaned away. Inside among various objects – including a small clay pipe and a pair of moccasins – stood an empty baize-covered plinth. Next to it was a broad clothes hanger, likewise devoid of its artefact. Besides it was a five foot high chief's war bonnet which was adorned by what must have been a hundred or more black-tipped eagle features.

'This,' Stephenson breathed heavily, 'is where until just before twelve noon there used to be a pipe belonging to the Indian chief, Sitting Bull, who I daresay requires no introduction. If the text is to be believed, the pipe was critical to working his magic.' Stephenson arched an eyebrow. 'And on that hanger there was a battle shirt of some description, also said to have supernatural powers. I am told that if you put it on it rendered you immune from gunfire.' The policeman offered a sarcastic smile. 'In which case we could do with a few of them down the Mile End Road.'

The inspector cleared this throat.

'The thief waited for the guard to exit the room over there, and then choosing a moment when no one else was in the gallery, he broke the glass, snatched the items, and made good his escape. The alarm was raised at eleven fifty-three a.m. We can only assume that the theft took place but minutes prior to this.'

Harris finished writing. 'Any leads?'

'We're investigating. No one conspicuous was seen in these galleries or in the museum before or after. As far as we know, no one else apart from the burglar was in the room when the cabinet got broken into. No one saw the stolen property exiting the building.'

'Are the items valuable?'

Stephenson's face contracted, his yellowing skin pulling itself taut. 'We're still trying to get a figure . . . Not *without* value, let's put it that way. Mind you, if money was your motive there would be plenty of other things to lift from the museum first.'

'So it's likely to be a collector of some sort?' suggested Harris.

'Precisely.' Stephenson lit a cigarette. 'Probably some crank who's desperate to complete his Red Indian dressing-up costume.' He glanced back over at the display case. 'Don't quote me on that.'

Harris crossed out what he had been writing and exchanged a glance with Drabble.

'Inspector, I was in Gravesend earlier today. Do you think there could be a connection to the Pocahontas robbery?'

'Who said there had been a robbery?' Stephenson spoke archly and then broke into a chuckle. 'I know about that, Harris. Look −' He shrugged. 'Who knows? But by Christ I hope not. Those gits down in Kent really get up my nose . . .'

Drabble peered down at the plundered display case and read the small card that stood on the empty plinth:

Smoking pipe or calumet (c. 1876) used for ceremonial rituals by Sioux medicine man and war chieftain Sitting Bull (c. 1831–1890).

14

Pipe bowl carved from red pipestone or catlinite. The three-foot wooden stem carved with a setting sun and bull's horns motif. It is adorned with twelve feathers, one for each moon or 'month'.

Then, beneath the empty hanging area, he read the next:

Cotton 'war shirt' decorated with embroidered raven and bull with flame motifs, worn by Sitting Bull at Battle of Little Big-horn (1876) and subsequently. Believed by Lakota Indians to possess sacred qualities and protect its wearer from injury . . .'

'Ah, Dr Yorke!' Drabble turned to see Stephenson address a tall, lean man well set in his years, dressed in a tweed sports jacket and generous brown corduroys. He had a fine mop of hair and a pair of powerful spectacles that made his eyes look enormous. He viewed Harris and Drabble with interest.

'Dr Yorke is the curator here –' Stephenson was saying, as he broke off to talk to a colleague with a camera.

'I thought it might be worth saying something of the arte-facts that have been stolen,' remarked Yorke by way of explanation for his presence. Harris had his pen poised:

'As you can see from the citation, the pipe was particularly prized for medicine rituals and elite conferences.' Yorke halted, his expression darkening, as though the impact of its loss was hitting him afresh. 'And that it should be the very pipe belong-ing to Sitting Bull . . .' He shook his head despairingly. 'We were most lucky to have had it in the collection.'

'Is it really believed to have magical powers?'

Yorke reviewed Harris gravely.

'Not as such. Rather it was for the sealing of compacts, and for use during religious rituals – the offering of prayers, and so on.'

'And what about the war shirt?' asked Harris pointedly. 'I see that was said to protect its wearer from injury.'

'It's certainly believed to have done so. Though as a society

I think we've rather moved on from believing in magic, in other parts of the world such beliefs have persisted and do persist. I know that there are examples held in collections in the United States that feature bullet holes, which indicates certain *irrefutable* permeability. As far as I know Sitting Bull wore our example many times in battle and lived to tell the tale. And he certainly wasn't wearing it when he was killed . . .'

'Perhaps he should have been,' suggested Drabble, though the bloodstains might have stopped the museum from putting it on display in that case.

Yorke smiled. 'Perhaps.'

Harris asked, 'Can you think of anyone who might steal these items, Doctor?'

Yorke plucked off his spectacles and began sucking on one of the arms. 'I fear,' he announced, 'it may be a particularly acquisitive private collector. These people know no limits and it means that the artefacts are virtually impossible to trace.'

Harris jotted this down in his bad shorthand, an act which Yorke appeared to view with distaste. 'I have said all this to the inspector,' he noted with a sniff.

'Do you suspect any collector in particular?' asked Drabble.

Yorke shook his head.

'If only I could –'

Harris cut in, 'I presume the items *are* valuable?'

'Oh, I should say!' Yorke lowered his voice. 'If memory serves, a similar pipe – owned by a chieftain of less renown than Sitting Bull – was sold for five hundred pounds at auction only a few months ago.'

That was a considerable sum, more than the annual earnings of several working men combined, and provided enough of a motive for a robbery, but if one wanted to obtain the sum illegally there would surely be less conspicuous or ostentatious ways of doing it. Harris caught Drabble's expression and cleared this throat.

'Do you know any collectors wh[...]
these pieces?'

Yorke raised his eyebrows, prompt[...]
furrow beneath the mop.

'That's what I'm rather hoping the insp[...]

Drabble and Harris were in another cab, bei[...]
their way back to the Granville for dinner. H[...] [...]re:
crime reporting was not really his oeuvre [...]nalistically;
hanging around with policemen was apt to make him start
feeling guilty about things – imagined sins ... But that wasn't
it, or all of it. The two crimes he had reported on today were
perplexing him ...

He was distracted by the sight of two men spilling out of a
pub and glimpsed the cheery interior. Lucky bastards ...

No, what bothered him was the possibility that a connection existed between the two robberies – a possibility
underlined by the timings of the two crimes and their undis-
puted cultural connection. It made it a possibility that did not
allow itself to be ignored. The trouble was that simply knowing
that wasn't helping much.

He broke the silence.

'It's got to be a spree by a nutty collector.'

The cab halted at the lights on New Oxford Street and Harris lit his pipe. Drabble immediately leaned across him and
snatched down his window, permitting a cold blast of damp air
to invade the warmth of the cab.

'Oh, must you?' cried Harris. He glared. 'It's only a pipe, for
God's sake.'

The cab set off. Up ahead he saw the lights of the Cambridge Theatre. *1066 and All That* was playing. Theatregoers
were queuing up outside. It was that time.

'I'd kill for a drink,' declared Harris gloomily. Smoke cas-
caded from his mouth.

.e no reply: instead he fetched out the newspa-
.e had been reading earlier and revisited Harris's
.t on the Pocahontas discovery. He hoped something new
might occur to him, but by the time he reached the end of the
story no thunderbolt had arrived. He admitted defeat and
began folding the paper away ... but then inspiration struck.
Drabble tore the pages back until he found what he was looking for: an advertisement just beneath Harris's story. He held
the newspaper up to the light from the window:

TONIGHT – LAST CHANCE TO SEE
Col. GRANT'S WILD WEST SHOW
Featuring
Black Cloud & the Lakota Sioux
Sharpshooter Fanny Howell
Ferguson's Rough Riders
Custer's Last Stand
Pony Express
& the Bison Hunt

Drabble handed Harris the newspaper and leaned forward to
the driver.

'The Earl's Court Centre, please – and don't spare the
horses!'

Chapter Three

Drabble and Harris alighted in front of the tall Art Deco façade of the Earl's Court Exhibition Centre. Much of the building, however, was unrecognisable because it was lost to a vast illuminated hoarding showing lassoing cowboys, galloping Indians, rearing horses, and charging bison before a horizon of cacti and tall natural steeples of red stone. People poured across the road from the Tube and side roads, converging on the entrances like it was match day at the Arsenal.

Their seats were near the back of the second balcony, looking down at the arena from some considerable altitude. There were more rows than could be counted by anyone of normal patience, and a vast painted backdrop was in darkness beyond the enormous stage. In the gloom Drabble could make out more sprawling cacti and high mountains – the sort you saw in Westerns. The air was heavy with an equestrian odour that lent the industrial setting a decidedly agricultural atmosphere.

Harris fidgeted excitedly in his seat.

'I read that they've been getting audiences of forty thousand a night,' he remarked. 'The King has been twice. They say he's enamoured of Fanny Howell – "very pert and feisty, with the hottest hips in town", according to the press. She knows her onions with a six-shooter, too.'

'Sounds right up your street.'

Harris gave a mocking laugh. 'More up yours, I'd say. She's an outdoors type.'

The lights dimmed and the noise of the audience's chatter fell away to a hush. Somewhere a horse bayed. Then the lights went up.

Arranged in a vast semicircle spanning the arena were dozens of figures on horseback in two rows. In the front were perhaps fifty white-feathered Indians in bright red warpaint. They were joined by cowboys in Stetsons, their polished leather chaps catching the drenching light. At the very centre was a white-faced patrician figure in a double-button military-style coat, with wispy grey moustache, goatee, and long silver hair, on a white stallion. To the right of him was a young woman with aggressively red hair and a green neckerchief – and twin white holsters – presumably, Fanny Howell. On the patrician's other side was a shrunken-looking Indian chief of advanced years, lost beneath his huge headdress of white eagle feathers, which ran down to his feet.

Lined up along the right side were what looked like half of the Seventh Cavalry. Rowed along the left flank were the Indians who would doubtlessly dispatch the aforementioned later. The fact that they were indigenous Americans of the Lakota Sioux tribe was what interested Drabble ... Sitting Bull was the greatest leader in the history of the Sioux nation – so if anyone was interested in the pipe and shirt stolen from the British Museum, it was them. And they might be a good deal more than just interested.

Back on the stage, Drabble saw the patrician flex his ankles and trot his horse out from the line-up, raising his hat to the audience's applause.

'Good evening,' he bellowed, his voice carrying across the auditorium. 'My name is Colonel Grant –' the cheering intensified – 'and this is my Wild West Show. Let the festivities commence!'

There was a mighty clash of cymbals and a blast of trumpets, leading straight into a sprightly tune that could have been 'Waltzing Matilda' if you squeezed your eyes shut. The double line of horsed figures immediately melted away, dispersing in every direction. They galloped up the aisles to the audience's roars, or peeled off-stage left and right.

The lights dimmed.

When they returned the stage was empty. Then there was a powerful drum roll – rising up like a locomotive and shaking the ground – and suddenly bellowing bison rushed on to the stage from all directions, pursued by shrieking, hat-waving cowboys. They discharged their pistols and started to circle the oval stage, sending the bison into a spiralling frenzy. The cowboys unsheathed their rifles and cracked off shots at the bison, and they continued to chase them into circles, like water cascading towards the epicentre of a vast bovine plughole. Just then there came another thunder of hooves and another human cry – this time higher in pitch and foreign. It was the Lakota.

Clothed in buckskins with feathers in their headbands, the Indians swept across the field, slicing through the vista in two diagonal waves. Cowboys were pitched from their horses – dragged along by their stirrups – arrows zipped through the sky, and the bison were chased away by the indigenous hunters. The cowboys gave chase.

The auditorium went dark again and when the lights returned a stagecoach with eight horses sped onto the stage, bleached in the magical yellow light of the West. It was teeming with passengers and topped with baggage and a driver with his mate riding shotgun.

Seconds later the cries of the Indians arrived and the native horsemen surged into the oval as the mate riding shotgun fired wildly – joined by the trigger-happy passengers. Soon the carriage was careening around the stage – tilting perilously as it cornered – chased by Lakota Sioux at full gallop, gunfire

21

peppering the air. Several fell in the melee – the crowd howled in horror – as braves trailed off from their stirrups, before – *yet more horror!* – one Indian caught up with the speeding coach and nimbly leapt onto its roof. The shotgun fired but missed and stowed his gun, then gave battle on the roof. They rolled this way and that – all the while the mass of the coach, the horses, and the pursuing dozen or so hostile Indians lapped the oval. Harris was on the edge of his seat.

The Indian on the roof suddenly rolled from the top, and clung on precariously – just as another horseman drew level with the driver and began to batter him. They wrestled as the coach cornered; now another Indian drew alongside the first in the team of eight horses and sprang onto it, leaving his own steed to run free. The crowd cried in collective angst: it was curtains for the stagecoach.

For all that Drabble disliked the caricature presented before them, the horsemanship on display was undoubtedly impressive – and could only be marvelled at.

Suddenly a bugle sounded – shrill, martial, and rising in pitch. Everyone looked . . .

Whoops, and howls, the cavalry arrived, in impeccable navy and pale blue, white and red pennants fluttering – and swords aloft. They strafed the stage, filling the scene with some hundred human figures in all, and then began to pursue the Indians in a vast circle, with the coach now immobile, centre stage: the whole mass was an auditory conflagration of hooves, neighing horses, gunfire, and whooping soldiers and Indians.

And then the Indians vanished, pursued by the cavalry. The lights went down.

Harris nudged Drabble's elbow.

'By Gad, that was thrilling.'

'If you like seeing the displacement of indigenous peoples.'

'Oh, don't be such a kill-joy,' sighed Harris.

Drabble's reply was lost to the roar of the crowd: the

Seventh Cavalry was here! In they came, riding side by side, and at their head a man who – judging by his flowing blond hair – was General Custer. He wore a tasselled buckskin coat and revolvers on each hip, their butts pointing forwards in frontiersman style.

'Ah.' Harris grinned gleefully over at Drabble. 'Custer's last stand. *This* should cheer you up!'

Somehow Drabble didn't think it would. Two dozen or so figures performed a stately canter around the perimeter of the oval. The pretty flags fluttered, and light sparkled off the cavalrymen's sabres and gold braid. Cheerful military music blared from the band. The crowd roared. Whatever Drabble might think, the citizens of Britain – based on this audience at least – didn't give a fig about indigenous people or their displacement.

The cantering of the troopers seemed to speed up ... and suddenly the music faded and there was a drum roll so intense it fluttered in your sternum. And then it all began: cheering Indians swooped into the stage from every corner, spurring their neighing mounts at full charge.

'*Hoka hey! Hoka hey! Hoka hey!*'

They fired wildly into the air as the bugle sounded, and began circling. The cavalry dismounted hurriedly and formed a square in the middle, also firing wildly. Arrows sprang up and clouds of smoke began to drift upwards to the ceiling ... one by one soldiers fell clutching their chests, and the Indians lapped the stage, their shrieking war cries intensifying. Every now and then a warrior would break loose from the long pack and curve towards the thicket of cavalrymen, swiping at one of the number with his tomahawk. Likewise a trooper's aim would find its mark and an Indian would tumble from his saddle and be dragged offstage by his sprinting mount – to rapture from the audience.

Soon just six or seven cavalrymen were left, amidst a pile of blue-clothed casualties: at their centre was the Stars and Stripes,

23

the regimental banner, and the man himself, Custer – puffs of smoke rising from the barrels of his busy revolvers.

The cheerful martial music had been replaced by something darker, a score that might accompany the defiant moments of a cornered quarry. Just then the clamour of hooves and saddlery, of arms and gunpowder, ceased and the neighing horses and ponies of the Lakota Sioux attackers paused, forming a ring around the final cluster of soldiers. The warriors raised their weapons, roared – and charged, lancing through the last soldiers . . .

The flags were snatched away and then there was Custer, staggering backwards, collapsing to one knee, but still shooting. A warrior fell from his horse, crying in agony. Just then a horseman approached Custer from behind – the crowd howled in outrage – and dealt the killing blow. Suddenly it was all over.

'Christ alive,' Harris leaned in, tears of outrage in his eyes. 'Did you see that? What rotters. They smote the poor sod from behind.'

Now the warriors returned to the stage, swirling around the mass of still bodies – equine and human – before forming a broad, theatrical semicircle around the fallen. From offstage, a trio of Indians now emerged, led by the elderly chief they had seen at the start. He rode a white and brown pinto horse and scores of black-tipped eagle feathers sprouted from the train of his long war bonnet. The man beneath the headdress was frail-looking but was steady in his saddle and held his spear firmly. He wore a decorated battle shirt and his arms were banded with scarlet cloths. The chief cantered forward. He was flanked by two figures, one of whom appeared to be wearing a bison for a hat. They stopped before the heap of bodies. The pinto horse's head dipped, bobbing to its rising foreleg, and it shook its mane. The elderly chief began to speak, his voice strong but somehow quiet at the same time. The entire audience was spellbound.

'My name is Black Cloud. I was yet two moons from my sixteenth birthday when the Battle of the Greasy Grass – that is the what you call the Battle of Little Bighorn or Custer's last stand – took place.' He swallowed and bowed his head briefly. Drabble wondered if the strain of addressing such a crowd was too much. After all, if the chief had turned sixteen in 1876, then he would be seventy-seven now. Or perhaps it wasn't age; perhaps he was instead receiving unbidden memories of what had actually taken place over sixty years before. The chief resumed.

'To this day, no one knows who killed Custer, whom we called Long Hair. He may even have taken his own life, fearing capture and what we Indians would do to him. Mighty war chief Sitting Bull told me himself that he never saw Long Hair during the battle. What I do know is that the blood of the Sioux people was hot that day and they took no prisoners. The *wasichus* fought like braves and died with honour. After the battle the whole land smelled of nothing but blood.'

He paused, as his horse bobbed its head once more. 'It made my heart hurt to see so much blood shed. I killed many enemies with my hatchet, as did my brothers. We fired many arrows. Looking back at this, I have regret for the war between my peoples and those of the United States. These many years since we have learned to live in peace and harmony, and this makes my heart happy …'

The stage door outside the exhibition centre was thronged with off-duty cowboys, cavalry, and groups of women in bonnets and bustles – enough people to populate a wild west town. Most stood around smoking, chatting and drinking. Drabble and Harris – 'The man from the *London Evening Express*!' – were led inside by a commissionaire, through narrow corridors high up into the building.

He finally knocked at the door, waited and then opened it up:

'Gentlemen of the press to see you, Mr Cloud, sir!'

He pushed open the door and withdrew immediately,

leaving a clear view of a poky dressing room: in the corner, seated before a mirror ringed with light bulbs, was the elderly chief. His head was now bare, and his long silvery hair was swept over the bowed shoulders of his tan-coloured buckskin coat. He was indisputably smaller and even more shrunken without his war bonnet, which lay inside an open chest. At first glance he looked rather pitiful. A half-smoked cigarette smouldered in his hand and he seemed oblivious to their arrival. The wide mouth was turned down beneath his aquiline nose and his expression was mournful – a cast of mind seemingly etched onto his face by ravines of sorrow and crevices of regret.

His heavy eyelids clocked Harris's notebook.

'If you want an autograph, it costs one pound,' he declared nobly.

'I'd like to ask you a few questions for my newspaper, if I may?'

The weary eyes reached Drabble and offered no opposition.

He indicated a pair of wooden chairs with a minimal shift of his head. Slowly the cigarette went to his mouth and he took a strong drag. Half an inch of ash slumped onto his hand.

As Harris introduced them Drabble took a seat and spotted the shirt the chief had worn after the battle re-enactment lying across the top of a chest beside him. It was adorned with a bull and a raven with its wings spread – fitting the museum's description of Sitting Bull's, though only Yorke would be able to confirm that.

'What a thrilling show,' offered Harris, breaking the silence. 'You must be exhausted.'

Black Cloud sighed, rather as if the sound of Harris's voice was the single most tiresome thing he had heard in his life. It probably was, thought Drabble, especially at ten o'clock at night at the end of a lengthy run of shows in London, Berlin, and Lord knows where else. Just how many banal journalists' questions could one elderly man have to put up with?

Harris pressed on: 'Is it true that each feather in your war bonnet relates to a single act of courage or an enemy killed in battle?'

They all looked over at it: if it were true then this elderly Indian had achieved perhaps several hundred such acts. For all his claims to the contrary, Drabble wondered if one of the black-tipped eagle feathers had Custer's name on it.

Black Cloud's expression softened – or rather, appeared to. Beneath the soft, loosened skin of the septuagenarian, Drabble saw his expression harden.

'I have fought more battles than I care to remember and count myself lucky to still be here – particularly after all this time.' His speech was laboured and Drabble realised that English was almost certainly a language acquired in adulthood. 'The white man is but one of the foes I've had to confront in a long life. Oftentimes the enemy has been plain stupidity, greed, and ambition in others – and it is a never-ending battle to keep them down, needing more courage than the taking of a life in battle. Mercifully, the Great Father has spared me and gave me the courage to continue.' He remembered his cigarette and finished it off with a long drag. 'What else, Mr Harris, would you like to know?' he asked as he extinguished it.

'How do you like London?'

He grimaced, showing neat, strong-looking teeth.

'It is cold. It is wet. That is the best of it.' He reached for another cigarette and lit it. 'From what I see, it is a place untroubled by nature. Even the air is tarnished. I do not believe that the Great Spirit above dwells here, and Mother Earth has been driven far, far away. But the people, I like.' He smiled as if surprised. 'They are warm. Many years ago, a man I once knew – an Indian like me – came here with the Wild Bill Hickok show and they performed for Queen Victoria. You know what she said? "You are the handsomest people I have seen. Were you mine, I would not let them put you on display in this uncouth fashion."' Black Cloud shrugged, as if to say, *bad luck*. 'I have long wondered what would have happened if we had all been born in Grandmother England's land, and not that of the Great Father in Washington.'

Harris noted all this down.

Drabble gestured towards the shirt lying with the war bonnet in the box, 'Would you mind telling us what this is?'

The Indian's leathery forehead wrinkled.

'That is my sacred shirt; it protects me in battle. That is why I wore it tonight.'

'Did you wear it at Greasy Grass?'

Black Cloud hesitated.

'Not that one. It is,' he paused, 'a *copy* of the one I had. But it is the same.'

Harris met Drabble's gaze and received a nod. It was time. He addressed Black Cloud: 'Did you know that a shirt like this one was stolen from the British Museum today? It had belonged to Sitting Bull.'

The chief frowned hard at Harris. But it wasn't anger.

'What was Sitting Bull's sacred shirt doing in a museum in London?' he said, after a pause.

'They also stole a pipe of his,' interjected Drabble.

Black Cloud turned to Drabble.

'His pipe? What was *that* doing in a museum?'

Drabble shared a glance with Harris – Black Cloud's question demanded the sort of answer that could not readily be summoned. Harris grasped the nettle: 'Chief, do you know anyone from the Wild West Show who might have stolen these items?'

Black Cloud began shaking his head, clearly outraged at the suggestion . . . his lips began to move, but he suppressed whatever it was that he might have to say.

'I would not speak it, even if I knew.' He glared from Drabble to Harris and an oaky power came to his voice, replacing the laboured gentility. 'I *knew* Sitting Bull.' He thumped his chest. 'He was my friend. His war shirt and smoking pipe should be with his people, not in London behind a glass screen being stared at by *wasichus*. These things should not be in a museum. They are living parts of our living culture.'

'And I couldn't agree more,' soothed Harris hurriedly, realising it was time for a change of tack. He smiled at the chief earnestly. 'What was Sitting Bull like?'

Black Cloud's clenched jaw relaxed, and the mouth dipped.

'He was a man of great spirit and wisdom. He died before his time at the hands of the *wasichus*.' The chief's lips lingered on his cigarette. They waited for more, but that was it.

Drabble leaned forward. 'Chief, if you could help us find the person who has taken these items – whether it is a collector or someone else – then we could help recover them and bring them to you and your people.'

'Exactly right,' interjected Harris, nodding a little too keenly to be quite trustworthy.

The chief turned to Drabble.

'Professor, I appreciate your thoughts, but they are of no help. I can not know who might have taken these things. Why should I? Because I knew Sitting Bull?' He shook his head. 'No ... but I appeal to you – and to you, Sir Percival. If you do find them, please return them to my people, whatever your museum says.'

It was time to leave. Harris folded away his notebook. Black Cloud frowned in thought.

'Sitting Bull *was* my friend. He was a great medicine man, and,' the chief raised a bony index finger, 'he had a good heart. He was also correct that the Great Father in Washington is not to be trusted. Never.' Black Cloud stroked back a strand of his long silver hair. 'We leave for the United States tomorrow – if the shirt and the pipe travel with us on the fire-ship across the seas, then the Great Spirit has willed it. You should not mourn the loss of these items from your museum. They *live*, and they *should* live with us.'

29

At the door, Drabble turned back to the chief.

'Out of interest, did you know that the grave of Pocahontas has been found, not far from London, and that it was disturbed yesterday?'

Black Cloud digested this and then swallowed, his face grave.

'It saddens my heart to be told of this. I know of Pocahontas. She is not one of my people but I hope she may rest in peace now.'

They went to leave, but Black Cloud wasn't finished.

'You should know, Professor, I am a Sioux chief of the Great Plains. A long-dead Powhatan princess does not interest me. My cares are for my people who are hungry and have no land. The sacred hoop of our nation has been broken. The bison are dead, and we are fast following them.'

Black Cloud shrugged and looked down at his lap, where the cigarette burned between two fingers. He spoke scarcely above a whisper. 'Hundreds of years and hundreds of miles separate Pocahontas and Sitting Bull. That they were both *Red Indians*, as you would have it, is all there is, I think.' He held the cigarette to his lips and inhaled. 'Was her grave robbed?'

His eyelids regarded Drabble and Harris.

'We don't know,' conceded Harris.

A mist of smoke spread across the space towards them, and Black Cloud shook his head.

'Let her be, I say. Let her be.'

In the corridor they met Inspector Stephenson. He was breathing heavily, doubtlessly owing to the six flights of stairs, and was evidently surprised to see them.

'Harris –' Stephenson grinned, showing his teeth. They were the colour of urine the morning after a heavy binge. 'I didn't think you went in for overtime?'

'Nor I you, Inspector.'

'So what are you doing? Paying your respects to the big chief?'

'He doesn't think Sitting Bull's artefacts should be in the British Museum.' Harris reported. 'Hold the front page. In fact, he was horrified to discover that they were there at all.'

'That *is* interesting.' Stephenson's eyes narrowed. 'Dr Yorke says that Black Cloud paid him a visit only the other day – told him that he wanted the stuff back. He said he was prepared to trade for similar items in his possession or pay him for them fair and square. But,' the inspector lit a cigarette, 'he was adamant he was having them back. When Yorke told him that was out of the question he was less than cordial.'

'Less than cordial?' Harris opened his notebook.

'Uh-uh-uh!' The detective wagged his finger at Harris. 'Not for publication.'

'What did he say?'

'Something of nothing.' Stephenson's gaze flitted to Drabble; he was clearly now thinking twice about his disclosure. 'Never you mind,' he added querulously.

Drabble stepped in. 'Black Cloud's not a suspect, is he?'

Stephenson cackled sharply and addressed Harris, 'I thought you said your friend was a sleepy academic.' He turned to Drabble. 'It remains to be seen, Professor.'

The inspector backed away as two cowboys approached, laughing loudly. They dragged heavy trunks covered in sea-going stickers – P&O, White Star Lines, and so on – and the trio moved aside to let them pass. It reinforced their parting.

'I'll be seeing you, Harris,' declared Stephenson as he moved off.

Drabble and Harris took a taxi back to Piccadilly, where the friends said good night. But if Drabble or Harris thought that was the end of their Indian summer, they were gravely mistaken.

31

Chapter Four

The telephone by the bed was ringing. The incessant peal fetched Drabble from a contented sleep. His eyes opened reluctantly as the persistent chime continued. What time was it? Pale crevices of light intruded into the darkness around the Granville club's dense curtains. It was early. The phone droned on. Drabble sighed. He knew only one person would have the temerity to ring at this time of the day. He was just baffled as to what *he* was doing awake – and in any fit condition to do so in the first place. Drabble lifted the handset from the cradle and barked into the receiver.

'Yes?'

'It's *me*,' boomed Harris.

'I know it's *you*!' Drabble rolled his eyes. 'Are you drunk?'

'Far from it, old man,' chirped Harris. 'Now look – tell me you've got your passport?'

'My passport?'

'*Yes*, it's Yorke; he's *dead*. Stephenson called me half an hour ago. They fished him out of the Thames at the top of the tide this morning. He had an arrow in his back.'

It was Drabble's turn to chirp up, 'An arrow?'

'Not very subtle, eh? Now look, Fleet Street will be over this like a rash. The public loves nothing more than a good *novelty* killing – and the murder of the curator of the American section of the British Museum by Apache-style arrow on the Victoria Embankment is just too delicious for words –'

Drabble cut him off. 'What's this got to do with me?' Fleet Street's dubious appetites did not appeal to him.

'Well – you're coming . . .'

'Where?'

'To Liverpool.'

'*Liverpool?* And why do I need a passport to go to Liverpool?'

'Because that's where the ship is leaving for New York . . .'

Drabble cursed under his breath and climbed out of bed. At the window, he carefully drew back the curtain to see out . . . thank God for that, Harris *wasn't* calling from the telephone box across the road. Mind you, he was still blathering away in Drabble's ear . . .

'Look here, Harris,' exclaimed Drabble, exasperated. 'I can't come to New York with you –' He yanked apart the curtains. 'We've only just got back from India, for goodness' sake. I have students to think of. The Michaelmas Term begins –'

'Oh, *shush*, Professor! Set them a couple of boring essays and tell them you'll be back before they know it. See that they're not chuffed as punch. Now look, I've got two return tickets – first class! One for me and one for my photographer. And I've borrowed a camera for you.'

Drabble broke into a chuckle. If Harris had a pound for every time he had talked someone into doing something they didn't want to, he'd be a millionaire . . .

'How soon can you leave?'

'You are insane.'

'No I'm not, *I'm in the lobby!*'

The taxi sped along Pall Mall towards Trafalgar Square. Unshaven, his hair uncombed, Drabble sat in the back seat beside Harris, being jolted by the rocking cab. In the moments since leaving the Granville, Drabble's initial wave of excitement had turned to scepticism as he started to see the usual holes appearing in any escapade involving Sir Percival Harris.

'Surely the police will apprehend Black Cloud and his followers before the ship leaves, so they won't even be on it?'

Harris waved this off. 'Stephenson blotted that one already: Black Cloud was at the Earl's Court centre from six o'clock last night – for the show along with the rest of the cast, and then with us, and then with Stephenson himself, until about ten thirty. That's when the charabancs carted everyone off to Euston to catch the night train to Liverpool.'

'Which presumably renders this whole trip a complete waste of time – if the Wild West Show's Indian members have already been cleared of any possible involvement in Yorke's demise, why are we bothering to go to Liverpool at all?'

'Because, Professor, there are no fewer than thirty-odd Sioux in the cast – and you and I both know that any one of them might very well have been working with Black Cloud ... and could easily have slipped away unnoticed.'

They sped up the Charing Cross Road, passing the shuttered bookshops; Drabble saw a drunk weaving along the pavement. Several women in cheap furs chatted, smoking, at one corner. It was getting late for them. The façade of the Cambridge Theatre came into view.

Drabble turned to Harris. 'Or it might be someone else entirely, someone who simply used the arrow to point the finger of blame at the American Indians – as if the poor bastards haven't had enough thrown at them by the so-called civilised world already.'

'It's possible. Does it matter?'

'I'll say it matters – quite apart from the ruddy injustice of it – why else are we bombing to Liverpool?'

Harris turned to him, his face full of concern, 'For the story, of course.'

The story ... Drabble scoffed. For Harris it was *always* the story. He should never have got the train down from Cambridge yesterday. Why had he even answered the telephone in the first place? No good ever came of answering telephones – especially to Harris.

Harris knocked his pipe imperiously on the windowsill.

'The fact is, my friend, that the truth will out. In the mean time I plan for us to have a fantastic fortnight ... plus, I'm hoping that Black Cloud might actually tell us who killed Custer.' He chuckled. 'Now *that* would be a scoop worthy of two first class return tickets to New York.'

The three-funnelled SS *Empress of the Atlantic* slipped her moorings at twelve noon precisely, the great ship coming away from the dock as the bells of the city struck the hour. She was not long from Harland & Wolff in Belfast and positively gleamed in fresh white and green livery. Colonel Grant's Wild Westers thronged the decks facing the shore, and his brass band struck up a jaunty Yankee tune: the crowds that had gathered to see the colourful company depart cheered and waved. Hats somersaulted in the air.

'What a view,' marvelled Harris, removing his pipe. His next comment was lost to the boom of the ship's horn as the vessel nudged out into the grey river. Drabble gazed back over the shore, over the long roofs of the dockside buildings and the high gantries of the shipyards.

The horn sounded again, and the great ship slipped further from the dock. They crossed to the far side for a view of the city, seeing the brick stack of the ruddy Albert Docks, and the twin spires of the Liver Building. There was a chill in the salty breeze that his overcoat did little to resist. Drabble was troubled by his lack of reading matter – if he'd known he was going to be confined with Harris for ten days or more, he would have brought something more substantial with him. *War and Peace* would be a good start. He sighed as the cityscape gave way to irregular timbered wharfs and dirty fields, scrub and small boats.

Harris clapped him on the shoulder.

'Fancy a drink?'

'What's the hurry?' Drabble checked his watch. 'The bars don't close until we reach Staten Island.'

'I know.' Harris beamed. 'It's heaven, isn't it?'

Harris lay on his back on his bunk, his waistcoat half undone and tie askew. A streak of golden light from the porthole fell across his open mouth, from which emanated a loud snoring. It reached a crescendo and then he fell silent, before appearing to choke, at which point the snoring resumed.

Drabble stared up at the ceiling. Christ alive. Four days and nights of *this*?

Harris's sleeping orchestration reached another pinnacle, one attenuated with a falsetto whistle from his adenoids. Drabble muttered and resolved to get up. Pulling back the bedsheets, he got to his feet and stretched, checking the time: knocking on six . . . Christ, *and yes* he had a headache.

'Goodness,' he groaned. And soon it would be time to dress for dinner. He shook his head and eyed his dinner suit, which had been supplied by the ship and hung in the doorway. *What a palaver.* Harris, needless to say, loved it. He had brought two of his own. 'Can't be too careful,' he had declared gleefully.

Especially when you drank like Harris did. What had they had during their lunchtime tipple? Two pints of Courage's Best Bitter followed by double gin and tonics. That lot had gone down faster than the *Titanic*. Then they had lunched; oysters with champagne, celery soup served with a cheeky white burgundy, followed by jugged hare for Harris and pheasant supreme for Drabble – all rinsed home with a bottle of 1932 Chateau Gevrey-Chambertin. That evaporated like an ice cube in the Sahara. Bread and butter pudding came to the rescue – preventing a second bottle of Gevrey-Chambertin, but instead heralding a chilled carafe of Sancerre. Then, of course, cheese was served with the port. They finished lunch at four with a small glass of Scotch to aid digestion.

Christ be born. Drabble stared out of the porthole from the bathroom; across a gently rippling grey sea. In the dark distance lay a tawny-brown landmass that must have been Ireland. At this rate he would have gout by the time they arrived in New York. Or sclerosis. Possibly both. He splashed his face with water. Why had he agreed to come? How had Harris talked him into it? Again? Drabble poured another glass of water – but it wasn't for drinking, not for him at all.

'*Harris!*'

He flung the glass of water over his companion.

'Whoa!' Harris sat bolt upright, droplets of water springing from his face. 'Wa-wa-what do you mean by that, Drab?'

'It's time for dinner,' stated Drabble coldly. He snatched up his shoes and started putting them on. Harris yawned, still taking stock.

'I say, what are you doing?'

'I'm going for a walk,' announced Drabble. 'And then I'm going to get dressed for dinner.'

Chapter Five

It felt much better to be outside of the cabin than in it. Drabble
filled his lungs with sea air and willed his headache away. He
wanted still more to will away the gnawing sensation in the pit
of his stomach that he was committing an abysmal error by
wasting his next two weeks on Harris's stupid escapade.

But the sea air was good, undeniably so. He strode along the
deck, taking it in. The sky was a grey-tinged pale blue and
faded to yellow at the horizon. Looking over the balustrade at
the navy hull, he could see the smooth water below passing by
at pace. It occurred to him that he must have looked a mess; he
hadn't shaved that morning, and he was without his hat. A couple were coming the other way – he in bowler hat and black
frock coat, the lady in a long dress and wide hat secured with a
gauze ribbon knotted beneath her chin. Drabble did a double
take. They looked like they were out to enjoy the Edwardian
sunset, not one in 1937.

Drabble followed the line of lifeboats suspended from their
davits overhead. Everywhere passengers huddled in groups at
the balustrade or sat in deckchairs reading or drinking. Soon he
passed the bulwark of the bridge and arrived at the foredeck.
Here, more passengers sat in sheltered booths or on deckchairs,
enjoying the evening sunshine and brisk breeze.

Drabble made for the prow – marked with a small, fluttering
pennant of the Green Flag Line. After waiting his turn, he took

in the panorama and attempted to commit to memory the view; the ocean and the setting sun before him, Ireland on the right, the Welsh coast on the left. In the unseen distance would be the north coast of Devon and Cornwall . . . It was a golden evening; he could feel his head clearing by the minute.

Drabble stepped down from the rail into the shade of the deck, and almost walked straight into a short, bespectacled man. They both apologised and retreated.

The man wore a neat black beard and whiskers that spoke of committed cultivation and lent him an anachronistic but important presence. A pale horn pipe twisted from his small mouth and the lenses of his spectacles became two discs of shimmering gold in the setting sun. He plucked out his pipe.

'Professor Drabble!'

The American drawl carried despite the wind, and the man raised his grey homburg. 'Wheelock,' he declared. 'You won't know me, but I read all about your exploits on the North Face of the Eiger a while back . . . When was it?'

'Last year —' They shook hands, and then awkwardly moved aside to allow a couple to proceed up onto the viewing platform. Drabble's climbing companion Hubertus had died during that attempt and eighteen months on he still found it almost impossible to think of it without being overwhelmed by the tragic loss of his life. Drabble forced a smile. 'Though it seems only yesterday.'

'I know what you mean,' declared Wheelock as he started off, now in Drabble's direction away from the bow and towards the seated passengers.

'What takes you to the United States?' asked the American.

'That's a good question . . .' Drabble shot him a smile that he realised immediately looked evasive, which it was. 'I thought it was time to broaden my horizons,' he corrected. 'How about you? Were you visiting England for work or pleasure?'

'Mainly work, but it was a pleasure.' Wheelock beamed

beneath the hirsute extravaganza. 'I also got to follow up on some ancestors; the Wheelocks go way back in Cheshire.'

They took another pace or two; Drabble registered the expense of the other man's garb: that felt homburg, the stiff wing collar and tie, and the long grey woollen overcoat that shimmered with cashmere. It piqued his curiosity. Elite species of lawyer, thought Drabble. 'And what of your professional exploits?'

Wheelock's eyes shifted behind his black plastic spectacles. 'Not bad,' he declared. 'Let's call it a work in progress.'

As that non answer settled they turned on to the starboard deck, arriving in the lee of the bridge, and the wind suddenly dropped. Wheelock removed his pipe.

'That's better.'

Drabble agreed. 'You don't know it's there, until it's not.'

'Precisely!' They took another pace. 'You're a historian, aren't you?"

'For my sins.'

Drabble grinned apologetically and Wheelock replied with a nod.

'I've a cousin who's a Latinist. You two would get on like a house on fire.'

'I dare say.'

'Well –' Wheelock gestured towards one of the nearby door-ways with his cane. 'This is my stop.' He raised his hat and bobbed his head in a polite nod. 'Time to go change for dinner, then it's cocktails o'clock. Cheerio, Professor . . . dare say we'll run into each other again.'

Drabble watched the small figure disappear inside. It *was* time to dress for dinner. The good news was that his headache had vanished.

Dinner was served in the Restaurant at seven o'clock sharp. The unimaginatively named venue was immensely large and decorated lavishly like a Venetian ballroom – all reliefs swathed in gold with elaborate swags and swirls framing scenes of classical nauticalia and rusticity.

Perhaps inevitably, they were seated at the captain's table. It dawned on Drabble slowly but he got there: the Green Flag Line was a major advertiser of the *London Evening Express*, so it was likely that their first-class tickets were not costing his host – Lord Axminster, the owner of Harris's newspaper – very much indeed, if anything. Naturally any stories that emerged from Harris's trip would be good publicity for the shipping line, too.

The captain, by the name of Rossiter, was a serious-looking fellow of about sixty, going to fat in places with whitish-ginger mutton chops. He performed the introductions with the gravity of a Presbyterian minister on Good Friday: either side of him were the Duchess of Montgomeryshire and her sister, Lady Ashley. Both were considerably senior in years, finely attired – that is to say, decked out in Kimberley's finest – and would doubtless prove formidable company. Harris, still recovering from lunch, had to be circumspect about looking *directly* at the Duchess's tiara – it prompted spasms of outrage in the frontal lobes. Next came Colonel Grant – on the Duchess's right – of the Wild West Show, who looked like he'd just stepped off his horse. Seated by him was a tall, slim Japanese man in a dark suit: 'Major Sakamoto of the Japanese Embassy in London,' Sakamoto offered a stiff bow, Rossiter moved on, 'and here it's my pleasure to introduce Miss Fanny Howell, equestrian sharp-shooter *par excellence*, and the first of those I've had at my table!' There was a ripple of polite laughter. 'Next, I'm honoured to introduce Mr and Mrs Tuchman of Budapest –' a tweedy couple in late middle age nodded genially. As Rossiter introduced Drabble, a new arrival pulled back the vacant seat separating him from Harris.

'And this is Mr Wheelock, of the United States government.' Wheelock, his hair parted fastidiously and resplendent in black dinner jacket nodded in reply. Rossiter now cleared his throat: 'Finally, I have some bad news: we have among us a distinguished gentleman of the press – so watch what you say!' He broke into what for him was probably his number one smile: 'Sir Percival Harris ...'

'Hello, everybody,' boomed Harris. At his throat dangled his gleaming Star of India decoration.

'Fancy us being seated together,' exclaimed Wheelock warmly. 'And mustn't we both be important to be on the captain's table.'

'Or just paying the most,' replied Drabble under his breath. He noticed Fanny Howell throw Major Sakamoto a flirtatious glance and then turned to Mrs Tuchman to introduce himself properly.

After a few minutes, Wheelock leaned in. 'I'm a Virginian, by the way – at least the family have been for the last two and a bit centuries. We left *after* the English Civil War.'

'Arriving in plenty of time for the American one ...'

Wheelock smiled sadly. 'What? The Revolutionary War. Unfortunately –' the waiter filled his champagne glass, 'we chose the wrong side.'

Rossiter raised his glass. 'Good health, ladies and gentlemen.'

'Of course –' Wheelock closed in again, talking from the side of his beard, 'I realised what you meant. We had two civil wars, really. The first in the 1770s that got rid of you lot, and then we had the one everyone thinks of. The Wheelocks got it wrong the second time, too.' His eyes pinched sadly. Virginia, of course, had been the hotbed of the Confederacy.

'Hindsight is a wonderful thing.' Drabble watched as half a dozen oysters on ice landed in front of him. 'I imagine it would have been difficult for a Virginian to stand up for the Union.'

'But what of the English Civil War, Professor? Then Virginia was in it for itself, right?'

'That's about right, I think. She was neutral enough, until she wasn't: they then got bludgeoned into submission by Parliament. Cromwell was good at bludgeoning.'

Wheelock replied with an amused smile and then cocked an eyebrow at the menu – it read, *Loch Ryan Oysters – Galloway*. He loosed an oyster and bucked the shell to his lips.

'What do you do at the US government, out of interest?' asked Drabble.

Wheelock laid down an empty shell and went for the next. 'That was good . . . I look after Indians.'

Drabble looked up from his plate – that was surely a coincidence too far. But he could tell nothing from Wheelock's face, which was cheerfully focused on his second oyster.

'There aren't many Native Americans in London. Don't tell me you went all the way to Europe to watch Colonel Grant's Wild West Show?'

Wheelock chuckled. 'As a matter of fact I have seen the show quite a few times. And I think it's fantastic, I mean, quite *literally* fantastic. But I also like it, a lot.'

Across the table Miss Howell was now conversing with Mr Tuchman. The Japanese envoy, meanwhile, beamed at her with an undiplomatic lack of restraint. Drabble had noticed Harris notice her a few times, too. Which surprised him a little, because she was not a beauty as such. But Miss Howell clearly had *something* – even if it wasn't immediately obvious to Drabble – and she was a woman with admirers. There were at least two of them right here. Drabble tackled another oyster, catching her expression mid-sentence: and then he saw it; there was a robust freshness about her, an alacrity of expression that cut through. And her figure didn't let her down, not by any means. Indeed, when her feather stole descended just so, you got a powerful display of compressed cleavage that made for compelling viewing. Drabble saw Harris staring at it again as the waiters replaced their starters with the main course.

Wheelock was saying, 'Actually I had meetings with various officials, and some work to do in the archives. As you'll know, there are quite a few important sets of papers relating to various tribal matters, still in the United Kingdom which pre-date the Divorce.'

This sparked Drabble's curiosity but Wheelock was mid-flow. 'I hope you don't mind my saying, Professor –' Drabble felt the man's breath on his ear – 'but I have to admit to being an admirer of your works – particularly your monograph on Cromwell . . .'

After a short discussion, Drabble steered the conversation towards the coincidence. 'May I ask, what is it you do for the Native Americans?'

Wheelock laid down his cutlery. 'I'm with the Bureau of Indian Affairs; we oversee the lands and reserves, given over to the indigenous peoples of the United States. There's about two and a half million acres of land held in trust for them, and that's exactly what we do.'

Drabble received this information with a silent nod, inviting Wheelock to continue. He started on his main course.

'Do you know much about the Indian situation in the United States, Professor?'

'Not especially.' This was true, although what little he did know he didn't like – and was sharply critical of.

'It's complex . . .' Wheelock stressed the second syllable and it contained the hint of an apologetic cadence. 'And *ongoing*. It takes active management . . .'

I bet it does, thought Drabble.

'Many would say that the Indians have had a bad time. I guess they would too.' Wheelock smirked, but not unkindly. 'The grim fact is that when we arrived in North America in 1607 – and I say *we*, because it was the Brits – there were perhaps five hundred thousand native Indians living in what became the United States. It's hard to know precisely. More

44

than three centuries later there are just three hundred and thirty thousand Indians. At the same time the immigrant population has risen from zero to more than a hundred and thirty *million*. As you'll know, the Indians didn't give up without a fight, but in the end they simply could not compete with our numbers, our diseases, and ultimately our arms. Their ways were old and inefficient. You can't feed a big population by hunting and gathering. It simply can't be done. And while you might choose to see the Americans as the villains of the piece – it's a highly attractive thesis, I confess – frankly, most of us are European expatriates; we're the product of excessive over-breeding and fertility success in Europe – pure and simple. You needed somewhere for us to go, and Indians are the ones who felt the pinch.'

It was one hell of a pinch. But Wheelock was right: without America, Dr Malthus would have had his wicked way in Europe. Yet the bison had been hunted to the verge of extinction in a wasteful fashion – probably as part of a deliberate policy to destroy the bedrock of the indigenous civilisations. And you only had to take a sniff of the story to smell the injustice. All in all it was an indefensible record.

Drabble addressed himself to his dinner. Wheelock, however, had perspicaciously read Drabble's thoughts.

'As I said, Professor, casting the Americans as the villains of the piece is a very attractive thesis. But look at the British record in Ireland – or indeed in any of the dozens of other places around the world where you rule. The unavoidable fact is that progress is progress. Might will prevail, rightly and sometimes wrongly.'

Drabble considered this piece of sophistry as he sat down his wine glass. Comparing the US record to that of British colonialism was a rhetorical ruse, not a response, notwithstanding the atrocities such as at Amritsar – which, rightly, had been condemned. 'I would like to think that we live now in more

45

civilised times, and that many of the massacres that have taken place – whether in British colonies, or at Wounded Knee or during the forced exodus of the Cherokee – would no longer be tolerated,' Drabble suggested. 'I might be being naïve. Wasn't it in 1834 that Congress voted to confirm that all the lands west of the Mississippi were Indian territory? Didn't last long, did it? What have they got now, a few reservations?'

Wheelock nodded, his lips pursed tightly. 'You know what, Professor,' he smiled, his voice relaxing. 'You clearly know a lot more about America's Indian situation than you let on.'

Dinner came to an end. As the party broke up, Drabble and Harris caught Colonel Grant and Miss Howell at the bar, where there was a good crowd enjoying a nightcap. The passengers had won their sea legs early and were fresh enough to make a night of it. Grant nodded genially at them both over his bourbon. Howell offered a smile. Amid the wider press of people were several other cast members from the show. Despite Harris's exhortations, they did not linger, just long enough to arrange an interview with Grant.

Back in the stately cabin, Harris poured himself a grown-up Scotch. Drabble began to undress and prepare for bed. He had had enough for one day – a week, more like. Also, his mind was working through the conversation with Wheelock and the coincidence of his presence aboard the ship – not to mention the chances of their encounter on the deck and then their placement at dinner.

Perhaps officials from the Bureau of Indian Affairs were constantly criss-crossing the Atlantic and visiting dusty archives in London? It didn't seem likely. Might Wheelock have been involved in the disturbance of Pocahontas's grave or the theft from the British Museum? That was even less likely, however. Or was it?

Counting in his favour was that he hadn't really attempted

46

to put up an actual defence of American behaviour. Instead, he had offered an explanation, albeit with some justified finger-pointing towards the old country. It was surprising, since one would expect a senior government officer such as Wheelock obviously was, to be rather less, well, *honest*.

Drabble brushed his teeth and looked out of the porthole – seeing nothing apart from the black ocean and sky. What he had learned from his time in India, in particular, was that it was perfectly possible to find decent individuals who were trying to do their best for the people in their putative care, even within the confines of a system that was itself malevolent. So Wheelock might be a decent cove after all. It was likely that over the next few days he would find out.

Drabble turned to the mirror. Of course, one of the principal culprits for destroying the Indians' way of life was steam power and not the Americans per se. It was that technological progress, intended to help increase output in manufacturing in the North of England, that had inadvertently wrought the destruction of this aboriginal way of life thousands of miles away. Not that it made it easier to bear.

He sighed. The fundamental point that Wheelock had failed to acknowledge was that it didn't have to be this way. Why leave the Native Americans with so little when the North American continent offered so much? They could have given them the equivalent of a couple of states' worth of land, and left them to it. Would that have been so unfathomable? Unfortunately life was rarely that simple, and people were rarely that magnanimous.

Returning to the bed-sitting room, Drabble found Harris slumped forward in the armchair, fast asleep. He teased the tumbler of whisky from his hand and helped him up.

'Come on, pal –' He got his arm around Harris's shoulder and dragged him towards his bed. 'Don't forget you've got your big pow-wow with Black Cloud first thing.'

Chapter Six

The next morning the sea was a shade of Oxford blue under a Cambridge sky. It was coming up to seven-thirty, Dabble set out for a walk, leaving Harris sleeping.

At this relatively early hour the decks were largely free of passengers, though members of the crew were abroad, mopping down the teak planking, polishing brass, and setting out furniture.

The *Empress of the Atlantic* appeared now to be alone in the ocean – and made stately progress, with a strict breeze running the length of her decks. After a cup of tea, Drabble was first into the ship's library, where he was lucky enough to find a copy of Kenneth Carley's *The Sioux Uprising of 1862*. Back in the cabin, he found Harris recently emerged from the bath mopping his hair with a towel. 'Still on for Black Cloud after breakfast?' he chirped. 'Don't forget the camera!'

Black Cloud, a chief of the Oglala Lakota, sat smoking a Player's Navy Cut cigarette in an armchair. His second-class cabin was less than half the size of Drabble and Harris's, and cluttered with possessions. His trunk filled a good portion of the floor space, but provided a useful seat for Drabble, who set to work with the camera. Harris took the other chair and got his notebook out on his knee. Black Cloud, seemingly more fatigued than the night at Earl's Court, embarked on the story of his life, which was what Harris had asked for.

'I was born in the moon of Black Cherries, the month which you call August, in the year 1860, on the banks of the Platte river in Nebraska. My father, also Black Cloud, was the chief of our band of Oglala Lakota. My mother was She Who Smiles. She gave my father four sons; I was the second, and the first to live to maturity. My grandfather was also called Black Cloud and was the first of our line to be chief of the band.

'We are a nomadic people, gentlemen, and before the coming of the white man, the cycle of our year followed the path of the bison – and the needs of our ponies. Fortunately, the prairies with their lush grass offered enough food for both, so we had plenty. We hunted in the summer and kept enough food to sustain us through the moons of Frost in the Tepees and Hunger.'

He waited for Harris to stop writing before setting off again. 'We worship and fear the Great Spirit, and we worship and fear Mother Earth. Nothing good can come from ignoring the commands of either of these; this we knew to be true.

'I saw my first *wasichu* when I was about six or seven. He looked like a good man and disposed me well to your people.' Black Cloud's mouth widened to a flat smile. 'He was dead, and covered in frost, for the snows had come and we were running from the Bluecoats.

'Years later I understood him to be among the number who died at the Battle of the One Hundred Slain, as we know it – the Fetterman massacre is what you call it.' He halted, revisiting a memory, before finding his way. 'I remember my people being happy at the sight of the dead men, but it saddened me, since I could not understand why they had to die. The way I saw it there was enough land and bison for everyone.' Black Cloud stubbed out his cigarette and then reached for the packet: he inched out another Player's Navy Cut, and then having decorously positioned it between his teeth, struck a match. His leathery cheeks formed hollows as he drew in the tobacco smoke.

'I soon learned that the white man was greedy, and he was many. What is more, this greed made him untrustworthy. Not long after the Battle of One Hundred Slain there was new peace with the *wasichus*. I remember because we travelled far to get there, and then there were hundreds of tepees and lodges. It was all of Lakota, as well as the Arapaho and Dakota people. It was an incredible sight – a vast circle of lodges, the national hoop, and it gave us great hope. This was at Fort Laramie, with peace signed by the Great Eagle Warrior Sheridan. After that I remember we had peace and everybody was happy.'

Black Cloud took a long drag on the cigarette.

'But the peace did not last. When I was yet fourteen the yellow metal that makes *wasichus* go crazy was found in the Black Hills. Soon, so many white people came and the government did nothing to stop them. They destroyed everything they touched, stripping the timber and killing the bison, often just for their skins. They left the meat to waste. I can still remember the stench of decaying bison . . .' He shook his head, his eyes squeezed shut. 'And now all the bison are gone, and with it my people's way of life.'

The elderly Indian drifted off to his thoughts.

Harris leaned forward. 'What happened next?'

'The *wasichus* offered us money for our land. But we did not want it. We wanted our lands, as had been promised and agreed at Fort Laramie. When we refused their bargain, the Bluecoats came to take our lands and drive us onto reservations. So my people refused to be moved, and there was another war. The Great Father in Washington had betrayed us and we had no choice.' Black Cloud took a deep breath. 'It began well. Crazy Horse led the Lakota and Cheyenne warriors against Eagle Star Crook and his Bluecoat column at the Rosebud river. The Bluecoats were driven back. We were happy but knew that there would be more to follow.'

Black Cloud knocked the ash from the tip of cigarette. 'At

the Battle of the Greasy Grass, there were hundreds of Sioux warriors – from different Lakota bands, including the Hunkpapa of Sitting Bull, but also the Arapahos and other Plains tribes. We had all prepared for the battle – I wore red warpaint on my face and chest. Early in the morning we massed in a ravine, near the Little Bighorn river, and waited. It was a hot day and we knew that the soldiers would come to the river. Then I remembered hearing that the Bluecoats were coming and that Long Hair was among them. We waited, and I remember now such a sickness in my stomach as I have never felt since. Then it began.'

Black Cloud looked over to the window. 'We surged up the hill – I had a lance and a bow – and there was much shooting and shouting. I saw a dozen or so Bluecoats lining up to fire their rifles into us, and then they vanished in a blur of Indian horses and dust. Suddenly a warrior was shouting at me and pointing to an injured Bluecoat. He had an arrow in his back and was crawling towards a rifle. "Kill him. Scalp him!" he shouted, before riding towards another soldier. I jumped down from my horse and stabbed him with my lance, and then I took his scalp.

'A Bluecoat shot at me, and missed, so I killed him with my lance. He did not want to die, and tried to stab me with his bayonet, but I killed him first. And I took his scalp. All the while the noise of the killing and the dying and the shooting filled the air and the grass was turned the colour of cherries. I cut the throat of an injured pinto horse that was kicking its legs in agony. The whole place smelled of blood. The waters of the Little Bighorn ran dark.'

Black Cloud shook his head at the grim memory. 'As I told you in London, I did not see who killed Long Hair. We were happy that he died, that's all. It sent a signal to the Great Father in Washington that the Sioux would fight for their lands.' He nodded solemnly, as if reinforcing the point. 'At sundown I went home to show my mother and my younger brothers my scalps. I was also hungry. We had fires in the camp, and the women sang tremelo. But then we heard that more soldiers were coming, so we broke camp and headed for the mountains.'

He extinguished the cigarette and then joined his hands in his lap.

'After that things did not go well. Crazy Horse surrendered at Fort Robinson in Montana and was murdered. I saw Sitting Bull at the Sun Dance in 1877, and my people surrendered at the Red Cloud Agency. The Sioux people then settled into a new way of life, one without buffalo or hunting grounds. The Great Father wanted us to live like white people. We wore pantaloons and hats, and became farmers.' He shook his head contemptuously. 'All the while the young bloods wanted to resume the fight with the *wasichus*. But our chiefs had all been to Washington, and they had seen the wealth of the white man, and just how many they were. There was no way that we could win. Sitting Bull understood that. Red Cloud understood that. But still it was hard for the young bloods to accept it. They were warriors without wars, hunters without buffalo.'

Harris looked up from his notes and nodded for Black Cloud to continue.

'We settled into the new way of life. For many years what we were endured in our memories. But then the memories started to go the way of the bison.' He reached for the cigarettes. 'We continued to live on the agency like this for many years. We were prevented from travelling to places that were important to us. The animals were all no more, and we saw the forests destroyed. The money that the Great Father promised us for our lands never came. And the people were not happy. They could not live, and many began to die. My father died and I became chief. But it was hard to lead when so much of what we were had been taken from us. I had problems stopping our

52

young people from fighting, but I was young myself and still learning my way. It was a dark time.

'But then hope arrived in form of the Ghost Dance religion. A man with powerful medicine, Wovoka, came among our people and promised that the world would change.' Black Cloud shook his head, his mouth turned down, as if he were dismissing the hope that had once gripped him. 'If the Indians danced, then the ancestors would be reborn and the white men would be destroyed and the bison would be plentiful once more. We believed it was true. Wovoka had had powerful visions which I did not doubt.' He turned back to Drabble, his expression pained. 'Across the great Plains the Indians began to dance, dancing in their thousands. But our ancestors did not return to save us and the white man was not driven from our lands. All that happened was the *wasichus* became fearful – they did not like to see Indians standing up and celebrating their deaths!' He emitted a lone, staccato chuckle. 'I suppose you cannot blame them. Much cruelty has been as a result of fear.

'Then the *wasichus* killed Sitting Bull, the last of the great chiefs, even though he did not believe in the Ghost Dance. His people, the Hunkpapa, then fled for safety; many headed towards our reservation even though it meant marching through deep snows. The big chief in our reservation, Red Cloud – no relation of mine – had been to Washington and met the Great Father Ulysses S. Grant. He knew what we were up against.

'But before the Hunkpapa could reach us, the Seventh Cavalry, still hungry to avenge the death of Long Hair and the shame of Greasy Grass, got to them first. It was three days after Christmas 1890, and the Hunkpapa camped overnight at a place that has since become infamous. Wounded Knee, it is called. Their people were hungry and half-frozen. The Army went in and gave them food and blankets, leaving a guard. Then the next morning, a fresh detachment of troops from the agency headed out to their location – so I and a few others followed. We had a sense of what was going to happen.' Black Cloud hesitated, as if confirming what he was about to say to himself. 'We arrived in time to hear the shooting. It was deafening. By the time the gunfire stopped, the Army had killed more than two hundred and fifty Indians, including over two hundred women and children. It happened in minutes. They left their bodies to the blizzard.'

He swallowed hard. 'We arrived to find a horseman coming the other way, fleeing. The gunfire was really loud. He told us what had happened. The Indians had been disarmed in the morning and during the search of the lodges one rifle was found. It was new and its owner refused to give it up, and there was a gunshot: the army then began shooting – including with a Hodgekiss machine gun. Bullets tore through the tepees and the warriors and the women and children. It was a slaughter.

'The man who I had seen fleeing, then rode on. But we went in to attack, and other Lakota by this time were moving up from Pine Ridge. We found the soldiers and charged them, but after firing they ran, and then we saw all the bodies of women and children, lying in the snow. They had been running away and were shot down. I saw a baby with blood from its head colouring the snow. These are things no one should see.'

Black Cloud's voice had fallen to a whisper and the only other sound in the room was that of Harris's pencil scratching across his pad. He turned the page over, and continued writing. Black Cloud was breathing hard. 'After Wounded Knee, I returned to Pine Ridge and settled down. I married and had children. I drank the whisky and the coffee. I grew corn badly, as my father had. I wore pantaloons and sought to keep the white man's peace. I did my best to make my people keep the white man's peace. It was a soulless existence.

'Looking back, I see now that my nation died in the snows at Wounded Knee. Where you kill children you kill the future.

The *wasichus* had started with the bison and then moved on to us. As a result, the sacred hoop of our people was broken for ever, and now we are relics, divided from our Father Sky and Mother Earth. Until the hoop is restored the Indian will not recover. It is too late for that now anyhow.'

Black Cloud looked up at the corner of the ceiling. 'You have not asked, but I should tell you. I decided to join the Wild West Show because I could not bear to see my people's deprivation on the reservation. Without weapons, without pride, and without their hunting or lands, they were dying. And then Colonel Grant came along and offered to pay me fifty dollars a week to gallop around the stage in his silly show.' He sighed and reached for his cigarettes. 'How could I refuse? At least this time I would be paid properly for my humiliation.'

Drabble found himself nodding. 'What is the condition of your people now? Do they have enough to eat?'

'They eat, Professor Drabble. But no food will satisfy their hunger. Life offers few joys. And I despair. There are less of us than there were. Yet the white man continues to grow in number. One of the few pleasures of this appalling "Wild West" show has been the warm welcome of the crowds. But it is not right for me. It is beneath my dignity.' He spoke this last comment rather as if he was repeating words told to him – not that that in any way invalidated the sentiment. 'Fortunately,' said Black Cloud, 'now I go home, and I will be with my people.'

They paused for a minute or two as Drabble took several photographs of Black Cloud with Harris's camera. The chief sat unblinking as the flash erupted into life.

There was a knock at the door, and a tough-looking Indian of about forty poked his head in through the gap. He saw Harris and then Drabble and his expression hardened. 'I'll come back –'

'No, no, Christopher –' Black Cloud reached out. 'We are finishing.' He turned to Harris and then Drabble. Drabble got his hat and Harris followed him to the door, where the new arrival stood sombrely. They each nodded at one another.

'This is my son, Christopher Black Eagle,' declared Black Cloud with majesty. 'He has been on the tour with us.'

'And how do you like Wild Westing?' asked Harris lightly.

'I don't,' he replied. 'It is beneath us.'

They emerged from the interview in sombre spirits. The contents of Black Cloud's narrative had made for depressing listening.

Harris shuddered and took out his pipe: 'How bloody awful ...'

'Well,' Drabble stated what he thought they must both already have been thinking – 'it plainly wasn't the moment to bring up poor old Dr Yorke either.'

'Oh, sod!' Harris had forgotten all about that. He lit up. 'We'll have to go back.'

Drabble agreed.

'The Americans –' exclaimed Harris, staring indignantly out at the sea. 'What a bunch of bastards. Christ alive. They're practically as bad as the Belgians, and I thought no one touched the Belgians for sheer bloody ruthlessness.'

'I'm not so sure about that.' Drabble sighed. 'We've all got blood on our hands, old man ...'

'True,' muttered Harris bleakly. '*True* ... but the poor old Indians. I mean, I've always understood them to be a bunch of wild savages. But it's obviously nothing like that at all. They're clearly a remarkable people.'

Drabble looked over at his friend: his frowning face a picture of mental anguish.

Suddenly the expression brightened and Harris pulled out his pocket watch.

'Now look at *that*!' He fixed a prepared gaze on Drabble and ineptly stifled a smug grin: 'Sorry, old man, I've got to ...' The sentence was left unfinished, Harris was already on the move, and exhibiting an awkwardness that was unmistakable.

It could only be one thing: a woman. And if it were a woman aboard the *Empress of the Atlantic*, then it could only be Fanny Howell.

Ten to one, that's what it was, Drabble thought. He drifted over to the rail, the pall of the interview hanging over him. Truth was, it had left him feeling altogether rather nauseous. Mankind's seemingly limitless capacity for inhuman awfulness was truly sickening, he realised. Drabble stared down at the sea and raised his eyes to the horizon: there was nothing out there, just the waves, peak and trough, peak and trough ...

The ultimate tragedy was that Black Cloud was right. The genie could not be put back in the bottle. Indeed, the genie was dead and the bottle had long since been smashed to smith-ereens. Such damage had been done and was irrevocable. The unique life and world of the Plains Indian, as it had been, could not be resuscitated. And nothing could be done to rectify the injustice, saving perhaps giving all the land back and magicking the bison back into existence.

But that was a fantasy.

He strolled on until he arrived at a deck café, where pas-sengers enjoyed the weak sunshine in relative shelter from the breeze, serenaded by a string quartet which was working through some Mozart. The place was filled mainly with elderly women in furs crouching under hats or couples – perhaps on their way to the New World for a new life – and those sitting down with day-old editions of the *News Chronicle* or *The Times*.

Drabble ordered a coffee and absently watched the waiter stopping at the next tables, overhearing them ordering. Just then the newspaper at the adjacent table creased to one side, and an attractive young woman in a soft, brown fedora looked out.

'Professor!' she exclaimed with pleasure.

Chapter Seven

Harris beetled along the deck, whistling. He had admitted to himself that Fanny Howell was not his type. Not quite. First, she was not English, and she wasn't stick-thin, two things that usually carried a lot of weight in Harris's sexual selection. In fact, he paused thoughtfully, she probably carried a fair wedge of timber on her – but fortunately the majority of it was in the most ideal of locations. Harris smirked and lengthened his stride – O, to be in the prime of one's life!

Miss Howell also had a certain authentic rusticity about her; whether it was the apple-cheeked smile or the equine scent that inevitably clung to her ... there was something earthily fecund about her. And that was exciting. She was not an ener-vated crisp of an office girl with a complexion the colour of the concrete of the Great West Road. Nor was she the first girl on horseback who had caught Harris's eye. Oh no. Those spurs of honour went to the jodhpurs-inhabiting honourable Laeti-tia Conway of the Barnstaple Conways – he took a deep breath as that full equine extravaganza revisited him. He couldn't help but smile. Mind you, that had been a very long time ago. He marched on – and puzzlement descended upon him. Whatever had happened to Laetitia Conway of the Barnstaple Conways? He sighed, half sounding like a horse neighing, and confronted an entirely blank mind. No, it was gone.

But he'd never forget those thighs. Like hams, they were.

Ruddy great things that were hewn from years in the saddle. Oh, the saddle! Harris chuckled and continued ... but then a sense of mounting vexation began to cloud the happy vista – what had became of her?

He shook his head, forcing Laetitia, and her jodhpurs from his mind, and focused on the matter in hand. Miss Howell awaited ... And then it came to him. Married. Laetitia must have got married. That's what happened to all those girls. You knew them one day, and then the next they got married and simply vanished from one's mind. That's right, it all came back to him: an androgynous Household Cavalryman with the underbite of a Habsburg hamster. Well, so long as she was happy ...

Turning the corner, he took in the foredeck, his focus flitting between the couples in sober shades – and then he saw her. She stood near the bow, in a long dress and short overcoat, in western style, her long copper tresses trapped beneath a broad-rimmed cowgirl hat. She was attempting to keep back the wayward strands of hair from gusting in her face, and she was talking ... *to a man*. Harris recognised him immediately: Major Sakamoto, the Japanese diplomat.

Well, well, well. Harris didn't miss the suggestive smirk on his slim, and damned handsome face. Oh, no. Harris could spot *that* look of imagined possession at a hundred paces. So be it, he thought, as he marched up to confront his enemy. May the best man win.

'Miss Howell!' he bellowed warmly and tipped his hat. 'How the dickens are you on this fine morning?' Next he nodded to the rival. 'And Major Sakamoto, what a *pleasant* surprise.'

The Japanese diplomat offered a stiff bow, and Miss Howell smiled.

'Oh, gentlemen,' she swooned, her eyes twinkling but her expression a perfect mask of civility. 'I'm sorry to have double-booked you, but you were both so ardent –' they began to stroll, and she took their arms either side, 'and I never could say no.'

'I'm surprised that you only had two suitors for your morning, Miss Howell,' declared Sakamoto winningly, in such flawless English that he might have been an old Etonian. She tilted her head towards him and giggled.

'Now, Sir Percival, I hope you don't mind sharing me with the Japanese diplomatic corps?'

'How could I possibly object?' Harris smiled at Sakamoto, even managing a few teeth. 'In any event, the British and the Japanese have long been friendly rivals.'

'And not just in south-east Asia,' quipped Sakamoto.

Miss Howell liked that and gave a throaty laugh. 'It sounds like you two are just going to get along perfectly.'

The breeze passed over the deck briskly – the ship was probably making north of twenty knots, and it blew Miss Howell's long hair forward so that Harris could not in fact quite see her profile as they walked. Her arms interlinked with theirs, she drew them both even closer every time she pushed back the delinquent locks.

'How did you like London?' asked Harris.

'Honestly, I preferred Berlin.' She softened this with a wink at Harris. 'I can't resist a man in uniform,' she gasped, 'never could, and there are simply *so many* of them in Berlin. A girl could go crazy. Oh … the boots – and you know, I love a man in a Sam Browne belt.' She stroked back her hair. 'It's just crazy. And then there's the Tiergarten … As for the Nazis? They may not have a finely developed sense of humour, but they sure are a hilarious crowd. You get laughs and lederhosen in equal measure.'

Sakamoto gave a polite chuckle.

Harris asked, 'Did you meet any of the bigwigs?'

'Meet them?' she fired an inviting glance at Harris. 'We couldn't avoid them! I think Grant was having dinner with the Führer every week.

60

'And I can tell you this, the best of them is Goering by far; now that man's got some stories, *and* he likes the ladies,' she cackled, 'but his breath is worse than a mule's. And you must know that Hitler absolutely *loves* the Wild West. I think if he wasn't chancellor of Germany he'd probably be a cowboy.'

Harris chuckled. 'Prefers chaps, does he?'

'You know what? I think he could probably take or leave it, actually.' She glanced meaningfully at Harris and then turned to Sakamoto. 'Sako, do you have any top secret information on the Führer's bedroom preferences?'

His reply was cut short by the arrival of one of Colonel Grant's troupe. 'Miss Howell,' he drawled. 'Sorry to interrupt, but the Colonel needs your help with a matter right now. It can't wait.'

The word 'Professor' hung momentarily in the air, suspended in an unknown female voice. Then the interlocutor repeated it with the deepening inflection of someone reassuring themselves that their identification was correct.

'Professor *Drabble,*' she said, smiling. Her blue eyes shone at him. 'You won't remember me,' she stated, her confidence rising. 'My name is Miss Moore, *Dr* Moore,' she added, correcting herself cautiously. 'I'm a research fellow at Oxford. I saw you lecture there on Cromwell after your monograph came out two years ago. What a talk!' She smiled and laid her newspaper to one side. 'In fact, we met very briefly.'

'Did we?' replied Drabble gratefully. He began scouring his memory.

'Yes, I was with my father, Professor Moore ...'

It was coming back to him: the crowded room, the elation of completing his lecture –

'*Professor Moore*'s your father? Goodness me!' Moore had taught Drabble when he was an undergraduate and was widely recognised as a towering figure in the field. Drabble now saw the face looking at him in a new light, though he struggled to alight upon any particular familial resemblance.

She smiled. 'What a diverting coincidence.'

Absolutely, thought Drabble, who immediately forgot Harris, Black Cloud, Pocahontas, and everything else that had been filling his mind. He smiled at the young woman before him, noting the way her dark blond hair framed her attractive oval face.

'Did you say that you were an *historian?*' he asked, fully aware that she had but still requiring confirmation of the point.

'Yes,' she brightened. 'My field is Early Modern British. Just like you.'

Half a space separated their small round tables in the press of the deck café, rendering it the sort of gap that would make a discreet conversation awkward under normal circumstances. They both arrived at the same conclusion.

'Would you like to join me?' she asked.

Harris and Sakamoto looked at one each other like two dog-foxes outwitted by the same hen. Sakamoto took out his handkerchief and blew his nose before stuffing it back in his pocket and looking back the way they had come, rather as if he was about to walk off. Harris took out his pocket watch. It was coming up to noon.

'Time for a swift libation?' He met Sakamoto's blank expression. 'A drink? I dare say that the bar's been open for hours in Tokyo by now.'

The watering hole they selected was a baroque affair that recalled drunken nights in Saint-Germain, back when the going was good before the Americans arrived, pushing up the bars and the prices in equal measure. Sakamoto asked if they served Pol Roger by the glass.

'What a good idea,' sparkled Harris, who ordered a glass of Gossett, antiquity always being an essential marker of quality.

They remained at the bar and examined each other silently over their drinks. Sakamoto blinked first.

'What takes you to America, Sir Percival?'

Harris blew through his teeth. 'Bit of work, but I've never been as a matter of fact, so I'm positively killing to see the place. You? On a top secret diplomatic mission?'

'It will be work, regrettably. But I am determined to enjoy it as much one can.'

'So I observe,' chuckled Harris.

The Japanese diplomat arched a neat, feminine eyebrow quizzically, seeming not to understand the inference. Harris retrieved his smirk.

'What do you do at the embassy in London?'

'I'm the defence attaché.'

'Ah, so you're a *spy*!' The words blurted from Harris's mouth, and several other drinkers turned to look. The diplomat lowered his glass and grimaced beneath the narrow Errol Flynn moustache. Harris moved on, 'Where were you before London?'

'Berlin.'

'So you've seen Hitler and his cronies, including that clubfooted cretin, up close too?'

'Herr Goebbels is a very effective operator.' Sakamoto removed a lacquered cigarette case from his inside breast pocket. 'But yes, I had the opportunity to observe all of the Nazi elite *intimately*. I found them to be a most impressive group of individuals. Certainly not to be underestimated, Sir Percival. I think the Führer is probably one of the most underestimated individuals in the world – especially in Britain, where people make fun of him. If I were British I would not be making fun of the Führer.'

Sakamoto slipped a long 'Hope' cigarette to his mouth, lit up, and inhaled forcefully. A cloud formed of an unfamiliar blend of tobacco filled the space of the table. Harris was still puzzling over Sakamoto's comment as he took out his pipe.

'Do you think the Germans want war?'

'With the British Empire? Definitely not.'

'Splendid!' Harris was cheered by Sakamoto's sudden lack of diplomatic equivocation.

'But you English must realise that you can no longer dictate to the rest of us how the world is run. As we have seen in the East, where my own country has forged a new empire in Manchuria, different nations have their own territorial aspirations, which must be accommodated by the world order.'

Harris set down his glass of Gossett.

'Now look here, we can't have various countries gallivanting around, willy-nilly, stealing vast tracts of foreign land and subjugating their peoples. It's just not on.'

Even as he said this, Harris realised the potential flaw in his position. Sakamoto shook his head.

'I'm afraid the English have no position of moral authority on this topic. And London is acutely aware of that.'

Suddenly they were back to being foxes negotiating the same chicken coop. After mutely eyeing one another, Harris asked, 'So what do you think will happen when we *refuse* to let, for sake of argument, you chaps, or the Italians, have their wicked way in a distant foreign field?'

'Simple.' Sakamoto tilted his head back and pecked at his cigarette, 'There will be undesirable and *unnecessary* friction between the great powers.'

'War, in other words.'

'I hope it will not come to that.'

So did Harris. The difference was that Harris meant it – but he wasn't at all convinced that Sakamoto did. For years the headlines had been full of the free-booting belligerence of Italy and Japan, in fields such as Abyssinia and China. These Johnnies, plus the Germans, were also building battleships like their lives depended on it, which of course they did, up to a point.

None of it boded well, but on an individual level Sakamoto seemed like a decent enough cove.

'Cheers!' Harris raised his glass.

The diplomat smiled. 'Let us drink to peace, Sir Percival!'

Harris drained his glass, 'Another?'

Sakamoto shrugged indifferently.

'Perfect, let's make it a bottle.'

Not very far away, Drabble and Dr Moore – Charlotte – had enjoyed a second coffee and then moved on to lunch. After that they'd taken a stroll and ended up in the palm court for tea. They now sat either side of a small round table, divided by the paraphernalia of tea – as well as an understood cultural bias against public displays of intimacy. But for all that, Drabble sensed strongly that it would be rather wonderful if something did happen between them. And why ever not?

On the dancefloor half a dozen couples shifted from foot to foot as the band played popular tunes. Drabble did not dance, as a rule. But he did want to dance with Charlotte, as she had become in the course of the intervening three hours. And, if nothing else, going to the dancefloor would remove a major physical hurdle between them, namely the table. Of course, he was going to have to summon the courage to . . .

'Shall we dance?' asked Charlotte. She swung her knees out from the under the table before he could reply. Drabble took her hand – and placed his other hand on her waist, and willed himself to relax his arms and avoid her toes. They started to move to the music and he met her gaze. There, he thought. *It wasn't so difficult.* He looked down at her lips, and wanted to kiss them. Returning to meet her gaze he found she was smiling at him, with an eyebrow raised. He found himself blushing – and then they both laughed.

Chapter Eight

It had gone four by the time Drabble and Charlotte parted company and he made his way back to the cabin; he did so in a strangely altered state bordering on bliss, but as he turned the corner and arrived on his and Harris's corridor that all changed. Black Cloud's son, Christopher Black Eagle, was sitting on the floor outside their door. He spotted Drabble and jumped to his feet, shouting angrily.

'Drabble!' He approached, his finger raised in accusation. 'I want to talk to you.'

And quite possibly more . . . Christopher glared angrily and the muscles in his face and neck were flexing alarmingly. Charlotte vanished from Drabble's mind and he readied himself: he squared his shoulders and met the insistent stare – it was always the best approach, he had found.

'What is it?' he stated coldly.

Christopher Black Eagle stopped before him, standing closer than one would like, his chest puffed out and his hands balled into fists. The veins in his powerful neck were still flexing.

'Where were you and your friend between eleven thirty and twelve noon – after your interview with my father?'

'I was walking with Harris –'

'You're lying!' Christopher roared, and lunged with his hands like talons.

Drabble saw it coming and stepped aside, throwing out his

foot. It connected with the Indian's shin and his rage sent him tumbling over, but he was up in a split second and span around, glowering at Drabble as he rose to full height. Humiliation now piqued his anger.

Drabble reached out and addressed him as calmly as he could.

'Christopher, Mr Black Eagle, there's been a misunderstanding –'

'Do not call me Christopher or Black Eagle! Only my father uses those names. My people know me as Speaks With Fists.'

Drabble again registered the man's clenched fists. They were broad and strong and looked like they could do a lot of talking – which given the man's temper, they probably had. But fisticuffs right now would get them precisely nowhere, especially since Drabble had no idea what he wanted. And somewhere, Speaks With Fists would know that beating him to a pulp, which he could, would do no good as well.

Drabble saw the man's neck and face muscles settling.

'Listen, I have tea and whisky in the cabin. Let's talk about this inside.'

'I do not drink the white man's poison,' Speaks With Fists spat bitterly. 'It has sedated my people long enough.'

Drabble nodded. 'Tea it is then . . .'

'Somebody broke into my father's cabin this morning, when he was walking on deck. They tore the place apart.'

'Was anything taken?'

'We don't think so.'

That struck Drabble as odd, particularly since someone had gone to the effort and personal risk of breaking in. But given the way that Speaks With Fists' eyes roved hungrily around the cabin – and his demeanour at their meeting – Drabble reckoned it was also perfectly possible that something *had been* stolen, but that he did not want to or simply could not acknowledge it.

'What do you think they were looking for?' Drabble asked mildly.

The Indian shrugged his muscular shoulders. 'My father has many artefacts that collectors would want, and some are valuable, very valuable. They broke into his trunk, but did not take anything from it.' He looked up from his dainty teacup, which he had drained quickly. 'His war bonnet would be highly sought after, but with thanks to the Great Spirit that was not taken.'

It sounded like they were after something very particular, thought Drabble, as he refreshed Speaks With Fists' cup from the pot.

'I assume you know about the thefts from the British Museum, which took place before you left London?'

He nodded.

'I know that your friend interviewed my father about it. So did the cop.'

'It must have made you angry to see those things in the museum,' suggested Drabble.

Speaks With Fists appeared to contemplate the teacup, which he cradled between his large hands. 'It filled me with a burning sense of injustice,' he said after a moment. 'They are ours, and should not be behind a wall of glass for people to stare at.' He drained his tea.

Drabble nodded with understanding and it occurred to him that Black Cloud had used almost identical words on Monday night at Earl's Court.

'Did you go with your father when he met Dr Yorke?'

Speaks With Fists frowned, and when he spoke the anger that Drabble had seen before had come back. 'I was not aware that my father had spoken to him.'

Drabble waited a moment before continuing, 'The policeman said that your father had offered to buy the items from the museum.'

The Indian's face cracked a smile – it betrayed surprising warmth – and he set down the teacup.

'I find that very hard to believe. My father has been nothing but supine in the face of the white man's aggression: he has repeatedly implored my people to accept humiliation in return for peace.'

'I see,' said Drabble, waiting.

'When compromise looks like this, Professor Drabble, then the two are no different.'

Speaks With Fists got up to leave. Perhaps he could see no further benefit in talking to Drabble. What he had said about his father had a ring of truth about it. But would Yorke really have lied to Stephenson about it? Perhaps it wasn't a lie so much as . . .

'Was it you who threatened Dr Yorke, then?'

Speaks With Fists turned back at the door. His expression had darkened and Drabble sensed his blood was up again.

'Who says I threatened him?'

'The police were told that your father threatened Yorke. But if it wasn't him . . .'

Speaks With Fists held Drabble's gaze, his expression giving no ground. He made no reply.

'You do know he was murdered on Monday night?'

'We went through this with the police. Yes, I threatened Yorke, but *kill* the man?' He shook his head. 'I was angry that he had refused to sell us Sitting Bull's things, but that was all. He is not responsible for the condition of my people. I do not hate him.'

'Well, someone hated him enough to kill him – using an arrow of all things.'

Speaks With Fists nodded thoughtfully. 'Dr Yorke was passionate about my culture, Professor. He wished to conserve and foster knowledge of it. Yes, we argued. But I would never strike down a man who had dedicated his life to the study of my people.' Speaks With Fists put his hat on, pulling it deliberately to just above his ears. 'Now, I say this to you, Professor. Be careful. I am of the view that you are a good man, which is why I have drunk your tea and spoken with you in a civilised manner when my temper told me to do otherwise. So be warned, Professor, deeper forces are at work here, perhaps even ... evil forces. I could not say who or what they are, but something is wrong and you and your friend are best out of it.'

Drabble locked the door, his mind puzzling over Speaks With Fists' revelations and the warning. Or was it a threat masquerading as a warning?

'Deeper forces, perhaps even ... evil forces. You and your friend are best out of it.'

Drabble turned the words over in his mind. It was impossible to know for sure, but regardless of what was intended, the practical effect was the same. Keep away. And let's not forget that Speaks With Fists just admitted to threatening Dr Yorke ...

Drabble checked his wristwatch but did not the register the time. Notwithstanding Yorke's death, it had not occurred to him that either he or Harris might be in any physical danger themselves. That oversight, if oversight it was, had surely now been corrected by Speaks With Fists. He looked at his watch again. It was gone five.

Where was Harris? If lunch had ended up in the bar, which it would have done, then Harris would be positively roasted by now. And that would make dinner a singular pleasure.

He started to clear up the tea things. Something was going to have to be done about Harris's drinking, but not today. Or this week. But it had all got a lot worse since their return from India a few months before, and his heartbreak over Princess Padmini.

Drabble shifted the tea tray and saw a copy of the *Daily Telegraph* from the day before. Taking it to the armchair, he checked the updates on the Hong Kong typhoon, and then

Spain and the bloody push on Saragossa. In Germany, Hitler — more good news! — had made an offer to join Japan in a 'defensive' fight against Communism.

Then beneath the fold a headline jumped out at him:

BREAK-IN AT PEER'S PALACE

The Metropolitan police was last night investigating a burglary at Syon House, the London residence of his Grace the Duke of Northumberland. The Duke's secretary said that signs of forced entry had been discovered at the house on Monday morning by the household staff, who were now conducting an audit to establish the extent of any thefts. The secretary confirmed that an oil painting of an American Indian princess, Pocahontas, had been tampered with in the Duke's drawing room. The painting, which dates from the 1620s, and has been in the family since the late seventeenth century . . .

The Syon House break-in had occurred on Sunday night, around the same time that the remains of Pocahontas were uncovered — and a few hours before Harris was tipped off and had then called him to jump on the train. The theft of Sitting Bull's pipe and war shirt, meanwhile, took place shortly before midday on Monday. And then Dr Yorke was killed at some point on Monday night. Assuming the same individual or individuals was responsible for all of this, then they had undoubtedly been busy. But it could all have been accomplished by someone working alone, that was clear.

Then again, it was a lot to undertake for one person, meaning a team might be responsible — requiring greater planning *and* resources. Drabble glanced over at the porthole, his mind working swiftly. All that said, there was no evidence that the incidents were connected. But . . . *but*, the power of coincidence weighed strongly against that.

At the very least, the events bifurcated neatly, with Pocahontas on the one hand and then Sitting Bull on the other. As Black Cloud had pointed out, hundreds of years and hundreds of miles had separated these two individuals in life, and that might just well stretch to whatever criminal intent lurked behind it all as well.

They needed to question Black Cloud and Speaks With Fists about the Pocahontas aspects, Drabble decided. Despite what they said, the Indians remained highly likely to be responsible for the theft of Sitting Bull's pipe and war shirt. (Quite possibly, Black Cloud had even worn the shirt – a red flag, one might say – at Earl's Court on Monday night.) But in the absence of Dr Yorke's expert testimony or photographs it would be nigh on impossible to prove, of course, that they had actually been Sitting Bull's. Could that in itself have been a motive for killing Yorke? It seemed far-fetched, especially since the theft had already been successfully executed.

If Drabble could search Black Cloud's cabin then he might shed some light on it all. However, if one believed Speaks With Fists – and he had seemed sincere – someone else had sought to do just that already, and who might that have been? Might that extra party be the same party interested in Pocahontas – or someone else? And was that someone the 'deeper ... evil forces' that Speaks With Fists had given him warning of?

Drabble sighed. Or was his mind simply trying to force disparate matters together, out of nature's love or need for pattern? It was possible. What didn't seem credible was that one could take Speaks With Fists and his father entirely at their word. One of them – or both of them – were lying.

Drabble sighed. He noticed the time again. Where *was* Harris?

Chapter Nine

It was not long before Drabble heard someone making a fist of getting his key in the lock of the cabin door. Then, after the amount of time it would take an able criminal to pick the lock, rob the entire premises, and be off again, Harris appeared in the doorway, grinning like an imbecile trying to befriend a fierce-looking dog.

'What ho, Drabble?' he declared merrily. But on meeting Drabble's gaze, his brows lowered, 'Everything all right, old man?' A gust of sea air followed him in. It was laced with booze, though precisely which Drabble could not tell. Harris closed the door behind him and fell into the armchair very recently vacated by Speaks With Fists. Drabble looked him up and down.

'Where have you been?'

'Oh, Christ,' exhaled Harris, searching about him under cushions. 'Is my mother here?' He stared hard at Drabble. 'Don't tell me my mother's aboard?'

'Who were you drinking with?'

'Major Sakamoto,' said Harris, with some difficulty. 'On reflection, more Poo-bah than Lord High Executioner.'

Drabble knew enough to know that this was a reference to *The Mikado*, but that was as far as it went. 'Explain,' he instructed gruffly.

'He's not a bad cove. Comes across as a bit of a militaristic, stiff-shirt type fellow, you know –' Harris located his pipe and continued to speak with the stem jammed between his teeth as the quest went on for matches. 'But actually he's rather a good human being. Sound, almost.'

'Almost?'

'Well . . . all that funny business the Japs are up to in China –' He shook his head, his face pinched like a man who has just levered open a manhole cover. 'Still, he's not as bad as you might think. He's an epeeist, for God's sake.'

Harris, Drabble would never forget (or be permitted to forget), was a half-decent fencer. In fact, if memory served, it was the only sport that Harris had ever shown the slightest aptitude for or interest in throughout their time together at Lancing. And in Harris's book epeeists were the best of the bunch – significantly more trustworthy than fencers who specialised in either of the sport's two other weapons, sabre or foil.

'Foilists are shifty and sabreurs closet sadists,' he would remark bitterly. 'And actually many of them aren't that closeted, either.'

Drabble told him about Syon House and then showed him the article. After a few minutes in silent contemplation of the *Telegraph*, Harris laid down the newspaper and made an announcement.

'Oh, Drab,' he wailed pitifully. 'My head . . . it's killing me.'

'You've only got yourself to blame.' Drabble gave him a hard stare and went back to inspecting his bow tie in the mirror.

'I know, but I was applying myself diligently to Anglo-Japanese relations – and finding out vital information.'

'Really?' He looked over. 'What vital information?'

'Well . . .'

'Such as troop movements around Shanghai?'

Harris shook his head. 'I say, a cup of tea would go down a treat!'

'You'll have coffee. And then we'll talk.'

74

Three cups later, Harris was in the bath. But he still felt no better. He called through to Drabble, wincing with each syllable. 'I say, old man, how long is it till dinner?'

'Same as when you asked me last, less five minutes.'

Harris nodded solemnly. Drabble was becoming rather ogre-ish. What concern was it of his if he decided to have a few jars over lunch? He was probably jealous, wasn't he? Probably feeling a bit left out ...

Harris leaned his head back against the tiles meditatively and gazed up at the porthole, trying to ignore the stabbing pains in the sides of his head. He called out again, 'What do you make of the non-burglary at Syon House?'

'Impossible to say without further information.' Drabble now stood in the doorway looking down at Harris. 'You look pitiful,' he said, handing him a glass of water and a pair of aspirin. 'We need to interview Black Cloud again. He definitely has more to tell us. We could also benefit from having that chat with Colonel Grant: fewer people will know the old chief better. And it might be useful to see if we can get word to Stephenson.'

Harris swallowed the tablets and drained the glass, which he handed back to Drabble. 'I could always arrange an interview with Miss Howell?' He smiled.

Drabble left the bathroom. 'Dinner's in twenty-five minutes.'

After a moment, Harris heard the lock of the cabin door turning. 'I say,' he called. 'Where are you going?'

The answer, strictly speaking, was nowhere. But Drabble needed some air and Harris was annoying him. Where was his sense of responsibility? Drabble knew the answer well enough. He didn't have any. And if he'd ever had, he'd drunk it all by now.

Tonight was their second night aboard, meaning they would be landing in New York in two nights' time, and that gave them a limited window to get to the bottom of the mystery – if they were ever going to. Which right now he doubted.

It was dusk and becoming fresh on deck. The sky was a powdery blue at the horizon, rising in grades to a full, star-specked black above. Passengers were strolling out before dinner, dressed in their evening finery, their gleaming white silk scarves catching in the wind. Drabble discovered he was wishing he would bump into Charlotte. He stopped at the rail to admire the ocean and smiled. They had arranged to have lunch the following day and he was already impatient to see her. He looked out over the water: black waves, countless, dancing and ceaseless, confronted him, and he felt his mind expand with a sense of possibility.

'It would appear that we are quite alone in the world, Professor.'

Drabble heard the warm, rich voice, and turned to see Wheelock replacing his horn pipe. 'However, I would estimate that there are at least four or five vessels of a similar size within a twenty-mile radius.'

Drabble smiled. 'Mr Wheelock, I didn't have you down as a nervous traveller.'

'I'm not, as a matter of fact. But it never hurts to appreciate the context – and the risks. Heading to dinner?'

They strolled in the direction of the Restaurant, Wheelock resuming the conversation.

'I take it you're dining again at Captain Rossiter's table?' He caught Drabble's slight nod of confirmation. 'He has his favour-ites, I have realised.'

'I fear you are right. I wonder if he's granted us the pleasure of being seated next to one another for the second night running.'

Rossiter was already forming his table when they got there. Drabble was seated between the Duchess of Montgomeryshire and her sister. Colonel Grant and Miss Howell came next, followed by a grand-looking American society couple, Mr and Mrs Henry Spes-Burchill of Long Island. Harris – who arrived a little late but looking plausibly fit – was between them and the Captain.

Over dinner Harris was circumspect over his alcoholic consumption – not that Drabble was counting. He presumed his bibulous friend was exercising self-control, *or* having it exercised for him by his corporeal sufferings. By the meal's conclusion, Drabble knew much more about the intricacies of the steeplechase than he had thought possible – as well as the alleged shortcomings of the Welsh.

'Abysmal creatures,' sniffed the Duchess. 'I married in.'

After an hour of belligerent xenophobia and equestrianism Drabble was ready for a drink, and accompanied by Harris, they headed to the bar. Colonel Grant and Miss Howell, having quit the Captain's table minutes before them, were already in situ, surrounded by a gaggle of performers and retainers from the show. They were instantly recognisable – the length of their hair and style of dress was unmissable.

'This place is bad for my health,' Grant breezed. 'Hell –' He necked a shot of bourbon and slapped the glass down on the bar. 'Thank God the crossing only takes four days.' He jabbed his finger at the barman, indicating drinks for Drabble and Harris too. 'I always knew drowning was a hazard of ocean travel, but I never figured you could drown *inside* the boat.' The drinks arrived, and he passed the shots to Drabble and Harris. 'Get that down you!'

The three of them – Drabble, Harris and Grant – then detached themselves from the throng and occupied a quiet corner of the bar. The Colonel offered round a tin of cigarillos, which Harris received readily before taking out his notebook. He began by asking Grant to fill him in on his illustrious career.

Those snowy eyebrows went up and Drabble saw Grant's throat constrict behind his frosted goatee. 'All right ... I was

77

born in Deadwood in the Black Hills of South Dakota in 1865 –'
Grant spoke with the air of a man who had injected that same
sentence with drama on more than one occasion. 'Back then the
stagecoach would arrive festooned with arrows – looking like a
porcupine. My parents were journeying west but ran out of
money, so got stuck there. My dad was a hard-working black-
smith but I wanted more from life. I also had a taste for adventure
and was pretty good on a horse, so I joined the cavalry as soon as
I could. That would have been 1882 or 1883.

'Life was hard and life was cheap, but I was lucky.' He smiled.
'The discipline was barbaric, but not as barbaric as the enemy.'
He cackled at that. 'Looking back, I'll never know how we did
what we did. But when you're young I guess you don't know
no better.' He drew on his cigarillo pensively and in that
moment, Drabble thought he looked all his seventy-odd years.

'I went wherever I was told to. I must have ridden thousands
of miles. I took part in the Crow War in Montana. Vicious it
was. I was lucky to live, but that got me promoted. Later I was
at Wounded Knee, less said about that the better.' His gaze
shifted towards the bar. 'Like a lot of things in war it looks a lot
different in hindsight. As a historian, I expect you'll understand
that, Professor.' His lips found his cigarillo, and then his tone
changed. 'After that I saw the Indians were a lost cause. They
were beat and their fight was all used up. The buffalo were all
gone – I shot no small number of them myself. And that's when
I decided that instead of fighting Indians, I'd celebrate them.
That's where the idea of the show came from. I just had no idea
it would be this successful. You can imagine!'

Drabble could indeed.

'How did you convince Black Cloud to become your star
feature?'

'I rode up to his cabin on the Pine Ridge Reservation and
just asked him.' Grant broke into laughter. 'He told me to fuck
off!'

Harris chuckled. 'But you persisted?'

'Absolutely. The man had nothing. He was miserable. After Wounded Knee his people were over and what they believed in – that new messiah, Wovoka – that was all exploded. It was a bad time.' He spoke with sympathy. 'And instead of taking government handouts, I was giving him the chance to earn a good living.' Grant sighed wearily. 'I do believe he despises it with every inch of his red body, but he keeps taking the money and putting on the warpaint. And that's good enough for me.'

Harris looked up from his notes. 'Why does he hate it – he's the star?'

'Jesus, Sir Percival – re-enacting your lost civilisation night after night for the entertainment of the very people who wiped it out? Come on!'

Grant broke into an amused, if slightly contemptuous, chuckle and reached for his drink. Drabble coughed in a way that conveyed a change of subject.

'Has it occurred to you that Black Cloud or his son, or one of the other native Americans in your show, might have been responsible for the thefts from the British Museum?'

A sudden commotion broke out at the bar. Grant looked over, irritated.

'I've already said all I can about that, Professor. We spoke to your police at length. If one of the Indians did it ... well, *hell*, it's really none of my business – and frankly, good luck to them.' He paused thoughtfully. 'I'm sure that if you analysed the path of ownership which took them from Sitting Bull all the way to London, then you might discover at least one or two unequal bargains along the way. And trust me, I know all about unequal bargains.'

Grant gave a snort.

'I'm not sure that's much consolation to the widow of Dr Yorke ...'

Grant scowled. 'Now that's a different matter, Professor.

Who can know why Dr Yorke was killed – *or* who killed him. To accuse an Indian simply because he had an arrow in his back is like insisting that a Frenchman is to blame whenever someone dies of food poisoning.' He emitted a barking chuckle, made all the more awkward because no one else joined in.

Harris looked up from his notes. 'Is this definitely your last tour, Colonel?'

'Absolutely. I'm past seventy now – I'm retiring. I've got a ranch in the Black Hills, and I'm going to raise cattle, and see out my dotage in peaceful solitude. Now, gentlemen –' He rose from the chair. 'I think there's time for just one more nightcap.'

At the bar the Wild Westers were several more bourbons further down the trail, and singing had begun. Suddenly there were shouts; two or three cowboys fell, wrestling, rolling onto the floor. A chair, then a table overturned and drinks smashed to the floor.

Grant beamed at the pandemonium and turned to Drabble and Harris. 'I really am getting too old for this.' He took out another cigarillo, cradled a match to its tip, and called across the bar, 'Miss Howell!' He strode into the melee and seized one of the wrestling cowboys.

Drabble nudged Harris's elbow.

'Come on,' he said.

'What about Miss Howell?'

'Don't waste your time.'

They looked over and saw Miss Howell loop her arm into Grant's and watched them head for the door.

'I don't believe it ...' Harris turned to Drabble. 'He's old enough to be her father!'

'And the rest.'

'Well I never.' Harris brightened. 'Still, it gives one hope ...'

Chapter Ten

The next morning they went to see Black Cloud, arriving just as Speaks With Fists was leaving. He reviewed them both coldly, and moved off without saying a word. The door to the cabin had been repaired but showed signs of the forced entry Speaks With Fists had told Drabble of.

The elderly chief was sat cloaked in a red blanket, gazing out glumly at the never-ending ocean through the porthole. His cabin felt more cramped than before, and its shabbiness showed on this second inspection. It was a far cry from the spacious accommodation they enjoyed on the deck above in First.

'Professor Drabble, Sir Percival —' He nodded stiffly, and lifted a hand to indicate the seat by the small desk at the end of the bed. He settled in the armchair and regarded them frostily.

'I understand from your son that your cabin was broken into yesterday ...' Drabble glanced over at Harris. 'Was anything taken?'

He shook his head.

'Do have any idea what the burglars may have been looking for?'

Black Cloud nodded towards his trunk. 'They broke into my case but took nothing.'

It had occurred to Drabble that had Black Cloud and his followers stolen the Sitting Bull items from the museum, then this break-in might have been staged to deflect any accusations from them. It was a faint possibility. Harris tested the water.

'Do you think they were looking for Sitting Bull's pipe and shirt?'

Black Cloud recoiled. 'Why would they be looking here?'

Drabble and Harris left the question unanswered. A further possibility occurred to Drabble just then: the chief and his son could still have stolen the artefacts, but simply taken the precaution of storing them securely elsewhere. That was common enough practice for passengers with valuables on a ship such as this.

'Black Cloud ...' Drabble waited until the chief gave him his full attention and eye contact was made. Now it was his turn to fly a kite. 'Your son says you were angry with Dr Yorke because he refused to sell you Sitting Bull's shirt and pipe.'

He left it there. Black Cloud's expression did not falter.

'I was angry,' he stated, 'at his stubbornness – stubbornness in the face of my justified request.' Nothing in his tone or expression acknowledged the fact that just forty-eight hours before he had convincingly claimed no knowledge whatsoever of the existence of the artefacts in the museum, let alone their curator. Neither Drabble nor Harris acknowledged it either. 'I offered to pay him the same money that the museum had paid for them, more in fact, but he refused. And yet this was a man who claimed to be a supporter of the Indians.' He shook his head. 'It made me crazy.'

Drabble glanced over at Harris. 'Did he mention any enemies he might have?'

'Why should he?'

'Why,' asked Harris, '*in particular*, did you want Sitting Bull's things? Why are they so important to you?'

A smile came to Black Cloud's lips. 'I knew Sitting Bull. I can remember him smoking that pipe, wearing that war shirt at Greasy Grass. When I was told they were in the museum I knew I had to see them. But soon my thanks at their survival was replaced by a burning sense of fury and anger. What were they doing there – behind a glass wall? They should be with my people, I said. They belonged to us. They should never have been sold.' His old leathery hand went to his breast. 'But it was Yorke that made me really angry. He claimed to be a friend of the Indian, but instead he was a betrayer.'

Black Cloud lit a cigarette.

'In what way did he betray you?' asked Drabble.

'By pretending to friendship and then refusing us basic kindness. He acted without honour.'

There was a pause and then Harris asked, 'Are you sad to be giving up the Wild West Show?'

Black Cloud lifted his chin, the skin of his neck tautening. 'No. I look forward to retirement. I have bought a cabin in the Black Hills – where I will be at one with the Great Spirit. I have had my fill of the world – and if you'll forgive me – of the *wasichus*. Now all I want is to be alone.'

Drabble and Harris went out on deck. As the sea breeze hit their faces they traded the same expression of gloom. Harris went first.

'I hate to admit it, old man,' he sighed, 'much as it's all very interesting, we really aren't making much progress, are we?'

'Any slower and we'd be going in backwards,' stated Drabble dismally.

They reached a crossroads where the deck continued straight on to the stern – but there was a route either way. Harris pulled out his pocket watch.

'Well . . .' he began thoughtfully. 'It's a touch early for a drink and I've got plenty for the paper. They'll love the eyewitness stuff about the Battle of Little Bighorn. Our readers love schadenfreude – particularly when it's American.' His eyes glistened behind his gold-rimmed spectacles. 'So, I think I'll head back to the cabin and start writing the story up now. They'll be hungry for copy in London and one should oblige.' He cleared this throat. 'We are travelling First, after all.'

Harris slipped away and waved back at Drabble. 'See you at luncheon, pal.'

He was gone before Drabble remembered he had already arranged to see Charlotte for lunch. Oh, well. Harris would figure it out. Which was more than they were achieving with this investigation, if such was the word for it. Perhaps it didn't matter all that much. Harris had enough for his newspaper, and Drabble ... well, he had found Charlotte.

'Excuse me ...'

Drabble turned and saw a sympathetic face; it was the lean face of a man who could easily have been a bachelor master at a half decent public school – one of those quiet sort given to surprising fits of exuberance when reciting extracts of the *Iliad* or the *Odyssey*. He raised his trilby, revealing a brush of sandy hair that was parted reluctantly.

'The name's Walberswick – do you have time for a quick cuppa?'

They found a table in the corner of the deck café where the day before Drabble had lunched with Charlotte, and Walberswick introduced himself properly. He leaned in close and spoke in a low, urgent tone.

'I'm with the Foreign Office –' He gave a sideways glance, enough to invite suspicion, and dropped two sugar cubes into his cup of tea. 'The reason we're here, *chatting*, is because something is going on that we rather need your help with.' He cleared his throat. 'I have it on authority that you can be a useful man to have onside in a tight spot, what?'

Drabble nodded, inviting Walberswick to continue.

'I was contacted a little while ago by colleagues in the

Dominions Office, in particular by some chaps in Manitoba, about a situation arising there that they are concerned with.' He looked over his shoulder at a couple taking up the seats at an adjacent table and lowered his voice. 'Something fishy is going on with the Indians. We don't know what, *quite*, but something's afoot.'

Walberswick set his teacup back into its saucer, and resumed.

'You are familiar, I dare say, with the Ghost Dance phenomenon of the late 1880s? Well, what we hear is something similar is going on now. It's just rumours really, but a theme is emerging. Whereas the message preached back then was essentially pacifistic – you know, you do the dance for three days, then all will come good – now they've got a rather more bellicose approach. The other major difference is that then it was all pretty much out in the open. Now, thanks to bitter experience, the new dance is being kept firmly under wraps.'

Walberswick coughed into his fist and then lowered his voice to a whisper. 'So what we're looking at here is the fanaticism of the Ghost Dance, but now it's clandestine ... and there's something else, too.' He paused theatrically. 'They've got guns.'

'Guns?'

Walberswick nodded distastefully. 'Yes. They're trying to arm themselves. And I don't just mean a few extra hunting rifles. We have it on good information that the Indians tapped up the Italians to see about getting some of theirs. Beretta said no, thank God. They tipped us off.'

'That was good of them ...'

'An informal channel,' he announced, tightening his lips. 'From what we can ascertain, this new Ghost Dance originated in the United States – it's not a Canadian show, which is a relief to our brothers in Ottawa, but obviously we are worried about the potential for trans-border *leakage*, which is why we are taking an interest in it. It could be very damaging for British-Canadian interests, so we need to ensure it's contained. From what we can tell it's likely the Sioux will be involved, not least since they got their fingers burnt so badly last time.'

Which meant that they suspected Black Cloud and his followers of being involved, otherwise what was Walberswick doing here? Quite how Black Cloud, or presumably Speaks With Fists, would go about trying to negotiate the assistance of hostile powers left Drabble at a loss. Moreover, from what he had read, the United States was awash with guns – mightn't it be simpler to source them there?

The Foreign Office man topped up their tea.

'So, a question, Professor . . .' Two more sugar cubes plopped into Walberswick's cup. 'Would you consider extending your stay in the United States? If you could square it with Sir Percival, I'm sure you would find a field trip to South Dakota most enlightening.'

Drabble knew Harris would be a pushover. He couldn't say the same of the Master of his college, Sidney Sussex, but he wouldn't ask for permission.

'I think it can be managed.' Drabble realised he would like nothing more than to see the Black Hills of South Dakota for himself.

They parted company at the doorway of the tea shop. Walberswick pressed an envelope hastily into Drabble's hand.

'You'll be able to reach me, day or night, at the embassy in Washington DC. That's got my details in it.'

Drabble waited for him to leave before finding a quiet corner to investigate the envelope. Inside was Walberswick's business card – 'Captain H. Walberswick, Cultural Attaché, British Embassy, Washington, DC' – and a slim wedge of US bank notes. Drabble slid the envelope into his pocket, and permitted his eyes to travel to the broad blue horizon. A new ghost dance, but this time with guns? Harris was going to have kittens when he told him about this.

Chapter Eleven

Harris freed the last page of his story from the typewriter and admired the closing passage. Not bad. Not bad at all … He topped up his Scotch. His editor was going to love it, especially the betrayal, the blood, and the detailed eyewitness stuff from Custer's Last Stand. He leafed back to the start and grinned as he took in the first paragraph:

> *Is this the man who killed Colonel Custer? He doesn't admit it, but you can't help feeling the Chief Black Cloud is a man of secrets, many held for decades … '*

Harris tossed the proofs down onto this desk, and cracked his knuckles. An excellent morning's work. He yawned and rolled his head, stretching his neck. He finished the whisky and spied the clock. It was time for a proper drink and a spot of lunch. Now … where did Drabble say they were meeting?

He was at the door before realising that he and Drabble had not specified where they were meeting. Come to think of it, they hadn't made a plan at all. Or had they? He closed the cabin door behind him and made his way out on deck. Had he imagined it? He had, hadn't he? That was a bit rum.

Harris scowled. He didn't much fancy lunching alone, especially not after such an industrious morning. And if Drabble wasn't having lunch with him, then who was he having it with?

Harris performed a one hundred and eighty degree turn – a half pirouette, so that he now pointed aft. It wasn't like Drabble to be so secretive, or, perish the thought, *underhand*.

He set off. What the dickens was Drabble up to?

Harris quickly arrived at the Restaurant – the one in which they had dined for the last two evenings. Here lunch was served, but Harris wasn't convinced it would be Drabble's first choice – it was too grand for his socialist pretensions – but you never knew. All those college high suppers might have turned him, if they hadn't put him off for life.

Harris swooped in through the heavy rotating doors, steeling himself for whatever he might find ... and was confronted by an impenetrable sea of heads and the powerful white noise of collective conviviality. His temper worsened as he scanned the room. A waiter approached.

'Is sir *looking* for someone?'

Harris scowled and turned to the waiter ...

Sitting at a table for two in the Café Bruxelles on B Deck not two hundred yards away, Drabble heard the door open and craned his head to see. It was not Charlotte. Again. He inspected the menu card and laid it down. He already knew what he was having. He looked about the room to distract himself ... the wicker-framed tables and accompanying chairs, and the very realistic-looking plastic ivy crawling across cream painted trellises.

What would they talk about today? The day before they had both done a fairly comprehensive trawl through their respective biographies, but there was doubtless still more to mine, albeit fresh topics might be preferable. For obvious reasons the investigation with Harris was off limits. His mind went back to the conversation with Walberswick just moments before. Now he thought about it, could he share the details with Harris? Could he really be trusted to ...

'Ernest?'

Charlotte was suddenly standing before him, dressed in a fetching olive green mohair suit, and stripping off a pair of tan leather gloves. She smiled. 'Hope I'm not late.'

Drabble drew out her chair – she slipped in – and he caught her perfume lingering in the air.

They sat looking at one another, taking each other in. Drabble broke into a wide smile.

'Oh, stop it,' she laughed. 'I'm an historian, I don't meet strange men on ocean liners.'

'Who says I'm strange!'

'The circumstances are. What *would* my mother say?'

'I'd be more worried about your father.'

'You shouldn't be.' She looked at him seriously over the menu. 'Now,' her eyes narrowed, 'do you think we should have wine? I don't have anything planned for the rest of the afternoon, do you?'

'Champagne?'

'Champagne? I didn't realise it was a special occasion. I'd have worn a new hat.'

He ordered a bottle of Veuve Clicquot and waited as Charlotte examined the menu.

Yesterday he had considered her to be a quiet beauty, but on second viewing, he realised that that was an understatement bordering on gross negligence. Charlotte was as handsome a woman as you could hope to find. She was blessed with one of those delicate autumnal complexions, the sort that would never quite prosper in the sun, and her wide lips were dark pink . . .

'What is it?' she asked, before reading the expression on Drabble's face. She giggled into her menu – and blushed. 'Oh, goodness. We're going to have to pull ourselves together, aren't we?'

'Speak for yourself!' He smiled. 'I'm having the devilled mushrooms.'

'We're having starters?' She frowned at the crisp menu card. 'Starters *and* champagne? I must be going up in your estimation.'

'There's also pudding, if you can manage it.'

'Pudding?' She smirked. 'My mother told me about men like you.'

'This mother of yours seems rather opinionated.'

'I did warn you.'

Drabble flashed her a smile – but then his face dropped, as his gaze settled on the space in the window directly above Charlotte's head.

Harris . . .

Drabble glared.

Charlotte turned immediately – but just as she did so, Harris bobbed out of view. She turned back to Drabble.

'Is everything all right?'

Before he could answer the waiter arrived with the champagne and filled their glasses. Harris reappeared in the window and scowled at the bottle, mouthing the words, 'Veuve Clicquot!'

Drabble raised his glass and smiled, 'Cheers!'

They touched glasses, and when he glanced back at the window Harris had gone. That was better. Drabble exhaled, feeling himself relax, and sipped his champagne.

Charlotte smiled at him, but then her focus shifted.

'What ho!' Harris clapped a hand on Drabble's shoulder. 'Don't get up –' He reached forward, shaking Charlotte's hand and then yanked over a chair. 'Veuve Clicquot –' He grinned, clicking his fingers at the waiter. '*My favourite.*'

Harris beamed at Charlotte and turned to his friend. 'Come now, Ernest, are you going to introduce us, or do I have to do that myself as well?'

Harris reached for his pipe. He had been 'interviewing' Charlotte for several minutes and already covered several of the essential details. Now he moved in for the kill.

'And how did you two meet?' He addressed only Charlotte.

'I'm afraid to say that Ernest has turned rather secretive of late and most rudely *not* mentioned he was lunching with you today, otherwise –' he now addressed Drabble, 'I would have made alternative arrangements.'

Harris dispatched this comment with a verve that made Charlotte smile. 'As a matter of fact, Harris, we met properly yesterday – but I recognised your friend here from a lecture he gave in Oxford a couple of years ago.'

'Ah, the famous Magdalen lecture. Does that mean that you are *an historian* as well?' Harris's tone made it clear that he had no expectation that this was the case. But then she smiled her confirmation and his mouth couldn't have fallen open further. 'Goodness me –' Harris shot a look of questionable courtesy to Drabble. 'Now I know why he never invites me along.' He smiled and so did Charlotte, evidently not offended. Harris took a sideways glance at Drabble. 'Didn't take you long to find your sea legs did it, did it, old man?'

The waiter approached with a menu for Harris – but Drabble waved him away. Charlotte leaned in, concerned.

'Oh, Ernest, please don't feel you need to evict your friend on my account –'

Harris beamed like a cat in aviary.

'Unfortunately, *Sir Percival* has forgotten that he actually has a lunch appointment with his good acquaintance, Major Sakamoto, who is sitting just over by the door of this very restaurant – and waiting for him.'

Harris looked over and clocked him. 'By Jove, Drabble –' He brightened. 'It's all coming back to me.' He got up to leave. 'Perhaps, Dr Moore, we could have a drink tomorrow instead?'

A little while later, Harris was struggling to give Sakamoto his full attention. Instead he found himself looking over at his old friend and the young woman in the fedora. It was a rum matter, make no mistake. What was Drabble thinking? Had he been drinking? The man hadn't so much *looked* at a female of the species since the sad and unfortunate business with Miss H more than a year before. And now look at him. He couldn't take his eyes off her. He was besotted. And look at *her* ... nice enough on a wet afternoon in Margate but no great beauty. Certainly *not* a beauty of the first order – and certainly not worth dropping your friend for.

Harris seized a piece of bread and tore it savagely in half.

Look at her ... She was scrawny for a start – no bust to speak of. Was Drabble blind? Had he been staring at the sun? Harris frowned and attempted to imagine making love to the willowy, dark-haired blonde before him. No. It just wasn't happening. He shook his head and made fleeting eye contact with Sakamoto, just to show him he was still listening. No, the sea air must have got to Drabble. Or perhaps the altitude from all that time he'd spent in the Alps had finally addled his brain.

Harris slurped down some fizz. Hmmm, perhaps she was *almost* attractive. But it was a struggle. He took another bob of his fizz and nodded at 'Sako' to demonstrate his attention.

The worst of it was Drabble's secretiveness, because it pointed in one direction. Look at him! Look at the ridiculous, cooing tilt of the head. The man was smitten, *smitten* like a love-struck puppy harpooned by Cupid and punch-drunk on Circe's lotus juice.

Harris was struck by a fresh realisation. Christ alive. *Drabble was falling in love.* And if that reached its logical conclusion, then it meant only one thing ...

Harris froze, resisting the penetration of the dread M-word into his grey matter. It couldn't be. No, *no*. The girl suddenly threw back her head in paroxysm of laughter – and Drabble followed suit, guffawing like his ruddy life depended on it. Christ alive, thought Harris. How happy the stupid sod looked ...

'Sir Percival?' It was Sakamoto, apparently concerned. 'Is everything quite fine?'

Harris met his gaze and forced a smile. 'Yes, yes . . .'

But it wasn't. After nearly twenty years of friendship – a friendship born on that very first day at Lancing in the autumn of 1918, when the two of them eyed each other suspiciously on the stairs outside the dormitory, Drabble was about to be lost to him. They were pals – brothers. Harris swallowed and blinked back tears.

But it hadn't quite been the first day at Lancing. No. Though they had shared the same corner of the same long dormitory in the same house for the first weeks and months, Drabble had been decidedly reticent about extending the hand of friendship to Harris. In fact, he tended to keep himself to himself.

Then came the fateful argument. They had been chatting after lights out on Armistice Day, and Harris had made a disobliging comment about the Dutch: well, why not – after all, they had remained neutral throughout the Great War. In reply Drabble had made some off-hand comment about the Dutch king of England, which had raised Harris's hackles.

'No Dutchman has ever ruled England!' he bellowed with contempt, before a bet was laid for five shillings on the facts. Then with the help of an encyclopaedia, the truth was out. That Harris, then aged twelve, had not heard of William of Orange could not be held against him. Unfortunately, he still refused to back down, instead insisting that by definition William's nationality changed upon his receipt of the English throne.

No one was convinced.

So when Harris continued to refuse to pay up it could have come to fisticuffs there and then. But Harris suggested something more romantic, and something that might suit him better; a duel at dawn the following morning.

'We'll fence Prussian style,' he fumed. 'Bare-chested, without masks – and to the first cut.'

It is a fair bet that Drabble could have soundly beaten Harris in a boxing match, and they both knew it. But fencing was Harris's bag – and that levelled the playing field, a little.

The next morning, as they stood there in the freezing cold in the school's grounds confronting the reality of their hot-blooded decision-making the night before – neither of them backed down.

When their referee called 'En garde!', they ghosted each other back and forth, keeping well clear of each other's points. Suddenly Drabble sallied forward with a direct attack that was frankly childish. He lunged, his arm extending. Harris beat his blade aside, performed a neat *prise de fer* – a taking of the blade – and then disengaged and extended his own arm. Drabble, still advancing, went to parry this counter-attack – and Harris saw his moment. Without thinking, he evaded Drabble's blade, and straightened his arm ...

Harris's point landed hard on Drabble's forehead, just between his eyes. But his joy of triumph vanished precisely as the point struck home. Harris whimpered in horror, dropped his sword, and shrank backwards. Meanwhile Drabble's mouth fell open and he stood otherwise motionless, his eyes blinking inside the goggles.

'Bugger!' he spluttered at last. '*Bugger* ...' Just then he collapsed to his knees, gripping his forehead, bowed in pain. 'You rotter, Harris!'

But Harris didn't hear him.

He was doubled over, being aggressively sick. He scarcely had the courage to look over at Drabble for fear of what might have happened.

'I'm sorry,' he wailed between convulsions. 'I just didn't think ...'

He felt a pat on the shoulder and looked up. Through tear-soaked eyes he saw Drabble standing above him. His hand outstretched holding Harris's shirt.

On Drabble's forehead was an angry red blot where Harris's

point had landed. But no blood had been drawn. *He wasn't going to die!*

Harris's heart surged with relief.

'It's a miracle,' he beamed, as he got to his feet.

Drabble smiled.

On the way back to the dormitory. Harris asked Drabble if he had ever fenced before.

'Not really.'

Harris clapped him on the back. 'You're a good sport, Drabble. Here —' He pulled out a five-shilling note from his pocket and handed it over.

And after that they became friends.

Major Sakamoto cleared his throat.

'So, what do you say to that, Sir Percival?'

Harris's brain managed to catch hold of the power of speech and suppress the imploding sensation of doom overtaking him. '*Fascinating!*' he pronounced with all solemnity. He turned his full attention to his luncheon companion: 'And something else, too —' He rescued the bottle of champagne from the ice bucket. 'But I do believe that the ivy in this room is real.'

On the other side of the restaurant, lunch was progressing well. Drabble and Charlotte had moved on to a half carafe of Beaujolais to accompany the lamb, which had held up nicely. Various episodes of their respective childhoods had been alighted upon, including Charlotte's upbringing in Cambridgeshire – 'I was a child of the Fens' – and they had emerged unscathed back in the present. Drabble asked: 'What did your father say when you told him you wanted to become a historian?'

'Not a lot, actually. I think he was quietly pleased. But he just wanted to be sure I wasn't doing it to please him.'

Drabble had known Charlotte's father since his undergraduate days and both liked and admired him. It must have been a brave decision to follow in the footsteps of such an eminent father. 'Were you?' he asked.

She didn't respond straight away. 'Perhaps it's inevitable that I followed my father into the past . . . if only to find him there.' Charlotte smiled a little sadly and Drabble believed he understood.

She brightened. 'And what about yours – what did your father say when you told him?'

'My father?' Drabble thought back. 'I don't think I ever discussed it with him, funnily enough.'

She lifted her eyebrows quizzically.

'Both my parents were in India, so I barely saw them after I was five. We exchanged letters, but my mother was the letter writer; still is.' He smiled. 'I might have discussed it with my aunts, who were my legal guardians. I think Aunt Dorothy was particularly keen. Aunt Olive had always wanted me to be a doctor. I'm certain my father approves now. Back then, he probably regarded university as a waste of time – and money. I'm sure he would have been happier if I'd followed him into the Indian Army but that was never going to happen.'

'When did you last see him?'

'In April, in India.'

'India? What were you doing *there*?'

'Ah –' Drabble reached for his wine glass. 'Now that's another story altogether . . .'

Major Sakamoto and Harris addressed themselves to two species of fish: plaice in the case of the former, and turbot for the latter.

'Tell me, Sir Percival – how are your journalistic probings progressing?' The diplomat leaned over. 'Is it true you joined the ship in the hope of shedding some light on the American Indian robberies that took place in London before we departed?'

Harris dabbed the corner of his mouth with his napkin.

How interesting to see Sakamoto fishing for information! He smiled. 'Major, I didn't know you were a devotee of American Indian affairs?'

Sakamoto shrugged and tilted his head, communicating a decided blitheness as to whether or not Harris answered. Harris chuckled and forked a slab of turbot and spinach.

Pudding dispatched, Drabble and Charlotte had coffee and she smoked a cigarette. It was gone three o'clock.

'Shall we have a walk?' he asked.

Charlotte smiled. 'Take in some sea air?'

She took his arm as they exited the brasserie, as naturally as anything – but it gave Drabble a thrill every bit as real as reaching the summit of a mountain. Emerging on to the deck the day now seemed colder, perhaps a little breezier too, but he didn't feel it. Charlotte pressed into him, her gloved hands were folded over his. He felt her breath on his face – noticing the faintest smudge of red wine on the corner of her mouth. It was a beautiful smudge. He caught her gaze.

'What are you looking at?'

'You . . .'

She smiled at him and laughed bashfully.

They walked arm-in-arm until they reach the foredeck. They then turned down the starboard deck, the wind now blowing over their backs. For a while they walked in contented silence. Slowly, Charlotte came to a stop by a doorway.

'This is me –' She smiled and looked up at him. 'It's been a wonderful lunch, thank you again.'

They broke apart and stood looking at one another. She stood before him, smiling, the stiff breeze blowing her dancing hair across her face. How he wanted to kiss her . . .

'It was a lovely lunch,' he said again, feeling the need to fight off the bittersweet prospect of their imminent parting.

Her smiled faded and she pursed her lips.

'Would you like to come in for a cup of tea?' The tone of her voice was almost formal but there was tension – Drabble could see it written on her face and in the way her throat constricted a little. And that was fair enough; under such circumstances, tea was potentially a very open offer indeed.

They started for the doorway, Charlotte's pace quickening. But then at her cabin door, she abruptly turned to him, her eyes filled with tears.

'I'm so sorry, Ernest. I've had such a lovely time ...' She smiled, shaking her head.

Gently, he took her hands and smiled. 'What is it?'

But he already knew what it was. She was having second thoughts about whatever it was she had planned for them, or where it might lead. Which was understandable. Under the normal laws of propriety a spinster such as Charlotte should certainly never permit a bachelor into what was effectively her bedroom, for tea – or anything else for that matter. And tea was the last thing on Drabble's mind, and, he assumed, hers.

Drabble drew her closer and she turned her head up, so that her mouth was but an inch or two from his. He saw her lips part and wanted to kiss them. And he knew he was going to. Her warm breath stroked his mouth and he leaned forward. Their lips touched.

Drabble shut his eyes as she returned the pressure on his lips, and he felt her mouth open ...

She broke away, wiping her lips.

'Charlotte?' He stepped towards her. He wanted to do that again. 'Whatever it is, I promise you it'll be fine –'

'No it won't be *fine*!' Her eyes flashed testily at him. She turned away, unlocking the door. 'It won't be *fine*,' she went in, leaving the door ajar, 'but it will have to do.'

Drabble shut the door behind him, hearing the latch click into place, and meeting the smell of perfume and lavender. He took off his hat. She had already removed her gloves and stood before the mirror unpinning her hat. Laying the brown fedora aside, she turned towards him, the faintest of smiles on her full mouth, and plucked his hat from his hand and tossed it across the room.

'Forgive me,' she said, though she didn't look like forgiveness was foremost on her mind as she put her arms around his neck. 'I don't know what came over me.'

Drabble pulled her to him and their mouths met once more. This time no one broke away and as their kisses continued, they moved, step by step, towards the bed. Falling back upon it, Charlotte smiled at him – her eyes bright, sunny, and confident.

'I think you should take off your overcoat . . .' She started unbuttoning her jacket.

The coat fell to the floor.

'What about my shoes?'

Some times in life a question needs no answer.

Drabble followed Charlotte hastily onto the bed. She wriggled free of her jacket and pushed it off the side of the bed, taking his face in her hands and plunging her lips onto his, taking gasping kisses. He was now on top of her and her blouse was free – he felt the bare, warm skin of her back with his hand. She pulled her mouth away and inspected his ardent face. She was breathing hard and her breasts were rising and falling beneath the blouse. Drabble couldn't take his eyes off her.

'Do you think, perhaps, you should take that off?' he asked

She smirked and began to unbutton her blouse.

'And might you remove your jacket and tie? This isn't the senior common room.'

He pulled off his college tie and slung his jacket to the floor.

'And now it's time for the shoes?' he asked, gazing at her nipples showing through the pale brassiere.

Charlotte shook her head playfully and gripped his waist-band, which she unbuttoned quicker than one might have expected a woman in her position to do.

Drabble felt her hand glide up his leg.

He exhaled – and leaned in to kiss her. His hand went to her thigh, reached the band at the top of her stockings – and then continued. Charlotte exhaled sharply.

'Oh, my God –' She broke into a giggle. 'Oh, Ernest, don't stop, whatever you do . . .'

Harris had watched the 'love-bores' depart. They had looked every bit as enamoured on leaving as they had throughout the gaudy display over lunch. He growled under his breath. Something would have to be done to prevent the match – and fast. He reached for the port and topped up his glass. Plus she looked boring. Probably frigid. I mean, for Christ's sake, *she was an historian*. You couldn't expect a thoroughbred in the bedroom – like Fanny Howell almost certainly was – under those circumstances.

He would talk Drabble out of it. It was as simple as that. Oh yes, that's the spirit, he thought. After the realisation, depression, but then the fight.

Sakamoto was looking pretty fresh despite his portion – a half bottle of champagne followed by a half bottle of white burgundy, then an equal share in the bottle of Bordeaux and then whatever they'd got through so far of the bottle of 1912 Warre's. Harris had spotted it on the wine list and despite the cost, had insisted so that Sakamoto could taste 'some of the very finest port wine ever artificed by man'.

'Do you always talk like this?' asked Sakamoto.

'Only when I'm tiddled.'

When the port arrived, Sakamoto had given it a good sniff and then took down a couple of inches like it was lemonade. He pursed his lips.

'It's not sake,' he remarked. 'But it's not bad, for port.'

'Not bad? Pitt the Younger would have given away York-shire for a thimble of this stuff.'

'If you say so.' Sakamoto put his cigar to his lips and smoke drifted from his mouth. He leaned in and spoke with delicious conspiratorial relish, 'Do you know that we are building four new aircraft carriers and two new battleships?'

Harris confessed that he didn't.

'The battleships will be the biggest, most powerful, and fast-est ever built. I have seen the aircraft carriers myself. They are so long, they make you go cross-eyed.'

'Impressive,' replied Harris, absently. He dabbed at his cigar, and wondered what Fanny Howell was up to. Eventually his mind went to the general thrust of Sakamoto's comments. 'You don't think there'll be war, do you? We don't want war.'

'Well why would you?' Sakamoto emitted a dry chuckle, like a small dog choking on chestnut. 'You British have every-thing you want already. Therefore war is the last thing you desire. But that doesn't mean it won't happen.' He noted Har-ris's expression. 'Don't worry, Sir Percival, I'm sure we'll all still be friends at the end of it.' Sakamoto took a sip of his port. 'You know it's not bad. What year did you say it was?'

'1912.'

'Ah, yes, the year your Captain Scott was beaten to the South Pole – *and* the *Titanic* went down.'

Harris frowned and came to a realisation: he and Major Sakamoto were not going to be friends – not now, nor at the end of it all, whenever that was.

'Ernest.'

Charlotte lay looking at the ceiling, still getting her breath back. Her chest was rising and falling and her head was in the nook of his arm.

'Yes.'

'Would you pass me my handbag?'

Drabble reached down from the bed and lifted up her small leather handbag.

'Thank you.' Charlotte propped herself up on one elbow. Several strands of her hair were matted to the side of her face, which was still flushed. She took out a packet of cigarettes and a lighter and then tossed the bag off the bed. Lighting one of them, she inhaled, her ribcage pushing her small breasts towards Drabble's face. As if invited he smoothed his hand across them, gently feeling the sensation of her nipples under his fingers. They were, he noticed, the same shade of pink as her lips, and he wondered if that was true of all women. His mind went back . . .

'What are you thinking?'

'Oh,' he looked at her adoringly, 'about . . . nipples.'

She smiled into her cigarette.

'Do you like nipples?'

'Definitely. What about you?'

'Yours are rather handsome, not unlike yourself . . .' She pursed her lips approvingly, and kissed him. 'It's nearly five. Would you like that cup of tea?'

'I thought that's what you invited me in here for.'

She raised an eyebrow at him. 'No you didn't.'

Charlotte crawled forwards, cigarette still in her mouth, and he watched, enjoying the view as she stepped from up from the end of the bed. She pulled on a dressing gown, and went into the adjacent cabin.

Drabble lay back down. Over the sound of an electric kettle and crockery, he heard another noise – that of wind buffeting the ship. A dullish, flat light now came in from the porthole, so the sunshine was gone. He repositioned the pillows and leaned back, waiting for Charlotte, basking in the sheer delight of what had just passed between them.

When she returned with the tea, the floor moved sharply as

the ship lurched. Charlotte recovered her footing, but one of the teacups tumbled from its saucer and broke on the floor. Drabble rescued the other and steadied the tray – as the ship pitched the other way. Through the porthole he saw dark clouds mustering on the horizon. A storm was coming.

Chapter Twelve

Harris steadied himself at the threshold of the restaurant and blinked down at the floor: the ground seemed to be moving of its own accord. No ... the ground *was* moving of its own accord. Feeling the fresh air collide with his face, he noted that where once the sky had been the azure blue of the Madonna's robes in a Sienese altarpiece, it was now an unforgiving, Boschian pewter. Not only that, but the bloody boat was moving about like a startled sheep on ice. Harris gripped the handrail and muttered to himself.

'Come on, old chum, you can do it.'

The ship lurched and Harris danced left, juddering to a halt just before the wall. He held on and bowed his head as if in prayer – but it was all concentration. It was only a couple of hundred yards and a flight of stairs, he told himself. He could make it. Keeping his left hand trained on the wall, he moved off, attempting to anticipate the roll of the vessel. There she goes ...

He staggered right, but he went too fast, and stumbled. Falling to one knee in the lee of the handrail, he braced himself with his hands, getting his breath back. The Warre's had been a bad idea.

Holding the rail – now *that* was a plan – Harris moved along the deck, slowly. He was, he realised, decidedly squiffy. In fact, he further realised, the last time he was this drunk must have been on the return voyage from Bombay – crossing the Indian

Ocean. Then he'd had the heat to contend with too. That *had* been an ordeal ...

The ship pitched – he lunged for the handrail, but missed and tumbled to the deck, his arms windmilling.

He came to a hard stop and lay still, his eyes closed, in pain but grateful. His shoulder was smarting but nothing had been broken. Slowly, he began to get up, reaching his hands and knees. A small triumph, he decided, as he waited for the ship's roll to come back the other way, and for more energy to come to his limbs.

Suddenly strong hands heaved Harris to his feet and an American voice boomed in his ear, cutting through the howling wind:

'Let me assist you, Sir Percival!'

Harris felt his feet slip limply underneath him as the chap lifted him along the deck. Harris looked over at his good Samaritan, but could see nothing except for the dark silhouette of the man's head looming over him. Despite the fog of booze – the one that denied him much of his physical dexterity as well as a fair wedge of his cerebral capacity – an unwelcome sensation dawned on Harris. He was afraid.

'*I say,*' he slurred, raising his voice to address the American. 'How did you know my name?'

At that very moment Drabble finally departed from Charlotte's cabin.

He ventured out on the deck – clamping down his hat to stop it being swept out to the Azores. The wind was every bit as ferocious as he had feared it might be.

Stewards were out securing seating and closing shutters in preparation for the worst of it, but already much of the deck furniture had been tidied away or tied down. Above his head the lifeboats jerked uneasily from their davits, buffeted by the gusts and thrown by the awkward roll of the ship.

But the storm was somehow life-affirming in its sheer enormity and vigour, especially after the afternoon he had had, and there was a majestic brutality to the moiling black clouds rushing overhead. Thunder cracked in the heavens above and rain began peppering the deck. Within seconds it intensified and Drabble broke into a sprint. He reached the passageway leading to their cabin before the deluge hit, and bounded in through the door.

'Harris!'

Harris awoke with a snort and realised he'd been snoring. His throat was sore and his head pounded. 'Oh, Lord . . . Lord have mercy.' His eyes remained steadfastly shut, the pain was simply to crushing. 'Water, I *need* water!' He tried to reach out, to grope blindly for an unseen glass, knowing that if he opened his eyes he would be overwhelmed. 'Ernest,' he whispered hoarsely. '*Help me* . . . I'm dying. Oh, God –'

The stabbing pain was positively savage. Harris grimaced, imagining himself to be Irving's dying Romeo, and lay still, his eyes watering. Don't cry, he told himself, shaking his head again. Don't waste it. Every drop is vital. 'Water,' he moaned. 'I need water . . .'

Suddenly, a great wave of water broke over him – colliding with his face and soaking him to the skin. His eyes opened and he realised he wasn't in darkness – not quite. He also realised that he couldn't move; he was bloody well tied down. Then, as the water cleared from his eyes and they adjusted to the low light, he saw a figure sitting in the shadows – and those last moments on deck came flooding back to him.

Harris was no stranger to fear, and it hit him immediately. His heart led the way, breaking into a trot that became a sprint, and then his stomach tightened like uncooked haggis. He caught his breath.

'I–I say,' he declared. 'Wh-wha-what-what's g-going on here?'

The voice that replied carried a calm, other-worldly quality. 'Why don't you tell us, Sir Percival?'

Harris recognised the neutral American accent from the deck – in fact, he doubted he'd ever forget those particularly neglected consonants. Then for some reason, the fearful pulsating of his heart ceased, and he realised he was angry.

'*Excuse me* –' he said, turning on his odious captor with all the imperious grandeur of a Knight of the Order of the Bath *and* a Knight – grand cross, for God's sake! – of the Order of the Star of India. 'How dare you!'

Another bucket of water slammed into Harris's face, washing over him. He caught a mouthful, and choked. Coughing hard, his chest heaved painfully and he strained against the ropes tying him down. His head pounded and his throat, already sore, now stung. As his breathing settled, though, he discovered that he also possessed a deep yearning for nicotine, one that was coalescing in the saliva gathering at the back of his throat and in the pockets of his cheeks.

'If you cooperate, Sir Percival, I can assure you this will be a much more pleasant experience,' the voice said placidly. 'We had no option but to tie you down after you blacked out, for your own safety. There's a storm going on out there, you know?'

'And who are "we"?' stated Harris acidly.

'The ones who are asking the questions.' The man lit a cigarette and in the flickering flame Harris saw a hard, broad face. 'You want a smoke?'

'No.'

This was not the moment to lose authority or to show weakness by accepting gifts. But catching the smell of the other man's cigarette – it was a Lucky Strike, Harris knew – he regretted his pride and had to fight the urge to inhale the delicious swirls of drifting smoke. Christ, he needed to smoke.

'Why are you on the ship, Sir Percival?'

'I'm not going to answer any questions until you identify

yourself.' Harris lifted his chin and held his lips together in a manner that indicated resolution in young children.

By Christ, he wanted to smoke.

'That's not gonna be possible, Sir Percival. Nor are we going to tolerate your refusal to answer questions.' The man inhaled, the end of the cigarette burned keenly. Harris could hear the tiny fire tearing through the rich mixture of tobacco and paper. He sucked in the air between his lips ... ohhh ...

'Sir Percival?'

'Yes –' He turned to answer the summons.

A switch flicked and a piercing light suddenly swamped Harris, blinding him. He yelped ...

'Sir Percival –' the voice was firmer now. 'Tell us the purpose of your journey to the United States aboard the SS *Empress of the Atlantic*.'

Harris squinted miserably towards his questioner, his head pounding, his throat fizzing from tobacco withdrawal. He was panting like a dog.

'I'm here to interview the Sioux Indian Chief Black Cloud,' he mumbled, feeling self-pity overcoming him. *Don't cry*, he told himself. *Have some ruddy dignity, you cur* – 'for my newspaper, the *London Evening Express*.' He swallowed, the saliva was massing on his gums and he knew he was about to blub.

'Are you sure you wouldn't like a cigarette, Sir Percival?'

'No,' winced Harris, his eyes brimming with tears. 'No!'

Something clicked in Harris's brain. It was the injustice of it all. And the sheer, ruddy *front*: to be kidnapped, to be restrained against his will, to be interrogated and tortured in such a fashion ... on board a British ship of all things! And don't forget that he was double knight – *a ruddy double knight!* – and a member of Her Britannic Majesty's press corps! Against this, such American aggression was not merely insufferable it was unconscionable. Countries had gone to war for less! Had this cur not heard of Don Pacifico, for God's sake? Harris turned to the light.

'Do you know who I am?'

The questioner said nothing. Harris heard the paper rustling of a cigarette packet and the man lit up. As he exhaled, he said, 'Just *fucking* tell us what you're really doing aboard the ship.'

'I've told you everything I am going to say.'

'OK, Sir Percival. That's fine. You should know that I have lots more buckets of water here.'

'Do your worst!'

'I also have other tools of persuasion at my disposal.'

Harris swallowed. 'Other tools of persuasion' did not sound good. The pitter-patter of his heart resumed, his stomach clenched – and he broke.

'Very well,' he blurted. 'I'll tell you whatever you want to know ...'

Drabble whistled to himself as he took a quick shower and then hurriedly got dressed. He was expected at the Captain's table for dinner in twenty minutes, so there wasn't time to dally – or dwell too much on the wonderful afternoon he had just had. Of Harris there was no sign, which was unusual, even for Harris. What Drabble did know, however, was that Harris hadn't already dressed for dinner and gone on ahead, because both his dinner suits were still in his wardrobe. This meant that they were most likely in for a repeat of yesterday's antics. But this time the post-lunch binge had stretched out even longer. It was gone seven already, and if Harris was still conscious, he'd be absolutely sunk by now ...

Drabble, still whistling cheerfully, departed for dinner, entirely unaware that this was truer than he could possibly have realised.

Delicious cigarette smoke was still clouding in the light. Harris lay gazing at the ceiling hoping it would all go away. The placid voice kept at it.

'Kindly confirm your plans for when you arrive in New York on Saturday?'

He looked over towards the light.

'I'm really not sure. I *think* we're just going to be in town for a few days, then we'll catch a ship back. It all depends on how I get on with Black Cloud.'

The man made no reply. Harris's eyes had adjusted and he could now perceive the outline of the interrogator's head and frame. Even sitting down, you could see he was a big fellow. The red dot of the end of the cigarette intensified and a fresh cloud of tobacco swirled towards him. *The bastard.*

'Describe the precise nature of your relationship with Major Sakamoto, the defence attaché at the Japanese embassy in London.'

Harris blinked.

'What?'

'Describe –'

'*No, no,* I heard what you ruddy well said –' Harris had adopted an unfortunately condescending tone. 'But I'm just baffled as to why on earth you would be faintly interested.'

A voice from the other side of the room intervened. It was also American but lighter, and certainly more refined.

'Kindly answer the question as comprehensively as you can, Sir Percival.'

Harris strained his head to look over but the figure was lost in shadow. He turned back towards the questioner behind the light.

'We are drinking companions,' he said bitterly.

'Had you made his acquaintance prior to boarding the SS *Empress of the Atlantic?*'

'Never.'

'You quite sure about that?'

'Absolutely.'

'And what about Black Cloud? When did you become associated with him?'

'*Associated?*' Harris's indignation flared. 'If you intended to mean, when did I first meet him, then it would have been Monday night. At the Earl's Court.'

Harris's tone had become decidedly testy. He did not like the line of questioning.

'Back to Major Sakamoto ... You both attended a dinner given by the Japanese Embassy at the Savoy on June the twenty-first. Do you deny that?'

'Did I?' Harris glowered at the questioner like he was a fool. 'How could I *possibly* ... I mean, I like the Savoy very much so it's perfectly possible that ... Yes, *yes* now you mention it, I *did* go, and the Japanese ambassador was the host. But, frankly, there were fifty other people there – and I had had a very, very, *very* good lunch that day at Simpson's. So I would struggle ... I certainly wouldn't remember every last Johnny who was there and Major Sakamoto certainly falls into that category, if indeed he was there at all, which I don't remember.'

'But you admit you were there.'

'I rather think I've done that, don't you?'

There was a pause. He saw his questioner turn his head towards the man in the corner. He cleared his throat.

'Just for the record, Sir Percival. Describe the precise nature of your association with Major Sakamoto.'

'For Christ's sake –' Harris's temper broke free from his tremulous hippocampus. 'The *precise nature of my association* with Major Sakamoto is one based on the mutual appreciation of alcoholic beverages when consumed in a convivial setting. Is that good enough for you?'

His words vanished into the silence. He heard a cough from the corner, then a second cough.

The questioner stood and approached him, his considerable bulk blocking out the light. He began unfastening Harris's feet.

'At last!'

The mighty hands – the sort that looked like they could

111

strangle a buffalo – next freed the knot binding Harris's chest. He sat up eagerly and reached out his bound wrists.

But they were pushed roughly aside.

'W–what?'

Harris was shoved forward from the bunk – and sent lurching to his feet. A chair scraped across the floor towards him and he was stuffed into it. He was about to protest when he saw the floor. Six buckets, each filled with water, were at his feet.

The questioner looked down and met Harris's gaze. This wasn't good news.

'Wh–wha–what's going on here?' stammered Harris. 'What are you doing?'

'You're going for a swim.'

'A swim!' roared Harris. 'You're going to have to do better than that! I'll have you know I've gargled in more U–bends than you've had hot dinners, you bison-strangling nitwit. A bucket of water doesn't frighten me. Go on, do you worst –'

The punch wasn't even a blur. Harris didn't see it coming. His stomach simply imploded, flipping him forward, his mouth wide open, gasping for air.

And that's when his head was plunged into the first bucket of water.

How long was he down there for? That was hard to know. It was an age. He pushed back, but the hand that pressed the crown of his head to the base of the bucket was stronger. Much stronger. Harris's legs started to twitch like a corpse dancing on a gibbet.

Then, suddenly, Harris was out. Coughing. Water gushing from his mouth. He *was* drowning, and he gasped for air, his throat making a long whooping sound that scared him. But it wasn't working. He still couldn't breathe. He tried to get air in – but instead of inhaling, he discovered he was being sick ... again and again. After each spasm, he attempted to draw breath, before being denied it by another spasm.

And that's when it dawned on him. Just as he got the first touch of air, and he realised he would live. He realised this was all Drabble's fault. If he hadn't been having lunch with the Moore woman, then Harris would not have had a four-hour luncheon with Sakamoto, which for reasons best known to these insane Americans, had thrown him into suspicion – a suspicion that merited ruddy water torture. Damn Drabble. Harris felt his wits returning and glared up at the Buffalo Strangler.

'Who are the dickens are you?' he bellowed. 'I've just vom-ited all over my best dinner trousers. On what possible authority are you doing this?'

There was silence. Harris, his breathing laboured, turned to the man in shadows.

'You …' he declared, realising his voice had come out a wraithlike whisper. 'Why the devil don't you show yourself? Come on –' he goaded. 'Show yourself, *you turd*. Sitting there, skulking in the shadows like some venal cockroach. Come on. Show yourself. Be a man!'

Once again Harris did not see the punch coming.

Chapter Thirteen

Most of the party had already assembled at the captain's table by the time Drabble got there. He saw Wheelock arrive but on this occasion they were placed on opposite sides of the table. Of Harris there was still no sign, and his place setting was removed after the first course, which Drabble regarded as a touch peremptory, if appropriate. It was gone eight o'clock now and Harris would be either be passed out or still drinking in one of the ship's bars – of which Drabble believed there to be at least half a dozen. He had resolved to visit them later if Harris had still not materialised, but he hoped it would not be necessary.

That's because instead of trawling the alcoholic crevices of the *Empress of the Atlantic* he hoped to visit Charlotte ... His mind drifted to the memories of the afternoon's surprising turn of events.

A waiter proffering a bottle of claret interrupted Drabble's reverie. He shook his head.

'Not drinking –' The statement came from the mature American woman on his left, in a tone that was both acerbic and mildly resentful. She adjusted her horn-rim spectacles and cleared her throat. 'I can't abide vegetarians *or* teetotallers.' A sliver of beef disappeared between her burgundy-painted lips. 'They make my skin crawl.'

Nodding, she chewed, and her ringed hand settled on her

mostly empty wine glass: 'You know we used to have Prohibition, don't you?'

'I read about it.'

'It was so boring.' She took a generous tilt of her wine. 'It lasted thirteen years but it felt like *fifty*. I mean, can you imagine – sober dinner parties? I had to stop going. In the end I told my husband that we would either have to emigrate or get a divorce.'

'What happened?'

'He died,' she erupted into laughter. 'Thank God! He never would have left New England.'

Harris came up for air. He realised he had lost consciousness because there was an inexplicable, foggy gap opening up in his memory. His eyes blinked as he gazed down at the buckets of water and he saw he had been sick again. His breathing was laboured. The wheezing was back. And there was something else rather pressing . . . It suddenly occurred to him that this might not all end up in a satisfactory manner. One really could drown like this, after all. One's remains could then be dispensed with over the side all too easily – and untraceably. Harris did not have a criminal mind. On the contrary, the rather embarrassing truth of the matter was that he suspected himself of being a touch guileless. Nonetheless it was beginning to occur to him that his life might be in some danger.

He turned to the Buffalo Strangler. 'Major Sakamoto loves to boast about the size of the Japanese navy – and their building programme. He says that a war won't be long coming. He also insists that the balance of power has shifted East. That I *can* tell you.'

'That's a good start, Sir Percival.' Harris saw his meaty hands rub together. 'Perhaps you would return to the original question and tell us more about your association with Major Sakamoto.'

Ah, yes. The association. Harris blinked down at the buckets. Think, man, *think*. He looked straight into the bright light.

'As you say —' He affected a sombre, dignified tone of defeat — thinking of Cornwallis at Yorktown. 'I met Major Sakamoto for the first time at the Savoy, at the aforementioned Embassy function. I remember being struck immediately by his impressive military bearing and his martial acumen.' Good, thought Harris. This was good. 'As you are doubtlessly aware, Sakamoto is an impressive individual with excellent vowels and punctilious consonants. Very quickly we were drawn to one another by our deep, mutual epicurean appreciation, but also because he was keen to pass information to me, which I could then make use of in my newspaper.'

The Buffalo Strangler nodded. 'Very good, Sir Percival. What information has he passed to you?'

Harris was afraid he might ask that . . .

'He told me that the Japanese ambassador's wife was a nymphomaniac —' He paused, letting the comment land, 'that she had attempted to seduce King Edward. I didn't get the sense that it was a political attack — rather, it was a flight of fancy. Unfortunately the closest the story got to making it into print was a sole reference to the ambassador's wife having "gregarious inclinations".'

'What else?'

Harris swallowed. 'Apparently, Emperor Hirohito is a massive fan of Ginger Rogers.'

'*Good, good* . . .'

'And Westerns in general — Oh, yes. The bloodier the better.'

The Buffalo Strangler appeared to weigh this up.

'As a matter of fact, has Major Sakamoto said anything to you about the Native Americans?'

Harris hesitated and was about to answer when the man started to repeat the question, more forcefully.

'What on earth would Sakamoto be interested in the Native Americans for?' Harris looked over at the unseen man in the corner and raised his eyebrows in withering dismay. 'For heaven's sake, the man is the defence attaché in *London*, there aren't many Native Americans there!'

Perhaps he ought to have concealed his utter contempt. The interrogator began to rise: 'You look like you could do with a drink, Sir Percival.'

'I say!' Harris brightened. 'And one of your Lucky Strikes would go down a treat!'

The Buffalo Strangler twisted the cap from a bottle of Famous Grouse and put it to Harris's mouth, which he gripped firmly.

'Here, let me help you . . .'

Escaping dinner at the earliest opportunity, Drabble returned to the cabin; Harris was still not back. Nor had he been to the cabin in the interim, unless he had been uncharacteristically tidy, which given his likely condition was incomprehensible.

So where was he? It was past ten o'clock, so not late for a night owl like Harris, but certainly late for someone who been drinking since lunchtime.

There was nothing for it. The time had come to search the bars and lounges. And after that, who knew? Perhaps it was best not to think about it.

After a fruitless tour of the ship, taking in various watering holes and umpteen smoking rooms, Drabble was forced to conclude that – whatever he was doing – Harris was not propping up the bar. Not propping up any bar, in fact.

Now he began to worry.

It was of course perfectly possible that Harris might have located some congenial female company. While it was improbable that Fanny Howell had submitted to Harris's charms, there were surely other women who might. After all, if Harris could be anything, he could be charming. At least for thirty minutes or so.

Yet as Drabble ventured once more out on to the open deck, he realised that it just didn't sit right. The simple fact was that Harris would surely have mentioned a girl if he had met one; he would have bragged about it. He would have shared his good fortune – with precisely the same relish that he shared his ill fortune. That meant that whoever *she* was, she was someone he had met in the course of the last seven hours since they had last seen each other at lunch. And that reduced the probably somewhat.

Because, to be perfectly frank, by the time Harris would have emerged from lunch he might well have peaked already on the charm front.

Drabble gripped the handrail and stared out at the black sea. *Seven hours . . .* There was no way that Harris would *voluntarily* leave Drabble alone in a confined space like a ship for that long – not unless he was delightfully preoccupied. But, as he had already established, that was highly improbable given the sheer quantity of booze that Harris was likely to have consumed prior to the conclusion of lunch. Therefore the explanation for his absence must be *involuntary*. Drabble checked that Harris had not returned to their cabin one last time. The cabin was in darkness and smelled of a salty dampness. He paused at the threshold and the words of warning spoken by Speaks With Fists the afternoon before came to his mind.

It was official. Sir Percival Harris was missing.

Chapter Fourteen

Drabble went to see the ship's doctor. If Harris had had an accident that merited medical attention, then this was the person who would know about it.

Arriving at the doctor's room, he found a tired-looking man in his late twenties at a desk doing paperwork. The wall behind him was adorned with a framed photograph of George VI, an eye test card with an inverted triangle of letters, and a poster that exhorted the virtues of fresh fruit.

The doctor stopped writing and gave Drabble an appraising look.

'The name's Dalgleish,' he drawled, in an accent betraying the mild steel of genteel Edinburgh. 'How can I help?'

He listened carefully as Drabble explained.

'I've not had anyone by that name come to see me today,' he said, checking his notes. 'I can see why you're worried. If you give me your name and cabin number I'll be sure to contact you if –' he hesitated, 'anything comes up.'

As Drabble went to leave, the doctor made another suggestion. 'Try not to worry, Professor. She's a big ship and there are plenty of places to end up – especially if you are the worse for wear. These sorts of things do happen from time to time. See if your friend doesn't turn up in the morning. If it comes to it, we can ask the captain to authorise a search but I'm sure it won't come to that.'

Outside, the wind had built up into a full gale and whistled in the spars and rigging. Drabble clamped down his hat and strode along the dark, empty deck in the direction of his cabin.

The doctor was right. There was nothing to be done now but to wait until the morning. That was true. After all, how on earth could Drabble hope to find Harris in a ship as big as the *Empress of the Atlantic*? And in the middle of the night?

But as Drabble turned into the corridor leading to their cabin, his mind reached a different conclusion altogether.

Five minutes later Drabble knocked on Black Cloud's door. It was gone ten thirty but that couldn't be helped. He waited. There was no sound over the background creaking and vibration of the ship. He tried once more, and held his ear closer to the door. Nothing. He knocked one last time, more loudly.

He waited. If the old chief was asleep, then it was a very deep sleep indeed.

Drabble stepped away, resolving what to do next. He should try to find Sakamoto. That was sensible – probably far more sensible that bothering an old Indian chief, now he came to think about it. He started off down the corridor.

'Excuse me –'

Drabble turned back and saw a narrow face poking out from the doorway of the cabin next to Black Cloud's.

'He went out about fifteen minutes ago,' said the face, which was cast disapprovingly. 'Not the first time, neither. If it's anything like last night he'll back at about two.'

The door shut abruptly before Drabble could ask a question. The communication left him with a dilemma but he resolved it rapidly: he knew that most of Grant's contingent were travelling Third Class, so there was a good chance that that was where the answer lay.

Three decks down Drabble found a steward manning the doorway leading to Third Class. He evidently did not think it quite proper that Drabble – as a first-class passenger – should be venturing into the realm of the Morlocks at this hour, but Drabble insisted. So he relented.

It really wasn't that different down there, he decided. The carpet had been replaced by brown linoleum, and the ceilings were lower and the corridors narrower. But apart from those small details ... Drabble peered into one of the dining rooms which was being prepared for breakfast. Long forms of tables with benches were crammed together in a fashion reminiscent of a Victorian workhouse. This was certainly a world away from the luxurious refinement and the degree of space upstairs. Then there was the smell – an unwholesome stench of boiled cabbage hung in the air, and he thought there might be a touch of effluent too. Drabble steadied himself as the ship rolled – that, too, was more pronounced down here.

He halted one of the attendants outside the dining room and asked, without much hope, where he might find Speaks With Fists. The man's expression showed Drabble that he knew him well enough – and didn't like what he knew. Drabble guessed he'd been on the receiving end of his temper.

'Cabin 563,' the man said tartly. 'Deck G.'

Deck G, Drabble knew, was the lowest on the ship, the last before you hit the engine room and God knows what else. They didn't have stokers anymore – ships like this had converted to oil in the twenties – but it was all in that territory.

And you could tell as much from the smell, which had grown steadily stronger as Drabble descended the stairs. The hint of diesel – or oily rags – was now pervasive. There was something else too: a constant, background drone and hiss of mighty machinery and combustion occurring close by, along with the faint tremor that he could feel through the soles of his feet. More than that, you could feel it in your heart, a foreign baseline vibration.

Together with the cabbage and effluent in the air, you could see how such accommodation would work its magic on Speaks With Fists' mood. No wonder he'd been grumpily appraising their cabin the day before. As a chief's son he would doubtless expect better treatment and he must have been cursing Grant's name all the way back to steerage.

At the foot of the stairs, Drabble confronted a green-painted wall, which he knew from the pulsating sound must enclose one of the turbine rooms. That in turn would lead to the base of one of the three great, green-painted funnels of the ship. He followed the narrow corridor around it, reaching a different section of the deck, set aside for Third Class cabins. Before long Drabble was standing outside cabin 563. He knocked.

After a minute he knocked again. Loud snoring emanated from the cabin door opposite and the sound of a hacking cough drifted along the corridor, mingling with the drone of heavy machinery.

Drabble knocked again. The last time, he told himself. As he waited the snoring from across the corridor reached a crescendo. Drabble cursed and knocked again.

If Speaks With Fists wasn't in his cabin, if Black Cloud wasn't in *his* cabin − then they had to be somewhere. Moreover, whereas Black Cloud had the luxury of a cabin to himself, his son would have been sharing, probably with up to five others, who were also either sleeping so deeply as not to be woken, or were somewhere else. Quite likely, with him.

The question was *where*, and whether or not Harris was with them, too. One thing was certain; waiting outside cabin 563 all night was not going to help. Drabble followed the corridor, turning left as it skirted another chamber. This time it was not a boiler room − rather, the smell of chlorine told him it was the ship's swimming pool and Turkish Baths, confirmed by a notice, which added: 'First Class Passengers only'. You can see how well that would go down …

After the pool, Drabble arrived at another stretch of Third

Class cabins, all crammed in, doors close to one another like on a railway carriage. These were numbered in the high five hundreds, so he knew he must be approaching the aft-most point of the ship. Sure enough, he reached another boiler room – the synchronous hum grew more intense – and he followed the corridor around it. On the right was a broad set of pale green double doors, labelled 'Post Room'. Then on the left was a set of doors marked, 'First Class Luggage'. He continued, no longer sure that he would find anything useful, but stubbornly determined to keep going to the bitter end.

Next he passed a storage space for second class luggage and then found himself between the last two doors, on either side of the corridor, marked 'Squash Court One' and 'Squash Court Two'.

Abruptly, Drabble stopped in his tracks . . . and then turned slowly towards Squash Court Two. He couldn't be sure, but he thought he could hear singing. He stepped closer.

But it wasn't singing, it was chanting. Not your sombre Gregorian, mind. No, nothing like that at all. It was certainly male – if not entirely, mostly judging by the low, guttural quality of the tone – but it comprised a series of repetitive, urgent cries. Of that he was certain. Drabble pressed his ear to the door. Now he could hear the voices rising and falling within a narrow vocal range. He listened, attempting to dissect the choral mass. It wasn't English . . .

Drabble glanced over his shoulder. His thoughts went to what Walberswick had told him earlier and the unavoidable conclusion reached him that the language being spoken was that of the Lakota Sioux. This was a ritual, without doubt – it couldn't be anything else. And quite possibly, this was the new ghost dance. Furthermore, it was highly likely that Black Cloud and his son were on the other side of the door.

Drabble focused his ears on the voices he could hear coming from within . . . the rising and falling cries and moans, all at once so impenetrable. But a word or phrase *was* emerging from the mass, one that was being repeated. He pressed his ear to the door and concentrated.

There it was, '*Bahi ... huska ... bahi huska ...*' Drabble mouthed the sounds in order that he might commit them more effectively to memory. If only he could see what was going on. If only he could open the door – very, very quietly – and peer inside. Perhaps he could just look – quickly ...

The sound of the chanting intensified and Drabble gripped the round metal door handle. It was worth the risk. He felt the cold touch of the stainless steel in his hand. *He had to see.* Seeing it would help him understand.

But just then, the door handle turned ...

Chapter Fifteen

In life Drabble considered himself lucky that he was seldom struck by what we might call fear. Nerves, of course, were only natural. But that searing, heart-clapping sensation of raw fear ... Hardly ever. Just once, he recalled, during his failed ascent of the North Face of the Eiger the year before had fear got hold of him. It was the second morning on the black rock, when they woke up at the foot of the White Spider – the vast arachnid-shaped ice field that leads to the summit. He had glanced casually down at the small town of Grindelwald in the valley seven thousand feet below and his stomach had just gone. Just like that. And then the hairs had stood up on the back of his neck, just as they stood up now – as he felt the door handle of Squash Court Two turn against his grasp.

Drabble let go ... and took to his heels.

Immediately a cry went up behind him. Then another.

Drabble charged past the First Class Luggage compartment at full pelt. His feet pounded on the brown linoleum and he bolted past the third class cabins. He dived left around the perimeter of the swimming baths and shot out into the next set of cabins. Now his full attention was on the end of the corridor and the next engine section. The distance fell away. He rounded the compartment and surged into the stairwell, hurling himself up three steps at a time, his hands greedily grabbing the handrail.

Deck F, Deck E, Deck D ... He saw no one as he raced up

the ship and then sprang from the stairwell out into the open deck, arriving into the storm that was now raging. His feet slipped on the rain-swept deck, as he skidded round the corner into the corridor leading to his cabin. He tore off his sodden shoes and socks – leaving wet footprints would make it all too easy to find him – and darted for his cabin. He bolted the door behind him, leaving the lights off, and sank to his haunches, his chest heaving.

Seconds later hurried footsteps arrived in the corridor. Drabble held his breath. The steps stopped outside his door. He made his breathing shallow and stayed perfectly still – suddenly conscious of the faintest sound. Then the door handle started to turn; whoever was trying it was doing so very gently. But it was locked.

Drabble knew it wouldn't take much to force the door and he braced himself for action.

He waited. If it was going to come, surely it would be now. It occurred to him to surprise whoever was out there, by springing the door open on them. But it would only confirm his identity, albeit they would already have a good idea of who it was, unless they were blindly trying all the doors in the section of the corridor.

Unlikely.

The door handle settled back in place, and the footsteps, softer now, departed.

Silently Drabble crossed the darkened cabin to Harris's bunk, which he knew already was empty. He reached over, found the decanter of Scotch and took a slug.

Bahi huska. The words *were* still in his mind. He hurried to the desk, pulled out a scrap of paper and wrote down the sounds phonetically. *Ba-hi hus-ka.* He would need to find out what that meant tomorrow. You never know, he thought, it might even help him locate Harris.

*

126

'Harris was found outside the Café Bruxelles on B Deck in a pool of his own vomit shortly after two o'clock in the morning . . .' Dr Dalgleish, looking tired, referred to notes. 'He smelled strongly of urine and –' the doctor cleared his throat, 'he had also soiled himself.'

Drabble grimaced. It was not uncommon for Harris to have a binge and even to pass out, but double incontinence marked a new low even for a man of his Falstaffian appetites.

Dalgleish took a casual drag on his cigarette. 'I took the liberty of speaking to the head barman just now and he confirmed that Sir Percival continued to imbibe generously into the evening.'

'What was he drinking?' asked Drabble.

'Everything, I should think.'

Regrettably, that sounded like Harris.

'I also found a mostly empty bottle of Famous Grouse whisky in his coat pocket.' Dalgleish nodded to the exhibit which now stood on his shelf. 'From what I could tell, he lost consciousness in the lobby and grazed his head when he fell. But it was the alcoholic intake that I think was probably the most concerning. Try as I might, I couldn't rouse him from his stupor. I'll be frank with you, Professor, I can't remember the last time I've seen a man quite so utterly incapacitated by alcohol – and I did my medical training in Glasgow,' he added with emphasis.

So far, so Harris.

'May I see him?'

'If you don't mind, I'd like to let him rest. He'll come to, soon enough . . .' Dalgleish extinguished his cigarette in the glass ashtray filled with dog-ends. 'Care to join me for a cup of coffee, Professor, while we wait?'

The doctor poured two cups, as Drabble contemplated his friend's mishaps. Harris had really over-cooked it this time. The only mercy was that it didn't sound like he had done any serious injury to himself, which was a minor miracle. The lucky sod could almost certainly count on Dalgleish's discretion in the matter too, so it wouldn't get back to Harris's paper – or its proprietor. But it was a worrying progression all the same.

And there was something else amiss too: Harris despised Famous Grouse. 'Bladder acid,' he called it. So there was no way – Drabble reframed this – *never yet* in Harris's drinking life had he plumbed the depths of drunkenness so low, as he would see it, to submit to the charms of a blended whisky. Harris might be a drunk, but he had standards. So in other words, this was serious.

Very serious.

They had scarcely dented their coffees when a nurse entered. 'The patient's awake, sir.'

Gathering up his stethoscope, Dalgleish led Drabble into the small four-bed sick bay. Harris, his face puffed and jaundiced, peered out of heavy-lidded eyes, which made him look like he was staring out through a pair of keyholes. The graze on his forehead was livid and around him hung a strong alcoholic pall which intensified with every step they took towards the bed. The smell reminded Drabble of specimens in a jar.

'Oh, Drabble . . .' Harris turned his head stiffly towards his friend and reached out with a weak, trembling hand. 'Oh, my dear friend.'

Tears swelled in his eyes, which he closed painfully. On the far side of the bed Dalgleish began checking Harris's pulse. Drabble sat down.

'Tell me what happened.'

'They forced me to drink . . . The bastards poured the juice down my gullet like I was some stricken Gallic goose. I didn't want the foul stuff,' he protested, the words rushing out. 'They interrogated me. Then they tried to drown me in buckets of water.'

'Open wide, please, Sir Percival –' Dalgleish pushed a wooden tongue depressor into his mouth. Harris waited, and then resumed.

'It was this huge American chap – the size of a ruddy

buffalo, he was.' Harris sighed, his strength was fading. 'Bigger, probably. I couldn't see his face too clearly. It was all very dark. And there was another chap, too. He kept out of sight but was clearly in charge – another American.'

'Hold it,' Dalgleish leaned in and shone a piercing light into Harris's eyes.

'Is that strictly –'

'Stay still, sir . . .' They waited. 'Very good.' Dalgleish nodded to the nurse, who withdrew. He started unbuttoning Harris's striped white and green pyjamas, then pressed the operative end of the stethoscope to the patient's chest.

Harris exhaled weakly. 'They tried to drown me in buckets of water. It was terrifying . . . Ernest,' he reached out. 'I thought I was a goner. I thought, *this is it*. No goodbyes, no farewells – just a face down in a sodding bucket.' Harris emitted a great sob –'They were trying to kill me!'

Dalgleish snatched away the stethoscope and shot Drabble a fierce glance.

'Sir Percival.' The doctor braced Harris's shoulders. '*You are fine*. You're in perfect health – somehow – except for a crushing hangover which many would say was well deserved, and a light graze to your forehead. Now, sir, do yourself a favour – drink the sweet tea that Nurse Powell is about to bring you – and then give your beleaguered liver a few days' respite.'

Dalgleish fed Drabble another thunderous glance and stalked out. Harris closed his eyes and exhaled slowly, his voice weak.

'I don't think he likes me very much.'

Drabble patted his leg. 'I'm sure that's not that the case.'

'Oh, I know how it must look, Ernest.' Harris sighed despairingly. '"Dipsomaniac drinks bottle of Scotch – shock". But you must believe me. They held the bottle of ruddy Grouse to my lips and forced me to drink it.'

Drabble nodded. He believed him all right, but he knew no one else would.

'There's something else, Drab –' Harris glanced over towards the door. He lowered his voice. 'There was something official about them, about the way they spoke. You know, it was all in *officialese*. And these chaps weren't thugs, notwithstanding what they did to me. If I didn't know any better I'd say they were policemen or – and look, I don't want to sound far-fetched – but I wondered if they might be, well, government agents *or spies* of some sort.'

Within a couple of hours Harris was sitting up in his sick bay bed and eating soft poached eggs on buttered toast with the crusts cut off. He didn't have much of an appetite, he said, but he was making of fist of it. His face was looking rather less yellow than before, too.

He was going through it all again as he forked in some egg and chewed heavily, like he was eating a tough steak. 'I'm trying to remember, but they were asking me about my association – yes, that was the word – my "association" with Sakamoto, that Japanese diplomat. They evidently think that the Japanese are up to something fishy.'

Drabble cleared his throat, announcing a minor shift of subject.

'The question is, who are "they"?'

Harris ignored the attempt, and added, 'They also kept asking me about my "association" with Black Cloud. Whatever can that be about?'

'I don't know . . .' Drabble eyed Charlotte, who was now sitting opposite him at the end of Harris's bed. He had begun to wish that he had not invited her to join them. That said, when she heard that Harris was hurt, she had commendably insisted on it. But he couldn't help but feel that the less he involved her, the better. Unfortunately, she evidently wanted to be involved.

Charlotte looked up from her book, where she had begun making notes.

'Can you describe the man again, Harris?' she asked.

'Not very well, I'm afraid.' Harris spoke in a doubtful voice. 'It was all very dark … He must have been six foot four. And his face … his face was, well, it was sort of rather thick-set, a bit Neanderthal. But that's really all I've got. But he's got to be somewhere on this ship. And that's the scary thing. He's out there.'

Drabble saw Charlotte write 'Neanderthal' in her book. He had not mentioned anything about his encounter in the squash courts – nor the chase to his cabin – and he was now sure that this wasn't the moment so to do. Then there was the Walberswick conversation. That would have to wait, too.

'Don't let your egg go cold, Harris.' Drabble turned to Charlotte. 'I wonder if we've got as far as we can with this for one day.' He switched to Harris. 'I don't think it's in our interests to raise this with the captain. He can't very well assemble every male passenger of American nationality who is around six feet four in height for your inspection – but nor do we want him to.' Harris was about to protest when Drabble raised his hand. 'Instead, I think we need to use this information to our advantage if we can. For now, Harris, I think you should keep a low profile and be grateful that nothing worse happened.'

'Nothing worse? They submitted me to water torture and then poisoned me with Grouse. Christ alive, man. These people are philistines!'

'I understand –'

'No you don't,' snapped Harris, surprised by his own vociferousness. 'You weren't there … you were off gallivanting …' His glistening eyes met Charlotte's, and he halted. She turned to Drabble.

'I should go …'

'Oh, I'm sorry,' wailed Harris. He reached out and seized her hand. 'It's all just been such an ordeal.'

Captain Rossiter stood at the end of Harris's bed, listening. The near empty bottle of Grouse stood in the corner.

131

'I see,' pronounced the captain, as his intelligent eyes flitted from Drabble to Harris, and then back again to the bottle. 'Sir Percival, you sincerely believe that these men wanted to kill you?'

'Absolutely.' Harris reached for his cigarette case. 'I really can't fathom *why* they didn't.'

Drabble lit Harris's cigarette, and interjected, 'Captain, we wondered if we might have a different cabin.'

Rossiter nodded, 'That's not a problem. Sir Percival, are you positive that you don't want me to try to find the man that did this to you?'

'Actually, I don't think I could even identify him – even if he was standing right in front of me. It's just all a bit of a blur, I'm afraid.'

Rossiter glanced sceptically at Dalgleish.

'Very well. Once you've been moved, I think it might be a good idea for you to remain in your cabin. For your own safety.'

Drabble was not under any great delusion that changing cabin would insulate them for long from unwanted attention. But it might help for a while, and in any case they didn't need long, since they would be arriving at New York inside twenty-four hours. What was essential, however, was that as soon as feasible, Harris should engage again with Sakamoto in order to attempt to find out more about whatever it was that his American interrogator may have been driving at with his questioning. Because evidently something was going on – something serious enough to inspire rough methods. Meanwhile, they would continue to assert that Harris had no memory of the identity of his attacker – the 'Buffalo Strangler' – which should offer some protection from a renewed attack from that department, since his stated ignorance offered immunity to the attacker. That at least was the idea. But it wouldn't offer Harris protection from others ...

Chapter Sixteen

Impeccably attired in black frock coat and brushed homburg, Sir Percival Harris entered the Britannia lounge on the main deck. To those that knew him well he would have appeared a little stiff in gait and his complexion might have aroused suspicion, but to the casual observer . . . he looked no different from the next specimen of upper-class urban manhood. In fact, squint a bit, and he looked like a English gentleman in the prime of life.

But inside he was crying; not only was he physically exhausted, but he felt like he'd been poisoned, which, of course, he had been. He looked about for Sakamoto. No luck. Half an eye was looking out for the Buffalo Strangler, too, mind you. Regardless of Drabble's planning, if Harris saw that bastard he would run him through with his sword stick – and he would gladly take the consequences.

Harris left the Britannia and made for the deck bar at the bow of the ship. Drabble followed at a discreet distance, watching Harris take in the view of the ocean before proceeding along the deck. Following the storm the sea was still running high, but the wind had dropped and the sky had cleared up.

Drabble glanced over his shoulder. As well as keeping an eye on Harris, he was hoping to see Colonel Grant again. Having spent many decades in the company of Black Cloud's Sioux band, he was sure that Grant would speak some of the language and might, therefore, be able to translate the words Drabble had heard repeated from the squash court.

Drabble watched Harris perform an uncharacteristically low energy lap of the foredeck. It wasn't *too* obvious that he was looking for someone.

'Professor?' A cheerful voice snatched Drabble from his observations. It was Wheelock.

'Hello, Wheelock,' Drabble smiled and the older man offered a courteous bow. Wheelock gestured with his cane towards the foredeck. 'Fancy a drink?'

They rounded the corner, the scene opened up and there were groups of people swathed in overcoats and scarves, sheltering from the brisk wind. Among their number was Harris. He looked like he was trying to manage his discomfort.

They took a table outside.

'I was sorry to hear about your friend.' Wheelock offered a smile of consolation. 'I'm afraid there are no secrets aboard the *Empress of the Atlantic.*'

'So it would appear.' Drabble acknowledged Wheelock's expression of care. It would appear that Dr Dalgleish, or perhaps the head barman from the Café Bruxelles, was not as tight-lipped about Harris's misfortunes as he had hoped they might be.

'Is he OK?'

'He'll live to fight another day. He's had quite a shock though.'

Wheelock nodded solicitously, 'Let me know if there's anything we can do to help.'

Quite what Wheelock could do to assist intrigued Drabble as their drinks arrived, and when the waiter left he was about to frame a question to that effect, but Wheelock cleared his throat into his grey-gloved fist.

'May I be candid with you, Professor? And may I count on your discretion?'

Drabble nodded. Wheelock did a left and right before leaning in. 'It's like this, Professor. We have an Indian problem.' He let that settle. 'Or rather, we're pretty sure we do . . .' He took a sip of his Manhattan. 'The problem goes like this. From time to time some foreign power or other party becomes sympathetic to the Indians' desire for greater autonomy and decides to dip its oar in.'

Drabble nodded. 'I didn't realise that such desires persisted,' he stated mildly.

'I'm afraid there are always mavericks and romantics waiting for an opportunity. We don't actually know *which* power is involved this time, but you can imagine that if one were it would likely be a power that is hostile to Uncle Sam, and that reduces the field of options somewhat.'

'I see.' Drabble sipped his sherry. 'So the Brits are above suspicion?'

'Absolutely. Those days are long behind us.'

They both smiled, but Drabble detected a new hardness in Wheelock's expression. It put him on edge.

'As a historian,' said Wheelock, 'I expect you can imagine how attractive it would be for a hostile power to think of the Indian option – you know, arm the Native Americans, foment a home-grown revolution. It looks remarkably neat. Especially when you consider the sort of bloodbath of a military response that it would draw. Just think how badly that would play internationally – as well as being a disaster for the Indians. God, it's unthinkable.' Wheelock shook his head. 'The United States would become a pariah.'

'What do you actually know for sure?'

'Not nearly enough.'

'I'm not sure I know what that means.'

Wheelock raised his eyebrows and exhaled. 'It means,

135

Professor, that we have suspicions but no proof. Therefore, we are urgently seeking –' his fingers went to his glass – 'to understand *any* relationships that the Indians have with hostile powers. For clarity's sake these would mainly be the obvious contenders – namely Germany, Italy, and Japan.'

Japan, obviously, had been high up on the hit-list of Harris's Neanderthal interrogator, as was the Japanese attaché's association with the Indians – Indians whom Walberswick also suspected of being involved in a new ghost dance. Did Wheelock know about that too?

'There are hundreds of tribes of Native Americans. Which are you concerned about?'

'In a word, the Sioux.'

'And presumably you've spoken to them?' suggested Drabble.

'It's not that easy. When you're fomenting rebellion you don't normally talk about it. But,' Wheelock's finger jabbed the table, 'at all costs we must stop this situation escalating. Otherwise it's going to be a very bad outcome for the Indians. And I tell you this, I fear we are running out of time to solve this puzzle. So if you and your friend have *any* information that has emerged from your extensive conversations with Black Cloud and his followers – I'm just saying – then I would urge you to offer it up now. You hear me?'

The hardness had returned to Wheelock's voice and suddenly the idea Drabble had of him slogging it out in dusty archives evaporated.

'Because there'll be hell to pay, if this gets out of hand . . . It could start with the Sioux and then spread.'

Drabble nodded. 'I'll make sure you're the first to know if we hear anything.'

Wheelock finished his drink and rose from his seat. 'I'll get this –' He slid a folded ten-shilling note under the ashtray. 'Thank you, Drabble. Remember, we aren't messing around.'

Drabble watched Wheelock walk away and pushed his half-full glass aside. Wheelock was evidently a man of many parts, and Drabble could no longer be sure of any of them. He made a visual check on Harris – who had a glass of champagne and a pipe on the go – and looked back over for Wheelock, seeing him turn the corner. Drabble hurried from the table. It was time to start eliminating the variables. He broke into a jog, reaching the corner in time to see Wheelock step into a doorway. Drabble dashed forward and followed him into the passage and out onto the far side of the ship. Peering out, he saw Wheelock reach his destination outside the starboard first class smoking lounge. Here a man was waiting for him and stood up to greet him: he was at least two heads taller than Wheelock and – just as Harris described – sported a plausibly Neanderthal cranium. Drabble's heart pumped – and he quickly stepped back into the shade of the doorway. So the Buffalo Strangler was Wheelock's man. That threw a whole new complexion on to the dapper Virginian.

Colonel Grant was in the Saloon Bar, which, despite its name, was not festooned with Wild West paraphernalia such as waggon wheels and barrels. However it did have a wide selection of bourbons, which it appeared the Colonel had been exploring.

'Howdy!' The American was smoking a narrow cigarillo and raised his glass. 'Drink?'

Drabble ordered a sherry and then met Grant's waiting, enquiring gaze.

'I hear that you used to have lunch with Hitler when you were in Berlin.'

Grant chuckled, 'Who told you that? Fanny? Sure, once or twice – along with about a fifty other people. He's a peculiar fellow, I'll tell you that. A vegetarian too.' He shook his head. 'Never trust a vegetarian.'

'Is he a lunatic?'

Grant shrugged. 'It all depends on how you define lunacy. To be honest I'd be more worried about Mussolini. He's seriously delusional.'

'They're all delusional.'

Grant raised his glass. 'I'll drink to that.' Smoke escaped generously from his mouth and nostrils.

'Cheers,' said Drabble.

They savoured their drinks in silence.

'Are you still planning to hang up your hat when you get back?'

'You kidding?' He adjusted his bandana. 'I've got a ranch in the Black Hills and that's where I'm gonna stay. Fanny has finally agreed to accompany with me.' He smirked down at his drink. 'Women.'

'Will you miss it?'

'No way. Touring is a miserable business. But I'll miss the cast ... the pleasure of entertaining people – sure, I will miss that.' Grant suddenly looked tired, like a man who needed to retire, perhaps.

Drabble pointed to Grant's near-empty glass.

'Another?'

'Sure.'

Drabble waited for the new drinks to arrive before carefully introducing the matter in hand.

'You speak Sioux, don't you?'

Grant nodded. 'I can get by.' Then he caught Drabble's eye and grinned: 'Try me.'

Drabble kept his tone casual. 'It's just something Black Cloud said ...' He feigned trying to remember the words precisely, as if he were mentioning the most inconsequential thing ever. Then the words popped out.

'*Bahi huska?*'

The Colonel immediately frowned at him, his voice raised. 'Bahi husker?'

Drabble felt wrong-footed and suddenly exposed. He began to flannel. 'If that's gibberish ... I-I thought he said something like it, but I couldn't be sure − I've never had a head for languages ...'

Just then Grant's expression switched and Drabble saw that suspicion was the last thing on his mind. He clapped Drabble on the shoulder.

'You mean *phehi haska*?' he growled triumphantly. 'It means "long hair". That's what the Sioux called Custer.'

Harris eyed the fizzing surface of his glass of Pol Roger dismally − watching the tiny, happy, white bubbles bursting out of its usually inviting surface. And he wondered how to start. But it wasn't only the drink he was contemplating. Across the small table sat Major Sakamoto, who sure enough had arrived for a five-thirty sharpener at the foredeck bar. As he viewed the Japanese diplomat's lean face, Harris realised that small talk was the imperative of the day. If he could manage it.

'I've been meaning to ask again, old man,' he began casually. 'But what's taking you to the United States?' He smiled absently. 'Is it a burning desire to gaze upon the visages of Mount Rushmore? I hear the Americans have nearly finished despoiling the landscape in furtherance of their national self-esteem.'

Sakamoto grinned at him. 'I'm sure that would be most distracting, Sir Percival. No, as I said before, I have some official business to conduct with embassy colleagues in Washington.'

'Ah, that's right.' Harris turned his glass and made a play of remembering. 'Sounds interesting. Is it "top secret" or can you tell me more?'

'It is confidential, I'm afraid, Sir Percival.'

'So it doesn't concern our Native American friends?'

The diplomat's gaze lifted from his cigarette and found Harris's − and then held it. 'Why on earth would you say that?'

Harris chuckled and immediately regretted it because it

sounded incredibly false. There was nothing else for it, he just had to dig in deeper. He leaned in. 'Come on, Sako –' he said gamely. 'You can trust me. *I'm very discreet.*'

An expression of marked incredulity visited Sakamoto's face, and he coughed on his champagne, even choked a bit.

'Sir Percival,' Sakamoto recovered, grinning. 'You are the least discreet man I have ever met . . .'

Harris stifled a smile – Sako was quite right, of course, but it hurt a bit – and he lowered his voice. 'Now look here. What I mean to say is you can *trust* me. I am no particular friend of Uncle Sam, nor do I harbour any particular animosity towards the Empire of Japan and its perfectly reasonable instincts for territorial expansion in the Pacific. However, I am very interested in our Native American friends, and – to be perfectly frank – I would like to do *absolutely* everything in my power to assist them in their struggles.'

He gave a nod loaded with sincerity and took out his pipe. Sakamoto seemed to be weighing his comments – not rejecting the errant nonsense outright, but considering it. That was something. Harris retrieved his leather tobacco pouch and began stuffing his pipe.

'It gladdens my heart, Sir Percival, to hear of your support vocalised for Imperial Japan. I'm afraid I am still forbidden from discussing my official business with non-diplomatic staff. I hope you will forgive me.'

Harris understood. He lit his pipe, bulbs of smoke pluming from the bowl, and discovered that Sakamoto was looking at him, most intently.

'Sir Percival, if I may ask you an impertinent question in return? Why did you think I might have an interest in the Native Americans? Where did you get this notion from?'

'Really?' Harris smirked as if such an idea was imbecilic, but his mind was racing behind his banal expression. Alas the racing was coming up with precisely nil. 'Well . . .' his feeble grin slid into a grimace, 'wasn't it something you said the other day, old chap?'

Sakamoto coolly extinguished his cigarette, his fine fingers twisting the stub into the ashtray. 'I have never discussed the Native American situation with you, Sir Percival. I have stated no interest in the Native Americans whatsoever in fact. So if you would be so kind as to answer my question, I would be obliged.'

Harris gave his pipe a heavy pull, hoping the smoke would conceal his awkwardness. The truth was, his mind had gone blank. All he could think of was Drabble's firm exhortation – that *he must not, under any circumstances, arouse Sakamoto's suspicions.* Across the table, Sakamoto stared at him with an expression conveying precisely that, waiting for an answer. And the problem was, Harris jolly well couldn't think of a single plausible response.

'Give me a minute, will you, Major?' Harris drained his glass and got up. 'I'll be right back!'

But Harris had no intention of returning. Instead, feeling Sakamoto's eyes burning into his back, he tottered towards the bar and entered. Once inside, rather than going to the gents as his comment implied, he stalked straight into the kitchen and demanded to be shown the back door.

Chapter Seventeen

'You did a what?'

'A runner,' repeated Harris as he reached for the next shirt stud. 'You know, I scarpered.'

'What part of making sure you didn't raise his suspicions was that?'

'Oh it was far too late for that, old man,' sighed Harris. 'He cottoned on immediately and he certainly wasn't going to drop it. These diplomats are obviously cleverer coves than we credit them for.'

Harris fitted the last of the shirt studs and began looking about for his cufflinks. Drabble, already dressed for dinner, watched him from the armchair.

'On the shelf by your whisky glass.'

Harris grinned in acknowledgement, rescued the cufflinks, and took up the Scotch.

'Did he give you anything, before you buggered off?'

'Nothing. But mark my words, he's up to no good – after all, why be so suspicious if you've got nothing to hide?'

Spoken like a true libertarian, thought Drabble sourly. Despite it all, however, he was inclined on this occasion to agree with him, but he didn't say so. Drabble remembered that he had still not told Harris about Walberswick, nor of the squash court incident. Moreover, he hadn't yet told him of the conversation with Wheelock, or shared the fact that he had almost certainly identified the Buffalo Strangler.

But right now, as he watched Harris failing to negotiate a cufflink, he wasn't at all sure if he had any intention of sharing any of it with him. Not yet, anyway.

'I just don't understand it,' protested Harris. 'Why pick on me? Out there are two separate groups of people who are either up to no good or think that the other one is. And for reasons unknown, they believe that *I* know something useful. Here ...' He held out his wrist for Drabble to do up the cufflink. 'We have to get to the bottom of this, Drabble. It's not on.' He scowled in the mirror. 'I bloody well want answers. More than that. After what I've been through, I *deserve* them.'

Drabble completed fitting the second cufflink and discovered that he agreed with him. 'All right, Harris. Charge your glass ...'

Harris listened quietly, without too many interruptions, as Drabble detailed all the salient points of the conversations and incidents that he had not yet disclosed, right up to his most recent exchange with Colonel Grant in the saloon bar. There was a pause as Harris appeared to be cogitating the mass of information, and then he spoke with a breathless intensity.

'So the US government believes that the Japanese – *most likely* the Japanese – have some barmy plan to supply the Sioux Indians with weapons to mount a revolution, while the British believe that a new, clandestine ghost dance or similar ritualistic, spiritual phenomenon is sweeping the Sioux people, which – *they fear* – could spread to other native tribes across both regions, thereby fomenting indigenous rebellion and unsettling the world order as it prevails in Northern America ...'

Drabble smiled. For a man who couldn't do a cufflink up, Harris could supply a surprisingly succinct précis.

'As improbable as it all may seem ... I don't think you've missed anything.'

'Well plunge my bonce into a pail of water –' Harris bounced up from his chair and reached for the decanter. 'What's the world coming to?' He began pouring whisky liberally into his glass. 'And naturally enough, it would seem perfectly possible that these two things could be connected, meaning that the aforementioned religious fanaticism is at the heart of the desire to secure weapons and mount the rebellion.'

Drabble nodded. 'What's more worrying is it's likely that we're the only people who have actually stitched all this together.'

'That is rather worrying,' agreed Harris soberly. He looked down at his glass and swallowed.

'So it's imperative that we learn more about the ritual – for which we need someone who understands Sioux to observe, or at least, *listen* to the ritual.'

'Colonel Grant?'

'I was thinking Walberswick . . .'

'Can we trust him?'

'Can't see any reason not to.'

'Good!' Harris knocked his pipe on the side table, clearing its ashes from the bowl. 'It sounds like an admirable plan.'

But first there was dinner to contend with. Once again, there was an elite cohort of the *Empress of the Atlantic*'s passenger list represented, with Captain Rossiter at the helm. The tedious duchess was not there this time, nor the American dipsomaniac, which was a pity. Instead there was a German couple – the von Ganshofs – who Harris assured Drabble were industrialists of some standing (and muttered as much rather conspicuously in Drabble's ear). Herr von Ganshof wore a monocle and the hard, taut features of a man who could commit acts of sadism rather lightly. His wife was in her forties and an absolute ornament. Her blond hair, arranged in a French plait, was adorned with a twinkling tiara, while her English was uttered with a flawlessness seldom found in native speakers. She wore a long figure-hugging dress of pale blue with a deep V exposing her svelte back, which prompted Harris's mind to wonder and his heart to hope. And he wasn't alone. Colonel Grant and Fanny Howell arrived after them; chatting affably and drinking quickly, and were probably drunk already. Next there was a bishop of the Russian Orthodox Church, who had a square black beard and an amiable countenance, but whom no one could understand.

'I see,' announced Harris, after several minutes' effort. 'Did you say Mount Athos, as in *The Three Musketeers*?'

Drabble had the German industrialist's wife on his left. She was telling him about the purpose of their trip to America.

'My husband's business – always my husband's business. We come over a few times most years – and he insists on my coming with him. Several of my husband's company's best customers are in the United States.'

'And what does your husband do?' As the question landed, Drabble noticed Herr von Ganshof wore a swastika lapel badge.

'Hydraulics,' she smiled. 'And industrial tools. I know, that's where the conversation usually ends.'

She laughed and Drabble changed the subject. 'Will you be in Manhattan long?'

'Just one night,' she replied, sadly. 'Then we will be heading to the Midwest, where my husband's clients are. We shall have a few nights in New York on our return. That I *am* looking forward to.'

'And where in Germany are you from?'

'Munich,' she stated, but then she brightened on seeing Drabble's expression. 'You know it?'

Drabble's gaze drifted again to her husband's lapel badge, and she noticed.

'Yes, *that*.' She shook her head. 'You have to have one of those to get on nowadays. We've never voted for Hitler, not – of course – that voting will do any good any more.'

145

She left her meal and lit a cigarette. Drabble watched her, his mind turning to Charlotte. The thought of her gave him a feeling of contentedness – which must have registered on his face, somehow. As bluish smoke stroked her full lips, Frau von Ganshof smiled. Her eyes appraised him.

'Are you married, Professor?'

'No.'

'Be sure you don't wait too long.'

He chuckled. 'What makes you say that?'

They met Walberswick in a smoking lounge on A Deck. He wore a black dinner suit and had evidently been in the very room that they had for the dinner with the captain. Drabble briefed him on everything right up to Custer.

'*Phehi haska,*' repeated Walberswick, becoming visibly more interested. 'Are you sure? You know what it means, don't you? Tell me again where this gathering took place.' He checked his watch. 'Do you think they might be meeting again tonight?'

'It's possible.'

'Good. I'll need to hear this for myself. Now, is there anything else you need to tell me?'

'Don't you want us to come with you?'

'That won't be necessary.' Walberswick raised a hand like a referee at a rugby match. 'Don't worry, chaps. This is what I do for a living. Now –'

Harris cut in, 'We've discovered that the Americans are *very* interested in this whole business.'

'Well, they ought to be,' replied Walberswick slyly. 'And that's where the cut came from, is it, Sir Percival?'

'Along with a few other invisible scars, too.' Harris gave Drabble a sideways glance. He wasn't finished. 'What about the Japanese, are they supplying the Indians with weapons?'

'Speculation and rumours –' Walberswick shook his head dismissively. 'Nothing more than that.' His gaze shifted between them. 'Very well. Thank you, gentlemen. Keep up the good work . . . I'll see you both in the morning.'

Back in the cabin Harris was pouring two statesmanlike whiskies when Drabble announced that he was engaged for the rest of the evening, with Dr Moore.

'I see.' Harris set down the decanter and replaced its stopper a little dramatically. 'It's not much fun drinking alone, you know. Especially after the ordeal I've been through.'

'I'm sure you'll manage.'

'That's not quite the same thing at all, old man.'

Harris said this in a surprisingly bitter tone that made Drabble momentarily reconsider his plans. He brushed at his hair with his fingers in the mirror, still in two minds, and then heard from the cabin a pair of ice cubes splash into a glass. *Harris would manage just fine.*

Drabble got his hat and paused at the door.

'Sleep well . . . See you in the morning.'

'You rogue,' Harris glowered. 'Cad!' He softened. 'Go on, go and make merry with your lady love,' he said, not unkindly as Drabble departed. 'Don't you worry about me. I'll manage – as you say.' He raised his tumbler. 'Bottoms up!'

Harris took a sip of his whisky and then set down the glass. He was perfectly happy to drink alone if he had to. Necessity, after all, was the mother of intoxication. But if he didn't have to, that was another story. As it stood, there were about a thousand thirsty passengers on the other side of that door, many of whom would be only too willing to keep the party going. One of them might even be Fanny Howell, too – part of the very reason that he accepted this assignment from his editor in the first place. (The other reason being that refusal would have prompted an unseemly riot from his editor – for all *that* mattered.)

Harris straightened his bow tie, and inspected himself in the mirror, glancing his fingertips through his blond hair. Yes. He didn't look too bad. Even the graze on the forehead looked rather distinguished. He took out his cigarette case and recharged it with Craven As. (One didn't want to go into battle without being fully armed, he thought.) He stopped once more in the front of the looking glass, and smiled. He looked the business. Whether it was Miss Howell or some other, he knew he would be lucky. There are times when a Harris just knows, he told himself, as he toddled out the door. And tonight was one of them.

He took a seat at the bar and ordered a Manhattan – in honour of the imminent landfall – and smoked a cigarette. Surveying the room it was, alas, a sea of unknown heads, bowed listening, chatting animatedly, or thrown back in laughter. Some glistened from wax in the muted electric light, others were softened by furs and feathers, or cloche hats and fascinators. Here and there was a delicious glimpse of flesh – a triangle of bare shoulder, or even an infrequent crevice of inviting cleavage. The tobacco warmed Harris's soul and the Manhattan looked after the rest. He felt like the million pound version of himself – roughly three million of your US dollars, he thought smugly. He tasted the intoxicating, sweetish, rusty flavour of the cocktail . . .

'Marvellous,' he declared. His ears drank in the scores of conversations all around him; the laughter, the flirtations, the energy of interaction. This was better than drinking alone, cooped up in the bloody cabin, he chuckled to himself. His eye fell upon two women in their pomp – a brunette with a razor-sharp bob, red lipstick and a face paler than snow, and her friend, who had her back to him but shimmered in silver, like a freshly landed mermaid. The razor-sharp bob raised a cigarette holder to her exquisite mouth. Harris gripped his drink and was poised to reach forward with his own lighter . . . when he saw her.

Fanny Howell appeared in a space beyond the wan bare

shoulder of the mermaid. Miss Howell's thick, voluminous copper hair had been pulled back from her face, showing it to be every bit as handsome as Harris had known, yet somehow more so. Perhaps it was the glow of the half-light and the flickering candles catching her bone structure, and those large brown eyes? Harris leaned forward to catch sight of her company – he couldn't quite see. But it was male, it was of middle height with dark, short hair . . .

Major Sakamoto.

The snake was at it again. Would he ever leave the poor woman alone? Harris clenched his fist around the stem of his martini glass. Now look at the expression on her face. It was positive rapture. Harris gritted his teeth. *Positive rapture.* He drained his Manhattan and ordered a second. Stubbing out the cigarette, he immediately lit another, hardly taking his eyes off Fanny Howell.

Sakamoto was leaning right into her ear, Christ alive, he was virtually *eating it*, the rogue. That was no way to behave. It was disgusting . . .

Harris started on the second Manhattan and puffed irritably. If she were romantically attached to Colonel Grant, as Drabble insisted, then the woman had a peculiar way of demonstrating it. Much more likely, if she were romantically attached to anyone, then it was to the Japanese defence attaché. At least his age was somewhat closer to hers. Harris muttered disobligingly under his breath. He wasn't sure who he resented more: Sakamoto or Grant – the old fox definitely living beyond his means, or the bright spark from the land of the rising sun.

'I don't suppose you have a light, do you?'

Harris turned to see the brunette with the razor-sharp bob standing before him. Her left arm, gloved in shimmering silk beyond the elbow, was bent, a cigarette proffered at the end of a black lacquered holder. A feather boa hugged her bare shoulders and her emerald green dress was cut down her bust, inviting a tilt of the neck. In the split second it took him to see all this – and to evaluate the expression of sexual availability implied on the pretty face – he had extracted his lighter from his trouser pocket and the flame was licking the end of her cigarette.

'Thank you.' The girl smiled, widening her mouth, as smoke drifted from her nostrils. Harris was about to compliment her velveteen choker, when something important caught his eye.

Fanny was on the move. In fact, she was striding towards the exit, the fox stole bouncing at her shoulders. And the other fox was just behind her.

Harris had a millisecond to decide. He smiled at the brunette – and hurried for the door.

Fanny and Sakamoto were proceeding at a good click along the port side sea deck, the wall-mounted lights catching them clearly. Their pace was perhaps indicative of an illicit coupling, Harris thought. But it was hard to say. Certainly they did not linger or gaze upon the stars as others with romance in mind were. But that made sense. If Grant got wind of this, he'd be liable to give Sakamoto both barrels of one of his six-shooters, so to speak. There would be no diplomatic immunity for this infringement.

Keeping well clear, Harris followed until they were near the stern of the ship, where they went into a doorway. Harris broke into a jog, reaching it seconds later. Stairs went up to the floor above and down – to the ballroom and Second Class cabins, and then into the Sisyphean bowels beyond.

It was a coin toss – above were First Class cabins, but below was the vast majority of the ship: six or seven floors of Harland & Wolff's finest – and who could know where Miss Howell and Sakamoto were bound? Harris had to guess.

He raced down the stairs, slowing at the end of the second flight where the next deck would be. He did not want to overhaul them. But of the duo there was no sign. He hesitated, contemplating running back up. But then he continued descending, passing a floor set aside for the Second Class cabins – where from the doorway there was again no sign of Fanny or Sakamoto in the corridor leading off. Harris kept on to the floor below and suddenly heard low voices. He held his breath and drew himself back ...

Peering around the corner he sighted the heel of Sakamoto's glossy black patent leather shoe before it vanished from view. *Hurrah!*

Harris's heart thumped thrillingly against his chest but there was no time for delay. Keep going, Harris, he told himself. *Keep going.* Before the next level he peered down, and then rushed the flight. By now the carpet had turned to teak – and from teak, as they went from E-Deck to F-Deck, to brown linoleum. G-Deck was the end of the line – after that was the keel, and then fishes all the way, till you hit the *Titanic* a mile and a half down.

Harris emerged on to G-Deck, finding corridors leading off in two different directions. He took the right fork and followed the corridor as it wound this way and that, encircling, Harris supposed, vast pieces of the ship's engines. He passed the swimming baths and Third Class cabins. This was sounding familiar. Perhaps they were heading for the squash courts? Could they be joining in the ritual, presupposing it was on again tonight? He checked his pocket watch. It was probably too early for that. Or perhaps Fanny and Sakamoto had come in search of privacy on neutral ground for an entirely different ritual? In which case, what was wrong with Sakamoto's cabin? Surely that would be more comfortable? But perhaps, Harris thought – with a mixture of envy and distaste – comfort was not what Fanny *liked*.

Just then, Harris heard a distinctive metallic *clunk*. He stopped. A lock had been turned. Harris stepped silently to the corner and peeked: Fanny was opening a heavy metal door, marked 'First Class Luggage'. Sakamoto stood close to her, waiting.

They went inside and then pushed the door to behind them.

So that was what they were up to, a trunk call of an altogether different kind!

Or was it? Harris hesitated as he experienced a conflicted rush of sensations – located between triumph *and* disaster. Should he go in and expose the lovers? And be reviled, but at least have the satisfaction of stymieing Sakamoto's pleasures or ... He needed to smoke. But this wasn't time for smoking, he told himself. This wasn't time to dally. He had to know what they were up to. Jealousy ... it didn't come into it. Well, not much. But there was an investigation to think of and this really, actually might be jolly important. Yes indeed. For all that it may just be two people responding to perfect natural human urges in the privacy of the First Class Luggage repository, it might also have a vital bearing on the case. And there was only one way to establish the truth. That it just so happened to also satisfy his jealous, thwarted sexual cravings for Fanny was something that he was just going to have to live with. But he couldn't let his personal conflict obstruct the greater requirement for clarity in the matter. Harris was fast reaching the point where he no longer cared what the consequences were because he was fed up with debating it. Plus, he simply had to *know*.

He pushed the metal door very gently until he felt it move. There came no sound of hinges, but there hadn't for Fanny and Sakamoto, either. He held his breath and inched it open a little more. He listened. The only apparent sound was the background drone of machinery from the engine compartment below. Harris pushed the door open wide enough to enter and leaned his head through the gap to get a better view. More of the brown linoleum met his gaze, followed by stacks upon stacks of suitcases and trunks arranged in a wall standing some eight feet high. This finished close to the ceiling, which was shrouded in pipes and cables. The wall of luggage continued in both directions. He crawled into the repository, pushed the metal door to behind him, and listened. He could not hear them – that was a bad sign.

Rising, he crept along the corridor until he reached its end, pausing every now and then to listen out. Whatever Fanny and Sakamoto were doing, they were doing it silently – rather too silently, in Harris's experience. At the end, he turned the corner and continued carefully down the next pathway in the maze formed of luggage, doubling back. He peered around the next corner and saw no one, so proceeded ...

There they were. He halted. At the far end of the next corridor. They were talking quietly and stood before an open trunk. Their backs were to him, but he could see most of Fanny's profile, the fox fur stole still wrapped around her exquisite shoulders. She bent down and reached into the trunk, lifting an object into view. Harris recognised it immediately. It was a rifle.

The stock of the gun went into her shoulder, expertly as you would expect, and she took aim at a point on the ceiling before releasing the trigger and the pulling the bolt back and then snapping it shut. She pulled the trigger again – it clicked – and handed the rifle back to Sakamoto, before bringing out another rifle for inspection.

So this was what the Neanderthal from the Bureau of Indian Affairs was so worried about. Small wonder they roughed him up. The stupid bastards. It wasn't the Indians they had to worry about, though, it was the cowboys. He heard a click, louder than the others, and looked up to see Fanny pointing the rifle along the corridor towards him. His heart stopped. He froze. She pulled back the bolt of the action and then drew out the long magazine, which she inspected expertly. She hadn't seen him.

'The fifty Type 99s have all been re-chambered, as you requested, to accommodate the .30-06 Springfield round,' he heard Sakamoto say. 'And as you can see they have been fitted with large capacity magazines to accommodate twice the usual quantity of ammunition, again as requested.'

'Very good.' She nodded. 'And where are the rest of them?'

'The ship arrives in San Francisco in four days.'

'The full consignment?'

'A thousand less this fifty, plus enough ammunition to start a war. Precisely as agreed.'

'Excellent work, Sako. I have to say that seeing *is* believing. The chiefs will be over the moon.'

The chiefs! A war!

Holy smokes. Harris's mind raced. A thousand rifles in the hands of the chiefs and their braves, inspired by a new ghost dance? But what could they hope to achieve with just a thousand rifles, even if they were fitted with double the usual ammunition? It was a drop in the ruddy ocean ...

Harris felt his throat begin to contract in panic. Christ and the angels! There *was* going to be a bloodbath. An absolute ruddy bloodbath of the highest order. He had to get out of here fast. Harris heard the trunk being closed and its locks snap shut.

Move, he told himself. *Move.*

He started for the exit, treading as silently and swiftly as he could. He rounded the first corner and then the second passed without mishap. The exit lay just paces away. He reached out to the door, his hand was shaking. He eased the door open and saw the corridor outside. Freedom was in sight. *This was it!*

Just then a heavy object found the back of Harris's head. He felt it land and would have cried out in pain, but for an unconscious cerebral instruction that muted his vocal cords first. A fraction of a split second later his knees gave way and he hit the linoleum, out cold.

Chapter Eighteen

The next morning Drabble was saying his goodbyes to Charlotte on B-Deck. It was taking longer than anticipated.

'I had better go –' he said again. He leaned forward and kissed her. After a moment they broke apart. He had to get back, he explained.

She looked him up and down doubtfully. 'If I don't see you before we make landfall, you know where to find me in Manhattan?'

'I do – the Aviemore. I even know the address off by heart.'

Her expression softened and they came together for one more kiss.

But as he went to set off, he caught a new look; she was worried.

'We *will* see each other again,' he said with meaning.

'It's not that. Look –' Charlotte summoned him back into the cabin and he shut the door behind him. 'There's something I keep meaning to tell you, something I think might have a bearing on this *situation*. For some reason I keep forgetting to mention it.'

'Go on.'

'It's Pocahontas. I've been wondering what the discovery of her grave might have to do with it all. Then eventually I had a brainwave.' She smiled. 'Well, a mini-brainwave.'

'This sounds like I need to take my coat off.'

'As you know, Pocahontas's father was Chief Powhatan, who ruled a stretch of Virginia, running perhaps one hundred and fifty miles and covering perhaps ten thousand square miles, between the James River in the south up to the Potomac in the North.'

'Yes . . .'

'He was also rich, though not necessarily in a way that we would immediately recognise today. His material wealth, such as it was, was in *wampum* – white and black beads fashioned from the inner spiral of *Busycotypus canaliculatus*. I'm sure you know what that is, *Professor* –'

'Enlighten me!'

'It's a predatory channelled whelk in the waters of the region.'

Drabble nodded. 'That's right. I've seen pictures . . .'

'Pocahontas's father did not have gold – except for the crown that it is believed the colonists foisted upon him – but he had hundreds, perhaps thousands, of these shells, and they were and *are* worth something. As you may know, Professor, they remained legal tender in many of the thirteen colonies well into the 1700s. Now, it might interest you to know that just one of these lengths of shells – a wampum belt as they're known – fetched thirteen hundred dollars at auction in New York last year.'

'So you wouldn't need too many of these before you've got yourself quite a fortune?'

'Precisely. What if I told you that he might have had as many as ten thousand wampum belts?'

Drabble smiled and kissed her. 'Charlotte, you're brilliant! So, you think this is a treasure hunt? You think that whoever disturbed Pocahontas's grave was looking for a clue to the whereabouts of her father's trove of shells?'

'It's just conjecture, but it might have been a factor. The reason I think so is the portrait of Pocahontas at Syon House. Were you aware that it has a map on its reverse?'

'A map? How on earth do you know that?'

'Because I've seen it. I examined it last year. And rather more pertinent to our conversation is what it shows.' Now Charlotte gave a broad smile: 'Werowocomocom, Powhatan's capital on the York River.'

'And does the map tell us where Powhatan's "treasure" is?'

'Do you mean,' she suggested coyly, 'is there a mighty "X" that marks the spot?' She let this land a little theatrically. 'Well, if you know what you're looking for . . .' She waited again and Drabble met her smile – he was seeing a different side to Charlotte and liked it very much. 'I can show it to you if you have time – I have a copy here in my notebook . . .'

After examining the map it didn't take long for Drabble to realise that Harris was missing again.

Once more he visited Dalgleish, finding the doctor at his desk, smoking a Woodbine and doing paperwork. He appeared to be pleased to see Drabble.

'As a matter of fact, I saw Sir Percival in the Brasserie bar last night at about ten thirty,' declared Dalgleish. 'He seemed well enough. If I remember correctly he was alone, but it's a sociable venue. I should add, I wasn't observing him *as such*, but I happened to notice that he only stopped for one drink, perhaps two at most.'

Such abstinence did not sound characteristic, but there were plenty of other bars to choose from on the ship where he could have continued to quench his thirst. 'Curiously I noticed that he left rather abruptly after two other passengers that have come to my attention – one was Miss Howell, from the Wild West Show, and –' the doctor lowered his voice – 'the other being Major Sakamoto of the Japanese Embassy in London. As I say, I happened to notice the two of them leave, then I saw Sir Percival hurry out, immediately afterwards. I half wondered if they had a mutual assignation of sorts.' Dalgleish chuckled. 'Nothing surprises me anymore.'

Nor Drabble. He watched the doctor stub out his cigarette and place the smoking ashtray in the top drawer of his desk. 'Let me a make a quick telephone call.'

Drabble could guess what had happened all too easily. And it was just what he feared might happen. Left to his own devices Harris had become bored, so had gone out for a nightcap or two, and ended up getting involved in something. That *something* was either a binge from which he would still be recovering, or an altogether less desirable happenstance, one that the previous night should have given him ample warning of. For now, it would seem that either Miss Howell or Major Sakamoto would be best placed to indicate the direction of travel. If they would cooperate, of course.

Dalgleish replaced the handset.

'I'm afraid he hasn't appeared anywhere else on the ship. Which in a way is good news, but doesn't help you much now.' The doctor offered a smile of consolation.

'Perhaps you could help me by locating the cabin numbers of Major Sakamoto and Miss Howell?'

Dalgleish nodded. 'I'll see what I can do. If it's permitted I'll have the details dropped around to your cabin as soon as possible. I can also ask the first lieutenant to begin a search.'

Drabble checked their cabin on the way to his next appointment – with Walberswick. It was coming up to ten o'clock, meaning the *Empress of the Atlantic* was due to make landfall in Manhattan in just a few hours' time. They were closing in on Long Island now and already the city was a dark outline on the grey horizon. It was getting bigger by the minute.

He arrived at Walberswick's cabin and went to knock – but halted when he saw fresh gouge marks and splinters in the frame by the lock.

'Walberswick?' He knocked, then immediately knocked again, but more forcefully. There was no reply, so he tried the chrome handle. It turned freely, and the door drifted open . . .

The cabin was in darkness; the curtains had not been drawn, and the room smelled – and not in a good way at all.

'Walberswick?'

He entered. The cabin had been ransacked. Drawers had been pulled from the chest and desk, and their contents had been strewn across the floor. A suitcase had been wrenched open and whatever had been in it scattered. Its lining had also been torn back in the search. Drabble swallowed and started to turn towards the bed. He experienced an uncomfortable presentiment, one inspired by unwelcome memories . . . a sickly, prickling sensation arrived at the pit of his stomach as he saw what appeared to be the clothed body of Walberswick lying on the bed, motionless. There was a nauseous residue at the back of his mouth.

He called out his name gently.

But Walberswick did not move, nor did Drabble expect him to. The curl of the legs and the twist of the torso were unnatural, and the left arm was somehow distorted and lost under the folds of the bedding. The head was turned away, but the unruly blond hair was undoubtedly Walberwick's, ending any doubt over identification. Drabble stood now above the body, recognising the conservative tweed of Walberswick's overcoat from the day before.

'Walberswick?'

He gripped the man by the shoulders and pulled him around gently, so that he could see his face. His head lolled over, showing his eyes fixed open. Drabble recoiled. Walberswick's throat had been cut just above his tie and blackish blood stained his front. A knife was embedded in his guts, beneath the ribcage. Whoever did this was leaving nothing to chance. And more to the point, they were quite possibly issuing a particularly strong warning.

The question was, who had done it?

Drabble pulled the knife free and drew the curtain aside to

inspect it: there was no mark to distinguish it; it was simply the sort of knife one might take fishing and was probably fairly universal. But he didn't need the knife to help tell him who might have a reason to do this. Each of the parties most likely to be responsible was known to Drabble already – and both he and Harris were known to each of them also. Particularly Harris. And that made the open question of Harris's whereabouts all the more pressing.

Drabble felt the hairs rise on the back of his neck. Harris . . .

Behind him, he heard footsteps.

Standing in the doorway was a ship's officer. He had a blunt-nosed Webley semi-automatic pistol pointed at Drabble.

'Put your hands up!'

Chapter Nineteen

Harris acknowledged consciousness through his nose. Usually, that was a job for his eyes, which would prickle or twitch irritably until they yielded to the insistent wishes of the great orb. But today it was dark, and it was a smell that woke him. Harris sniffed, like a rabbit catching an alien taste on the breeze – and recoiled, his face pinched. *Manure*. And something else ... horses. It was horses. *Ruddy horses*.

Harris realised he couldn't move. He was lying on his side on a thin bed of straw and his left arm and hip ached. His wrists were bound behind his back – that was disappointing – and he was gagged. He tried lifting his head – and very soon connected with a wooden surface close above. His feet, he realised, were tied at the ankle.

He nudged his head forward and it clunked against a hard wooden surface. *Ouch*. Next, he tilted his head backwards, meeting another timbered barrier. If he didn't know any better, he would have said he was in a coffin. Certainly it seemed to be about the right size. *A coffin!* A wave of anger seized him, tensing his shoulders and causing him to shake his fists behind his back.

The *bastards*. Damn them! And why. WHY? *Why* was this stuff always happening to him? For God's sake. And that ruddy smell of manure. He *hated* manure. How could they have known that? God damn it. He lashed out with his feet but without the space he couldn't even get a decent kick in. It was pitiful. Damn them. He let himself fall slack. Damn it all. He had been careless. He had overreached himself – dare he say it, he had even been a little bit brave. And now he was paying the price. It was a consequence. Damn it, consequences were boring . . . And not for the first time.

Harris closed his eyes and turned onto his back, to take the pressure off his left hip and left shoulder. Before he could complete this manoeuvre, however, he remembered that his hands were tied behind his back. He also discovered – *ouch!* – that there was a spicy new bruise on the back of his head. He got onto his right side, and remembered how it had got there.

Yes . . . as he settled into his new stress position, the closing moments in the First Class Luggage repository revisited him. Christ alive. What an utter fool he'd been. What an idiot. What had he been thinking? Harris realised to his horror that he had no option but to examine his conduct. It was Dutch courage, or rather Manhattan courage, in addition to the double whisky back in the cabin and whatever else he had drunk over dinner. He was aware that he had been drinking a little more since their return from India. The . . . he struggled even now to form the thoughts in his mind, but he forced himself . . . the *rejection* of his overtures to – He halted, finding he could not name her. But he knew it. The rejection had hit him hard. It had positively knocked him for six. And he'd been knocking it back ever since.

Salty tears raced down Harris's cheeks in the darkness of the manure coffin as a new unwelcome truth dawned on him.

He had to cut down. If not for his liver, then simply to stop him committing reckless acts of bravery. He would have to cut down. What was it Drabble suggested he do to take his mind off things? Play squash. Bugger squash!

Harris got himself together and decided to move on to practicalities.

What time was it? How long had he been in the horse-shit coffin that he now found himself imprisoned in? Harris closed his eyes. He had to think. *Think.* There was always a way out of these situations; it was simply a question of *thinking* of it. He halted, seeking to pause the rush of thoughts and urges pulsating through his mind. He took a deep breath in through his mouth; the gag didn't make it easy, but it was preferable to the stench. Beneath him he could feel the faint vibrations of the *Empress of the Atlantic* and hear the massive, mechanical orchestra of her vast engines. So he was still very much aboard, and evidently he was being kept amongst the horses and wagons of the Wild West Show. Establishing that was relatively gratifying.

Of course, what he had no grasp of was just how long he had been out of it for. His throat, he did know, was parched and his stomach ached from hunger. Fortunately, the sickly stench of manure had done for his sense of appetite, which made for a strictly alimentary quandary. He would have to solve the question of food and beverages before long, however. But for now, there was a more pressing issue.

It was imperative that he remained calm. This is what he told himself. To suffer some sort of anxious episode – a fit of panic, say – under these closed circumstances would not be advisable. He took another deep breath and exhaled slowly through his nose. Yes, panic would be the worst thing. And what's more, if he – Sir Percival Harris, KCB, GCSI, MA (Oxon) – succumbed to panic, then he would be letting the side down. And that was unforgivable. Not only was it not the done thing, but it was frankly un-British.

Therefore, *he must not panic.*

Harris breathed in and then exhaled like a Buddhist monk, willing himself to remain calm. And then again. Alas, it was not very relaxing with a gag in his mouth.

The major unknown was what on earth was going to happen to him? Where would he end up? Would they kill him? Would he be imprisoned indefinitely? The voices in this brain suddenly started to turn all falsetto. Yes, he realised, they *were going* to torture him, if nothing else than just for the pure sadistic pleasure of it. They *were going* to tether him to two pairs of horses by his hands and feet and tear him to pieces for the entertainment of crowds. No, no, no. They would then feed him to crocodiles or alligators (or whatever the beastly things were in the United States) and gamble over which would eat him first. Oh, God!

Harris's feet began trotting in the confined space of the horse-shit coffin. *He was too young to die.* And, more importantly, he hadn't had any children. Oh my God, I can't die childless – his brain wailed. *I must pass on my seed.* It is my sacred duty. As a Harris. The line cannot end here!

He did have a younger brother, of course. But could Francis be relied upon to produce a son and heir? Not on his present trajectory . . . Nothing wrong with that, of course – each to his own, as his mother would say – but it wasn't conducive to carrying on the bloodline. Harris felt the weight of generational failure crush down upon him.

He sobbed and realised he was attempting to stamp his feet. Tears traced down his cheeks. I can't die . . . Not like this. Not in this pitiable fashion. Oh, God. He was panicking. And not just that. He was having a full-blown *crisis*.

I won't tell anyone, he beseeched. Not a soul. *Please . . . just release me.* You will have my lifelong discretion – on my honour as a gentleman. I'll be as silent as the grave – suddenly the hot tears were coming too thick and fast. Harris began to whimper. The grave. Yes. That was it. *Their plan for him.* The tears pierced his clenched eyes and forced their way painfully free, as Harris sobbed in the darkness.

And now he needed to urinate. His bladder was full and tensed. It was. How it was. And once the notion had taken root it could not be forgotten. You can't un-need to pee, particularly when you're trapped in a coffin-shaped box with nothing but your imminent demise to distract you, he realised. He lay fighting the urge to pee, and resorted to shouting through the gag. He kicked at the timbered wall of his box prison. But the pain in his lower abdomen was winning.

In the end Harris gave in. He emitted a deep, pleasurable sigh, panting somewhat, as the warmth spread across him. Tears continued to trace down his face, but still the urine flowed. If the box were watertight, he wondered, would it be possible to drown in one's own outpourings?

His bladder eventually ceased its disgorgement and he lay groaning, his eyes firmly closed on the horror of the world. Into the rich odour of horse manure was added the fresh spice. Christ. The places one's brain went in a life like this . . .

The *Empress of the Atlantic* was closing in on the city fast. Through the small porthole of the cabin Drabble could now discern individual buildings within the dramatic Manhattan skyline. Wisps of smoke occasionally obscured his view – from a tugboat perhaps – and the great quay was in sight. The buildings in the distance towered high above the ship and he realised that the photographs he had seen had not prepared him for the peculiar, rectilinear majesty of the spectacle before him. From high up above a powerful horn sounded, then gave a second longer blast. That would be the ship's, he told himself, and sure enough it was answered by distant-sounding calls, presumably from pilot vessels or a harbour master. Seagulls scattered between his vantage point and the shore – Drabble saw teams of dockers in unfamiliar oilskins positioning a vast rope, probably a foot thick. The rain was falling and they waved signals at one another. The ship turned away from the shore – making a final adjustment perhaps – and then the dockers disappeared from view, as the ship closed in on the jetty. Beyond the dockside of warehouses, tall buildings soared into the sky, meeting smoke and soot.

Suddenly the great monotony of the ship's engine faded and for the first time since leaving Liverpool on Tuesday, Drabble rediscovered the absence of the noise. They were here.

And he was tied up – his hands bound behind his back, locked in his own cabin. Guarding the door outside was a sailor, posted to prevent anyone entering to help him or his escape. But who was going to help him? Charlotte was not going to visit. Harris might emerge from whichever bedclothes he had passed out under – although the jury was out on whether he might prove helpful under such circumstances. A bloody hindrance more likely. And that was only if Harris had emerged from said bedclothes. If he hadn't, if he'd been detained by one of Speaks With Fists' 'dark forces', then he would need Drabble's help.

The crew had swept the cabin of anything that might be of use to aid his escape – for instance the decanter and a heavy, wide-based table lamp. And they had taken his belongings, and Harris's. But Drabble knew this wouldn't stop him. And now was the moment to prove it.

He went into the bathroom and contemplated the mirror. That would do nicely, but he had to be quiet. He turned his back to the rail and dragged off a towel, pressing it into the washbasin. Next, he looked around one last time for an implement that he could use – but then simply leaned into towards the mirror. One sharp jerk of his elbow, then another, and suddenly the mirror splintered into angry portions.

Withdrawing his elbow, they fell silently from the brass frame onto the towel. Drabble picked through the mass and drew out the best contender.

Back in the main room he slid the shard into a drawer of the dresser and jammed it shut. Then, very carefully, he began sawing at the rope binding his wrists. He had the knot severed in a minute and quickly separated the mass of rope, before reforming the length with a simple reef knot.

Next he fished out Walberwick's envelope and his passport and fountain pen from their hiding place and pocketed them. He then banged forcefully on the door of the cabin – summoning his captor – and continued until he heard the door being unlocked. It opened a couple of inches: Drabble snatched the handle, yanking it open – and hauled the sailor into the cabin.

The startled mariner cried out as Drabble side-stepped, leaving his foot just where the sailor would trip over it. The man went down, hitting the floor hard, and Drabble pounced; pinioning the small of his back with his knee and lashing his wrists together.

'You won't even get off the ship, you murd'ring bastard,' spat the sailor. 'And if you do, the Yanks will make mincemeat of you. You'll get the electric chair!'

'We'll see –' Drabble jammed one of Harris's socks into the sailor's mouth, and shut the door behind him, locking it and tossing the key over the side. Ernest Drabble was free. For now.

The question was, for how long, and how would he get ashore? Once the alarm was raised the entire ship's company would be looking for him. And to get ashore required clearing immigration in the terminal – clearly not an option available to a wanted man. If he were captured, then whatever it was that Walberswick had died trying to prevent would likely occur.

Drabble hurried along the deck in the grey light. If he could get to the British Embassy in Washington, DC, where Walberswick and his mission were known, then he stood a chance of being listened to and raising the alarm – as well as avoiding the electric chair. But Washington was a long way from New York – and no small distance from where he needed to be in South Dakota.

Passengers were now assembling for disembarkation. Luggage would also be on the move, too – and luggage meant porters. He retraced his steps down to Deck G and the First

Class Luggage repository. More than once along the way he had to move aside to let green-coated porters, pushing trolleys and handcarts piled with baggage and trunks, hurry by. These men were too busy to give him a second thought, and just as well. Entering the repository he found a row of hooks with green shop coats and spare trolleys. Bingo.

Drabble emerged into the weak light of the day, pushing a cart loaded with a trunk across the gangplank onto the jetty, his face feeling the rain on it. In front of him a snake of porters led towards the terminal building. The route was marked with officials in dripping oilskins, barking periodically at the porters through speaking trumpets. Drabble saw several caped policemen positioned along the dock, keeping a proprietorial eye on the movement of passengers and goods.

He entered the terminal, following behind the porter in front, into a cold, electric-lit concrete corridor that smelled of damp. On one wall was a round lifebuoy and a coiled hose, with an axe on a bracket. Porters came pushing empty trolleys the other way, chatting loudly as they returned to the ship.

Drabble did not want to go back that way, but he undoubtedly would have to if no option of escape presented itself in the next minute or two. It would, of course, be easier to escape under the cover of darkness, that he knew. But all things being equal, he would really rather not return to the ship. He had had enough of the *Empress of the Atlantic* to say the least.

Drabble followed the luggage trail through a double doorway into a large room with a low ceiling. Here a counter ran the length of two of the walls, on the far side of which navy uniformed port officials were checking the luggage. Each porter loaded the bags onto the counter and then returned to the ship.

Drabble heaved the trunk onto the counter and then wiped his forehead with the back of his hand. 'I don't think they come any heavier than that –' He caught the eye of the official on the other side of the counter, who, promptly jabbed one of the red diplomatic badges pasted over it.

'Well, we'll never know what's in this one.' He slapped a customs clearance label onto it. 'On you go, there's a thousand more pieces of luggage to clear before this ship is done.'

Drabble headed out of the tunnel, back out into the shadow of the ship. There had to be something. *There had to be a way.* Glancing left and right he saw another lifebuoy, this one mounted on a post near the water's edge . . . the water, of course, remained an attractive option. But not *that* attractive. In late September the Hudson River was liable to be cold and it would dangerous at the best of times, what with the currents and the traffic. But what were his other options? The Hudson was certainly preferable to taking his chances with the forbidding, barbed-wired topped fence that encircled the dockyard.

Amidships a broad gangway now stretched to the dockside from a doorway in the side of the hull, and horses were being led down in pairs by the Wild West Show cowboys. There would be fifty or more horses in their baggage, in addition to a handful of carts, and then sets, scenery and costumes. *That* offered a promising opportunity for escape – if it could be achieved. It would mean he also ended up where he needed to be; namely with Colonel Grant somewhere in South Dakota, where the Lakota Sioux were.

The returning line of porters cut through the equine train – Drabble saw that they were being led up to the railway sidings. Head bowed, he pressed on, pushing his baggage cart towards an opening at the stern of the ship and the First Class Luggage repository.

Just then the air was pierced by a long, low wail – a siren. There was shouting and a horse shied, its steward reined it to get the beast under control. The porter in front paid no heed to the sound and plodded on. Drabble followed suit, keeping his eyes trained on the cobbled dockside directly ahead. But whatever his outward appearance, a knot had formed in his stomach. And rightly so.

The alarm had being raised. The sailor with Harris's sock in his mouth had been found – and Drabble's escape was now a known fact. He arrived at the gangplank as two dozen police-men with truncheons drawn charged out onto the dockside in formation – half peeling off to reinforce those already there and the rest running straight up the passenger gangway and into the belly of the ship.

Drabble could not hope to pass as a porter for much longer under the these conditions. He pushed his trolley across the gangplank into the ship, catching the play of light on the sliver of rippling waters below. He didn't want to have to chance swimming for it.

But if it came it to it . . .

Inside the First Class Luggage compartment about half of the room had now been cleared of baggage. Porters arrived every ten to twenty seconds, briskly loading their trolleys with the next bags, and then exiting through a second doorway. Under such circumstances tampering with a bag was out of the question, even if one could manage it without help. Drabble loaded his trolley with a trunk and then hurried out after the man in the snake ahead of him, closing the gap and putting more distance between himself and the man coming after him.

When the porter in front of him turned left towards the gangway, Drabble shot forward, carrying on straight ahead. He broke into a sprint, charging along the corridor and did not stop until he reached the swimming pool. He dumped the trol-ley into the water and kept moving.

Still in his porter's coat and cap, he headed for the stairs, stopping at various doors along the way to see if he could gain admittance. Every cabin was locked but there would be a thou-sand hiding places on a ship like this. Though hiding wasn't a durable solution.

170

Reaching the stairs he began to ascend, aware that every step quite possibly took him closer to one or all of the dozen policemen who had just streamed aboard. But there was a lot of ship to cover between them, and Drabble knew he would pass muster at first glance – especially if that person were not in the ship's company. He passed a sailor on A-Deck at the foot of the broad staircase that led to the ship deck from outside the ballroom. The man didn't give him a second glance. He was surrounded by Third Class passengers asking questions and looking for the way out.

That's when Drabble remembered Dalgleish.

Dalgleish barely raised an eyebrow at the sight of the wanted man – and perhaps this should have made Drabble suspicious. He calmly extinguished his Woodbine and placed the ashtray in his top drawer, and listened as Drabble explained his situation.

At the conclusion of Drabble's narrative, he locked the door to his room and announced casually that he had a scheme.

'Are you of a squeamish disposition, Professor? I anticipate not.'

Dalgleish took Drabble into the mortuary. 'It's not as uncommon as you would think for us to lose a passenger or two on the crossing – much as we try to avoid it. Throwing bodies over the side isn't deemed acceptable any more. More's the pity, it was much more hygienic.' He unbolted a narrow metal door which opened on large hinges: inside Drabble saw the outline of a corpse – presumably Walberswick's – under a thick white sheet laid out on a trolley. Adjacent to him was a second trolley. Dalgleish beckoned Drabble inside genially.

'My suggestion is that we take you out on the spare trolley. I'll mock you up a death certificate under the name of whatever you like. You'll need to undress and put on a gown but we could conceal your clothes underneath.' Dalgleish showed

171

Drabble the small compartment. 'I'll be accompanying the remains to the terminal where I'll hand them over to the city mortuary officials in about an hour and a half. Then you'd just need to play dead for a bit, before picking your moment to come back to life. What do you think?'

'Is this room air tight?'

'Aye, more or less, but you'll have plenty of air to breathe – there's certainly several hours' worth in here. And poor Captain Walberswick won't be needing any.'

That would suffice, Drabble thought, as he looked down at the empty trolley. It might just work.

'Thank you, Doctor – I'm much obliged to you ...' He reached out and shook Dalgleish's hand. The doctor hesitated before receiving his hand ... then Drabble discovered why. His palm was wet with perspiration. As Drabble registered this, he simultaneously noticed beads of sweat glistening at Dalgleish's hairline.

'Now –' announced the doctor, turning away. He leaned down to a small cabinet. 'For complete verisimilitude, I would advise popping one of these on your right big toe –' He turned, holding up a brown cardboard label dangling from a piece of string. 'You'll just need to make sure that the name corresponds to whatever I write on the –'

His voice trailed off as he saw Drabble edge towards the door.

'What are you doing?'

Their eyes locked.

'Drabble!'

Dalgleish lunged at him – a scalpel in his hand. Drabble leaped back, evading the strafing blade, and got his grip to the door. He slammed it shut just as Dalgleish's hand got to the jamb. The doctor howled in pain, and his hand shrank from sight.

Drabble bolted the door.

He cursed himself as he returned to the doctor's room. He

should not have been so trusting and now he knew he had no option but to swim for it. Drabble found a sealable container suitable for preserving his passport, wallet and money, as he contemplated his next step. It was only four thirty in the afternoon, so there was plenty of time to kill before darkness fell. That meant it was time for a diversion.

Drabble removed his porter's coat and cap, and then went to the corridor, where he retrieved one of the orange lifejackets mounted on the wall. Back in the surgery, he put this on the porter's coat, opened the porthole, and shoved them out. They dropped from sight. Within minutes they ought to be bobbing along the Hudson and catch someone's attention, buying him time until he followed suit.

Chapter Twenty

Harris woke abruptly and looked around himself with alarm. It was still pitch black, and there was that dreadful smell of manure – and not just manure – which he now recognised. But then he shivered, realising that he was cold *and* damp. He hadn't felt cold earlier. Then the rest of it all suddenly came back to him ... The bastards. Rage gripped him and he began shouting through the gag, and kicking out with his bound feet at the sides of the box. But the effort involved – especially when weighed against the pathetic output – was too much and he quickly gave up. It was useless. He was going to have to wait, wasn't he? Eventually they would open up the coffin – unless they meant for him to die in it. He pushed that eventuality from his mind. God damn it. He was starving.

Poetry, that was what he needed. But, God he *was* hungry. His poor, neglected stomach was positively devoid of matter. *It was an alimentary emergency!* And his throat was bone dry – drier than North Wales on Sunday in Lent. Oh, Lord, please, *please* get me a drink, he moaned. He'd give up everything he owned for a single glass of Dom. And he'd give everything Ernest owned for that glass to be chilled. Ah, he shut his eyes ... poetry. Some Lewis Carroll would suffice. And then he began, his voice low and timid, and all the words rendered a nonsense by the gag filling his mouth:

'*The bun was bithing on the bea,*

Yes, that was good ...
Bithing with all his bight,
He did his thery best to ache
The billowth bmooth and bright.
Harris cackled.
And this was odd, because it boz
The biddle of the ...

Suddenly Harris lurched forward, almost butting the side of the box. He was moving. They were moving. He heard horses neighing, then a loud metallic *clonk*, and then the faint *thump-thump-thump* of an engine. Then he felt another nudge from the world outside, shoving him in the box, and then another. If he didn't know any better, he would have said it sounded just like ...

He was on a train. And this could mean only one thing: that he was now heading West with the show to South Dakota. *That must be it.* His heart sank. That was a long way from the bright lights of Manhattan – and his belongings for that matter. Bloody hell. And where was Ernest? Why hadn't he come to Harris's rescue?

Perhaps he wasn't coming. Harris's eyes began filling with tears. That's right. He was alone. He swallowed hard, and scrambled to return to Lewis Carroll, blinking away droplets of fear water from his eyes.

'The boon was thining bulkily,' he continued, his voice rising to mask the sound of the engine, 'Because thee thought the bun ... Had thot no thizness to be there –'

In the distance Harris heard the cry of the train's whistle and beneath his shoulder he could feel the vibrations of the wheels striking as they reached the end of each rail. The timber of his box evidently lay either on the floor of a railway carriage or close to it, just inches from the bogies themselves as they jerked and played above the spinning wheels.

Oh what a wonderful life it was, thought Harris. South Dakota here I come! He closed his eyes. Buggeration, he was bored of Lewis Carroll. Bored to tears. He started sobbing. He had to get out and get home. But no one was coming to his rescue. I'll happily tell the bastards anything they want to hear, he vowed. Just let me out . . .

'BEASE,' he shouted. 'BLET ME OUB!'

Drabble did not know how well he would do in the water in an autumn-weight tweed suit and a pair of brogues. But he would need them on the other side, and he had a lifejacket, which would make a small contribution to flotation. You would hope so, anyway. In addition, he reasoned, the waters of the Hudson were likely to be brackish if not essentially salty, offering some extra buoyancy. Drabble looked out through the port-side porthole at the New Jersey skyline, etched out of the gloom by lights in high windows. Lamps twinkled on the shore and occasional lanterns showed shipping active on the river. It was dark enough now out there to stand a chance of not being seen from the ship, though that made the swim additionally hazardous from the perspective of water traffic.

He inched open the door of Dalgleish's office and slipped out into the corridor, finding his way to the port side deck without meeting a soul. The evening air was cold and the water was only going to be colder. He cheered himself with the observation that he would have to survive the drop first.

Drabble looked neither left nor right, but gripped the handrail – and jumped.

Falling through the air, he remembered thinking it was taking longer than he thought it would to reach the . . .

Drabble slammed into the water. His feet were together, and he kept sinking. It felt like he was sinking for ever. Then he lingered in the murky depths – before finally rising, seemingly slowly, bubbles of air trailing him. Finally he burst through the surface, gasping for breath, just as a steep wave towered above and began to break. He splashed frantically away as it crashed over him, temporarily disorientating him. But as his vision cleared he saw he was just yards from the steep hull of the ship, which rose up out of the water like a mountain of metal.

Drabble paddled out into the river, quickly feeling the tide grip him. It was in his favour, drawing him inland, past Manhattan Island. Thank God it wasn't going out to sea, he thought again. Soon Drabble left the shadow of the hull of the *Empress of the Atlantic* behind him – a first landmark of sorts – then rounded the end of the dock against which she was berthed. On his right, in pitch black, would be shuttered wharfs and warehouses. There were steps up, but he would likely find himself confined to their compounds, just as he had been earlier in the liner's dockyard. The water was tolerably cold for now, so he pressed on – part swimming, part drifting with tide.

He knew he would have to get out of the water soon. He was keeping count. He had been five minutes in the water already, and it could not be advisable to risk more than twenty minutes at this time of year. At the most. Up ahead he saw a portion of the shore where there were lampposts at regular intervals, connected by chains of lanterns, with riverside bars and the wholesome sound of drinkers and drunks yelling at one another.

His tired arms slapped down inexpertly into the water with each stroke. He knew his strength was leaving him – it was being eaten by the cold and the additional effort of swimming fully clothed for an English autumn. A large inky black triangle appeared ahead, cutting into the dancing landscape of silvery ripples of the water. At first he couldn't decipher it, but then he realised – it was a slipway.

Drabble splashed towards it, kicking doggedly with his spent legs. He had long stopped feeling his fingers so when he gripped the brittle, encrusted timbers of the slipway it felt like they were in someone else's hands. Drabble edged along to where the slipway was lower in the water and then beached himself up it. Rolling onto his back, he lay, arms outstretched, gazing up into the overcast sky.

I've made it, he thought. I'm in America.

Without warning the horses got spooked. They neighed, whinnied, and stamped their hooves – a cacophony that appeared to come from all around him. Then there were heavy footsteps, possibly more hoof-steps, and a loud, creaking sound directly above him. The sound was very close. In fact . . .

Harris experienced the stomach-departing sensation of moving through the air – and then a painful jolt as the coffin was dropped and landed hard.

Suddenly a hammer slammed into the side of the coffin, splintering the timbers of the box by his head. Harris yelled. Another blow landed and a narrow wedge of light shone directly into his eyes. There came a further chewy wrench of the chisel, followed by the sound of it being hammered – and abruptly the lid of the coffin was off.

Harris squirmed under the piercing light as unseen hands reached in and hauled him out – tearing off his gag and hurling him aside into a heap of straw. Harris landed heavily and scuttled backwards, suddenly feeling like a cornered spider, his eyes jammed shut.

'Leave me . . . leave me!' he pleaded.

He lay panting in the straw and the muck, as he heard the box – a narrow packing crate – being dragged and then dropped back into the compartment from which it had been lifted. Then there was a creak as the trapdoor was closed. Gradually Harris opened his eyes. First he registered that the wagon was in fact feebly lit – notwithstanding the impact of the light on his hibernating eyes. Next he saw that the further half of it was home to six or seven horses of various descriptions. Finally he saw two men, whom he didn't recognise, other than knowing them to be Grant Wild Westers by the looks of them. He glared, and gave voice to his anger.

'Where am I?' he shouted. '*Where* am I?'

One of the men – his bearded face lost in the shade of his hat – stepped over and kicked him. 'Shut up!' he growled.

Harris whimpered, bringing his knees up to his chest and squeezing his eyes shut. ('*Make it stop!*' wailed a tiny voice from his hippocampus. '*Make it stop!*')

'Give me your hands!' barked the cowboy.

He grabbed Harris's wrists roughly and sliced the rope that was binding them. The two men then headed for the door. 'We'll be back with your food,' one of them shouted. 'If you mess us around you're going back in the box. Got it?'

Harris nodded into his hands, daring not to look up. *Make it stop. Make it stop* . . . He heard the door of the wagon slam and being bolted, and he exhaled. That was better. He lowered his hands from his eyes and looked out. So this was it, a step up at least from the coffin of excrement. He stared up at the single electric light bulb, then over at the horses which were tethered to the walls, feeding bags placed before them. They stood in a layer of straw and manure about a foot deep.

It could be worse, Harris told himself. He sighed and patted his pockets, locating his cigarette case – also he still had half a dozen Craven As left, and his lighter. Thank the Lord for the simple pleasures, he thought. He crawled over to the wall and made a heap of straw to lean against. He eased his head back, stealing his eyes from the bulb and its inviting radiating waves of light. He kicked away some of the straw – dying in an equestrian fireball of his own making was not his idea of a good way to go – and lit up, filling his lungs. In that instant the Craven A transported him from the tyranny of horses and manure to a new, ethereal plain, one of Zen-like contentment. It almost made him forget that he was a prisoner on a train heading West – but something stronger than tobacco would be needed for that. But by Christ tobacco *was good*. Oh, Christ, thank you for the gift of tobacco. He looked heavenwards. Beneath him he felt the metallic beat of the wheels striking the next rail, a rhythm taking him further from where he wanted to be, but perhaps closer to answers that he was searching for. He had five more cigarettes left, and possibly enough tobacco for a pipe or two. And he didn't hate horses. Not really.

Harris inhaled strongly on the cigarette. And he was still alive, which had a distinct advantage over the contrary state. Neither had he lost any body-parts, but he wasn't counting his chickens on that score yet. But having been allowed to live this far, he might yet still be alive at the end of the process. Granted, being carted off a thousand miles or so into the West was not necessarily convenient. Nor was it optimal to have almost certainly lost all his possessions, but the very fact of still being alive, well, that should not be underrated.

He sighed and looked down at his clothes. Not that his best dinner suit would ever recover. That was a loss. But hardly an insurmountable one. The fact was, everything would be well so long as he didn't run out of ciggies, which meant he had to pace the five he had left. He cursed; he hated pacing himself with anything, particularly tobacco products. And if only he'd had the presence of mind to have gone out last night fortified with a hip flask . . . Now a drink would be good.

He gathered himself. What day was it? He couldn't be sure, which wasn't a nice sensation. But he knew it was night-time, because no daylight had come in when the Wild Westers opened the door. What he knew for sure was that he had been biffed on the head on Friday night, so it could easily now be Saturday night, meaning he had spent most of the night and day in the dreaded box. That fitted. It ushered a distasteful thought: so, if they were on the Pacific Union hurtling west, then they would right now be travelling through some backwater of the United States, one that no Englishman had any business being, probably nearing somewhere like Chicago, or Minnesota – places that did not figure in the geography lessons of a self-respecting British schoolboy. More's the pity, thought Harris. A basic appreciation of the layout of the United States would be incredibly useful right now. Damned sight more useful than the *Lays of Ancient Rome*.

He emitted a long withering sigh. But not, in many ways, any more help than a fully primed hip flask of cognac. Now, if only he had one of those.

Chapter Twenty-one

The rain came down with a determined vigour, reflecting the light from the tall buildings as it fell, making it all rather beautiful. The downpour had turned the gutters into fast-moving tributaries and overfilling drains formed swelling lakes at street corners. Drabble passed unnoticed amongst the sodden landscape of humanity, plodding stiffly towards his destination, among the puddles and the breaking waves of spray being sent up by the motorcars.

He could express only gratitude for Manhattan's grid system. Not for New Yorkers the questionable serendipity of medieval street nomenclature and randomness. And not for Drabble the need to ask for directions, which suited his purposes. He stopped to admire what he recognised to be Times Square, momentarily permitting himself to be a tourist, and contemplated what it would be like to be here under different, non-fugitive conditions. He then crossed the road and made his way along pavements busy with pedestrians striding purposefully underneath streaming umbrellas. Assuming he had understood her properly, Charlotte's hotel, the Aviemore, was not much further on.

It was now half an hour since he had crawled out of the Hudson and lain gasping on the slipway, and he still hadn't begun to feel any warmer yet. On the contrary the cold might have been making its grip all the tighter. He had confirmed that his paperwork and money were still dry, which was a god-send, but for now, his priority was getting himself dry and warm. Nonetheless he had to be careful and so kept to the shadows.

His working assumption was that the authorities would keep looking for him until his body washed up. Therefore he could not very well go to the hotel that he and Harris were due to stay at, and where he assumed Harris would currently be propping up the bar. That would be among the first places the authorities would look or have under surveillance.

Hence Charlotte's hotel was the preferable choice, but it was also a good choice for other reasons . . . And now he could see it up ahead: its name, The Aviemore, was emblazoned in warm yellow light, the same light which spilled out invitingly from the foyer across the pavement.

Drabble saw a liveried doorman outside, umbrella held aloft, protecting guests arriving by car from the elements. An older couple – a grey-haired woman in fur and her husband in top hat and cape – emerged from a yellow taxi and entered, and Drabble realised suddenly that there was no way he could simply walk in. Not like this, anyhow. His appearance alone would be enough to raise suspicion.

Fortunately it was all nothing that a hot bath and a thorough laundry service couldn't put right. But that didn't help him right now. Then as Drabble got closer another thought struck him. Surely, just as he was wise to avoid his own hotel, he ought to observe the same caution here? After all, he and Charlotte had made no secret of their relationship aboard the *Empress of the Atlantic* and so it was perfectly possible for their association to have become known to the authorities. As a result, if there was any doubt over his whereabouts then her forwarding address would also be among the first places that any half competent police force would put under surveillance. It stood to reason.

183

This dawned on Drabble just as he saw a pair of policemen arrive at the street corner outside the hotel. He immediately broke right up a dark side street. It was too risky. He needed somewhere else to stay – preferably a smaller hotel, a less grand establishment where a man of his dishevelled appearance might not be so remarkable. But also one not connected to himself in any way. The wind funnelled down the side road, buffeting him, and he pulled his sodden coat around him. In the distance he saw another hotel – it looked distinctly cheaper – and might just do the trick.

Just then a door ahead opened and two men spilled out into the road, the bright light from inside making their crimson Aviemore uniforms all the more brilliant. An umbrella went up against the deluge and a flame lit two cigarettes . . .

Five minutes and twenty dollars apiece later, Drabble emerged from a service stairwell on the third floor of the hotel and knocked quietly on Charlotte's door. He waited, and knocked again. When, after a few minutes, there came no answer, he began to contemplate his next step. If she wasn't in, could he wait or should he head to the less salubrious hotel he had already seen?

Just then the door opened and Charlotte looked out.

'Oh, Ernest!'

She threw her arms around him.

Nothing more was said at first. Drabble had a hot bath, accompanied by a double whisky. That thawed him out. Then he had dinner in the room, and that was when he started to explain what had happened to him since leaving her cabin that morning. After dinner, he lay in the large bed wearing a luxurious bathrobe, feeling immeasurably better about the world, and drifted back and forth across the margins of sleep. Charlotte washed his underclothes and shirt, which were now hanging up to dry in the bathroom, and announced that she would take his suit to a cleaners in the morning. The use of the hotel

184

facilities would certainly advertise his presence. After all, what would a spinster travelling alone be doing having a man's three-piece suit dry-cleaned?

He awoke finding her climbing into the bed beside him, her body warm and soft and entwining. This time it was different from the last time, the night just before aboard the ship. A different location, a different continent ... Perhaps it was his exhaustion, or the very real relief they shared at the dangers avoided. Or was it the sense of the dangers yet to come? It all confirmed something in both of them, Drabble realised, as they lay afterwards holding one another.

A little later Charlotte was sitting up in an identical hotel dressing gown, smoking. Drabble stroked her thigh, which pressed against his shoulder.

'I really ought to telephone Harris.'

'I'll do it –' She leaned over and lifted up the heavy telephone set, bringing it to her lap.

The telephonist at The Duke hotel was confused by the enquiry and it took several minutes to determine the reason. 'I'm afraid we have no such person of that name checked into the Duke, ma'am,' said the voice at last.

Charlotte replaced the receiver.

'So where is he?' asked Drabble. He added but then regretted saying, 'He can't just disappear.'

'Perhaps he decided to stay at a different hotel?'

'Unlikely. Harris doesn't like change. And his newspaper is paying, so he'd have no reason to swap, since it's about the most luxurious place in town.'

Harris's deviation from the plan was uncharacteristic, especially when you connected it to his disappearing trick on Thursday night. It confirmed in Drabble's mind precisely what he had feared. Charlotte put her arm around him.

'We have to go to South Dakota – and not just for Harris's sake.'

185

Drabble turned to her. This was all true – for him. But he had no intention of letting her go anywhere near South Dakota. It was far too dangerous, and he could scarcely hope to look after his own skin, let alone be responsible for dragging an innocent third party into this. Especially a third party he was in …

'And it will be far easier for you,' Charlotte was saying, 'to travel there incognito, if you did so as a husband with his wife rather than as a single man – a single man that every police officer in the United States is looking for.'

She was right.

'What about your research in Virginia?'

'Oh, that can wait –' She waved it away, and he knew from her tone that she meant it. 'I'll get the coffee …'

Drabble watched her walk around the large bed and over to the dresser where the coffee things were laid out on a tray. 'There is another option,' he said. 'I could simply throw myself at the mercy of the British Consulate in New York – explain everything – and hand the matter over to them?'

She shook her head. 'If you want to experience the American penal system first hand and surrender all hope of stopping a bloodbath in South Dakota, then I support you one hundred per cent.' She turned to him and smiled curtly before pouring the steaming coffee. Drabble realised, of course, that Charlotte was absolutely right.

Chapter Twenty-two

It was too cold to sleep. And anyway, Harris did not know if it was the right time of day to sleep. The train wagon had no windows and the single electric light bulb was never switched off. The cold, meanwhile, had worsened, leading him to suspect that it was that point before dawn when the absence of the sun is most felt and has been most prolonged. All the while the train continued its remorseless progress West, away from England and the coast that would get him there once this whole ghastly business was over. The Wild Westers had also returned to give him a thin blanket and an enamel mug of soup.

The soup was brown and as foul as the blanket was rough. But both were welcome. If only he'd had whisky he might have been comfortable. He drained the soup, fishing out the meagre lumps of vegetables with his fingers, and huddled into the blanket for warmth. His mind then began to drift off.

The soup course concluded, Sir Percival drew the horse blanket over his shoulders, and progressed to the tobacco course.

Taking a Craven A from his cigarette box, he lit up, feeling surprisingly uplifted, and leaned back against the wooden wall, his eyes half closed. It really wasn't so bad. Yes, he was still decidedly peckish. *Yes indeed* ... He began to visualise a table groaning with his favourite dishes, but stopped himself. He grunted. *No, Harris.* No. Instead he focused on his Craven A and determined to settle his mind. But for the lack of booze, and the solitude, it might have been rather enjoyable. A retreat, even. And the horses were decent enough coves, once one was acclimatised to the odour. He'd had pals who smelled worse, for God's sake.

Perhaps it was this brief respite from self-pity, but Harris was becoming aware of a latent curiosity starting to shake itself awake within him. It was growing in confidence, enough to arrive at the forefront of his mind – what *was* going on? What *exactly* had he observed in the First Class luggage repository on Thursday night – and why had it caused him to be kidnapped and imprisoned with such equestrian aplomb?

The Craven A was working wonders. Hang it that there were now only three left. Something would turn up to rectify the situation. It always did. He returned to his line of inquiry and his predicament.

He took a deep drag of the cigarette and then enjoyed the sensation of the smoke escaping from his nostrils, watching it play in the light while he corralled his observations. He was surprised to discover that Fanny Howell was involved in the arrangement, however unlikely, of the transmission of a thousand modified bolt action rifles from Japan to the US. And on that note, he could only presume that the first cache of fifty rifles was aboard this very train heading west. If they had smuggled him out, then a couple of Japanese pop-guns shouldn't be beyond the wit of man.

The satisfying aspect to all this was that it cohered: it fitted with what Wheelock had told Drabble about a 'hostile power' supplying weapons to the Indians. The Japanese were undoubtedly antithetical to the United States. It also fitted with the line of interrogation he had received from the Neanderthal. The implication, therefore, was that Fanny Howell and Grant were intermediaries. True, they weren't entirely satisfactory intermediaries for high-level – and highly sensitive – governmental discussions. But hadn't Grant been rubbing shoulders with Hitler? Who else had they broken bread with?

And then there were the Indians, or, perhaps more precisely, the Sioux.

Fanny had mentioned 'the chiefs' but that spurred the question of which chiefs?

Say what you like about him, but the role of revolutionary leader did not appear to fit with Black Cloud. While he was undoubtedly aggrieved over his people's treatment at the hands of the United States and the US Army – and fair enough – he did not seem to be the sort to start a war over it. Bitterness and regrets, yes. Slaughtering women and children in revenge, no.

Yet he might very well be the spiritual leader of the new ghost dance. That was all too credible. Harris took another deep drag of his Craven A, a sense of certainty rising within him. Yes. Black Cloud was part of the dance. That was certain, and it had something to do with Sitting Bull's shirt and pipe – Sitting Bull, after all, was the Johnny who orchestrated the victory of the Sioux over Custer at the Battle of Little Bighorn – and Custer was mentioned repeatedly in the ritual that Drabble had overheard. So perhaps the war shirt was something to do with it, like the cross or body of Christ at the Eucharist?

And any bellicose spirit that Black Cloud lacked, Speaks With Fists possessed in spades. Oh, no . . . He had inherited none of his father's spiritual equanimity. He just had anger. Speaks With Fists wouldn't think twice about taking Jap rifles to strike at Uncle Sam. In fact, he'd be sharpening his bayonets and polishing his bullets at the very prospect.

So let us suppose it was all true, thought Harris. Let's suppose there are a bunch of aggrieved Indians who have now got a thousand guns and God knows what else. They've also got a new spiffing dance which makes them feel invincible and the war shirt of the man who led them in their last great victory against the evil oppressors to buoy them along. That could work. And you could see why the Japanese were in to it: they got to destabilise one of their arch rivals – meaning they could focus on us without worrying about the Americans on their backs. Everyone knew they didn't like the Royal Navy ruling the Pacific roost, and Sakamoto had made that clear enough too. Harris took a last drag of the Craven A and ground out the stub on the floor.

But what was in it for Fanny – and Colonel Grant? Why would they help, especially a crusty old Indian hunter like Grant? He took out another cigarette and lit it. Why would they be sympathetic to the cause? Harris pondered it. It was possible, of course ... Spend enough time with another crew and sooner or later you either ended up hating them or seeing the world their way. And frankly, it was hard *not* to admire Black Cloud. Harris did – up to a point at least. The old man had seen a lot and been through a good deal more – and reacted with a rare magnanimity that was rather humbling.

The problem was a thousand or so Japanese rifles were not going to be enough to wage a rebellion. Ten thousand wouldn't be. Whatever they got would never be enough. All it would do is lead to a massacre – probably *plural* massacres on both sides but mostly on that of the Indians. And when the dust settled the Indians would undoubtedly have come off much, much worse. There would certainly be fewer of them around. Many fewer. And they must know that. So why do it?

Harris shook his head as the scale of the horror formed in his mind. He visualised the smoke and the blood and ghastliness of the whole thing ... stopping his mind from progressing beyond the mental image of burning tepees. It had to be stopped. Black Cloud had to be told – and warned explicitly. If necessary he had to reach Speaks With Fists and reason with him. Somehow, this madness had to be stopped. Moreover he had to get word to Drabble – or to Walberswick at the Embassy in Washington. The alarm had to be raised as soon as possible.

The next question was, how long did he have to avert tragedy? Sakamoto said the rifles would be arriving in San Francisco in four days, which was Tuesday, now probably the day after tomorrow. However, logic dictated that it would then take a couple of days to get the arms from the port to South Dakota. Then it was probable that whoever was using the weapons would require some elementary training in them – unless that's what the first fifty were being used for. It all meant that with a good wind behind them the Sioux could be on the warpath by the following weekend. Easy.

Harris heard the door being unbolted, the cowboys were back. 'Get up,' one of them barked. 'You're coming with us.'

Drabble and Charlotte were on their second train of the day, having left New York City shortly after dawn. Outside was a landscape of steaming and smoking stacks and chimneys stretching out as far as the eye could see. It felt like they'd spent an eternity passing through America's industrial heartland, and to Drabble's mind it was comparable to a train steaming through the West Midlands – for eight hours straight. They were due in Chicago in an hour. After that they had another train to catch to St Paul, Minnesota, which would take up another day. Whatever else you might say about the United States it was big, too big probably ...

Drabble was trying hard not to worry about Harris. It would do no good, after all. But it wasn't as simple as that. He picked up his newspaper and attempted to read it.

And it wasn't just Harris on his mind. There was *tomorrow* to consider. If they made their next connection they would reach Rapid City – the stop closest to the Black Hills – at about four o'clock in the afternoon. From there they would drive to Grant's ranch, which remained Drabble's first option. Quite what would happen once they got there remained to be seen. He simply hoped to find Harris there – or as a result of going there – and then to emerge with their liberty thrown into the bargain. He looked over at Charlotte, who was reading *Moby Dick*.

He swallowed and looked out of the window. The challenge would be keeping her away from the danger. Whatever fate befell Harris was, in honesty, none of her concern. And by that, he meant he had no intention of letting her put herself in harm's way for Harris's sake. To that end he planned to convince her to remain in Rapid City at all costs. Then she might be all right. But he would never forgive himself if anything happened to her. Drabble already held himself responsible for the death of one innocent woman during the affair that he and Harris had become embroiled in around the time of the abdication. And he wasn't about to repeat the mistake. But who could know how dangerous the next seventy-two hours were going to be?

Drabble picked up the newspaper again, and tried to read.

'Something troubling you?' asked Charlotte mildly.

He lowered the *New York Times* and met her enquiring gaze. 'It's nothing,' he said, smiling.

Her reply was a tart pout of the lips – communicating an amused yet respectful disagreement – and she returned to Melville.

Drabble scanned the newspaper – and suddenly wished he hadn't. Turning the page he discovered his own face staring out at him:

Diplomat murder sparks hunt: 'resourceful killer' at large

POLICE ACROSS four East Coast States are hunting Professor Ernest Drabble, a fugitive British historian suspected of the murder of a British diplomat on Saturday aboard the steam ship Empress of the Atlantic.

Drabble, suspected of stabbing diplomat Captain Hubert Walberswick to death, escaped custody and is believed to be at large, having jumped ship. A life-vest from the ship was located in a trash can on West 50 just hours after he went missing.

District Police Commissioner Patrick Morrency said the authorities would be releasing a new photograph of Drabble to aid his capture. 'Drabble is a resourceful killer and should be approached with extreme caution,' warned Morrency.

The police have issued a photograph of Drabble taken in 1936 during a climbing expedition in the Swiss Alps. They stress that he no longer has a beard and appeal for any sightings to be reported immediately.

Capt. Walberswick, 30, was a cultural attaché at the British Embassy in Washington, D.C. according to diplomatic sources. He was on his way back from England where he had recently become engaged to be married . . .

Drabble shook his head. Poor Walberswick. It might have been what he did for a living, but he surely had no idea what he was getting himself into. As for Harris . . . Drabble's focus settled on the words 'resourceful killer' in the caption under the bearded photograph of himself. That was probably American English for 'shoot to kill'. Probably. He could have laughed if it wasn't all so deadly serious. Drabble went to the next section:

Reporter 'missing'

In a related development police are still searching for missing Briton, Sir Percival Harris, who was also a passenger aboard the Empress of the Atlantic. *Sir Percival was last been seen on the transatlantic crossing on Friday night. He did not clear immigration in New York City and no remains have been found for the man, who is a close associate of Drabble. Police are not ruling out foul play and a source told the* Times: *'We could be looking at a double homicide.'*

Drabble exhaled and laid down the newspaper, his heart sinking. So Harris *was* missing, meaning he was either in South Dakota with Grant and the rest of them, or . . . or . . .

Drabble could not bear to think about the alternative. More

193

importantly – he rallied – he didn't need to; the information he had about Harris's last known whereabouts, namely, seemingly in pursuit of Fanny Howell at the Britannia bar, pointed towards the possibility that he would be with the Wild West Show.

This gave Drabble hope – and not the idle hope of blind, naïve optimism, but one founded soundly on the available evidence. All that was required now, was for Harris to keep his mouth shut and not to provoke his captors into doing anything he might regret. Because – and here Drabble was worried – why would you need Harris alive? If you planned a clandestine operation, and Harris knew about it, then he represented a clear danger. He was the enemy of discretion.

If only he could keep his mouth shut, then he might stand a chance . . .

Chapter Twenty-three

The steward, his pungent waxed hair immaculately parted, placed a cup of tea on the shelf next to Harris's bunk, and coughed politely into his hand.

Harris yawned and reached for his spectacles.

'What time is it?'

'Just after eight, sir.' Harris detected a notable whiff of lavender in the air – a step up from the equestrian experience – as the steward raised the blind. 'When you are ready, sir, the Colonel desires your presence at breakfast in the state car. There's water in the basin for you to wash, if you want. A clean suit of clothes has also been put in the wardrobe at your disposal, sir.'

Harris sat up and saw they were passing through a broad, hilly landscape that could have been Herefordshire – if the county had been afflicted by gigantism. The broad sky was pale blue and seemingly bigger and wider, too. Harris grinned. Things were looking up. And breakfast in the state car sounded like it had arrived just in the nick of time, too.

Ten minutes later he followed the smell of bacon like a starved bloodhound and arrived in the state car. Every surface was wooden and varnished, and in this tinted wonderland was Colonel Grant, Major Sakamoto, Speaks With Fists, along with another man he didn't recognise. He looked about forty and possessed the grizzled features and lean frame that spoke of an active life in the saddle.

'Good morning –' Grant spread his arm towards the counter where food was laid out on hot plates. 'You must be hungry, Sir Percival – please ...' Harris didn't have to be asked twice, even if Grant was the principal cause of his hunger in the first place. But right then, under the circumstances, that struck him as churlish, self-defeating observation. He heaped rashers of bacon onto his plate, before shovelling on fried potatoes and scrambled eggs. Toast was on the table and he saw a jar of marmalade. The American interior was certainly not entirely untouched by civilisation.

'Coffee?' It was the unknown Wild Wester, who was introduced by the Colonel as 'Ferguson'. He reached over and poured Harris a steep cup. Harris began to eat – ravenously. He chose not to acknowledge Sakamoto.

Grant was the first to address him. Harris eyed him as he chewed, looking like a dog worried you might steal its bone, occasionally nodding to show that he was listening.

'Sir Percival,' drawled Grant. 'I think it's only fair to appraise you of the developments of which you are now inextricably part.' Grant made a sidelong glance at Speaks With Fists, then slid out of the booth towards a shrouded picture on an easel. He pulled away the curtain, revealing a map showing a section of territory that Harris did not at first recognise. No coastline was visible and it was threaded with rivers and geometric lines, which Harris guessed were state boundaries.

'This is a map covering most of the territory of North and South Dakota, Montana, Wyoming, Colorado and Nebraska. This area here –' Grant hovered his finger over a shaded quarter at the centre of what Harris later learned was South Dakota – 'is, or rather *was*, what was once known as the Great Sioux Reservation.' Grant nodded meaningfully towards Speaks With Fists. 'That is to say, Sir Percival, that it *is* the land which was promised in perpetuity to the Sioux under the terms of the Treaty of Fort Laramie in 1868, signed by all paramount chiefs and band leaders – as well as the United States government. It furthermore came with firm assurances over adjacent territories set aside for hunting and spiritual reasons – here, here, and here, all shown in pencil.' His hand danced across relevant swathes of the rest of the map, covering especially the Black Hills. Harris now noticed the pencilled outline, encompassing a vast area probably the combined size of South Dakota and Wyoming.

'Now, these –' Grant declared, pointing to several small rectangles and chunks of land dispersed across the core shaded area – 'these are what became of the treaty of 1868. They are what the Sioux Indians have left after more than half a century of further treaty-making and larceny by the United States government. Not much, eh?'

It certainly wasn't.

'To the victor, the spoils,' suggested Harris, chewing.

'Precisely.' Grant nodded. 'The Sioux ended up with barely a tenth of what was agreed in 1868 – and that, my friend, was significantly less than they deserved in the first place, which,' he paused theatrically, 'if you were familiar with the terms of the 1851 treaty, also signed by the paramount chiefs at Fort Laramie, you would know.' Grant now indicated a black-inked dotted perimeter line outside of the pencilled border, enclosing still more land. 'This line is what the Oglala Lakota people and the rest of their Sioux cousins were promised in 1851. And that, Sir Percival, is what they're gonna get.'

Harris looked up from his bacon, still chewing, and found Grant's waiting gaze.

'So, you're probably wondering, what's this got to do with you?'

Harris nodded earnestly – he hadn't been, not in the least, but he definitely was now. He reached for his coffee.

'On Thursday we are going to begin the reconquest of all these lost lands on behalf of the Sioux people.' Grant's hand swept across the map with grandiose flourish. 'From the Missouri River in the east to the Powder River and Bighorn Mountains in the West; from the Yellowstone and Heart Rivers in the north, to North Platte River in Colorado in the south, we're taking it all. What you are looking at here, Sir Percival, is a new country – the Sioux Republic. We will begin by taking Rapid City, then we will take Pierre – seizing the railway stations and airports, the newspapers and radio stations. And then we will declare independence.'

Harris's chewing slowed to a halt and he swallowed and pushed away his half-finished plate of food. There was an exultant glint in Grant's eye that turned his stomach; it was the undoubting spark of a fanatic. And he wasn't alone. Looking across the party, they all had it, the same fervour in their faces. As unreal as it might sound, to these men the Sioux Republic wasn't a bizarre fantasy. And Harris realised that they were all looking at him, and waiting.

'What is it?' Grant smiled goadingly. 'Cat got your tongue?'

Harris tossed down his napkin in an act of defiance.

'How the hell do you hope to take an area the size of – I don't know, let's say for argument's sake, *France* . . . how in God's name are you going to take that from the United States government – and then to hold on to it – armed with only a thousand iffy Jap rifles? You'll be wiped out and you know it.'

A peculiar smirk arrived at Grant's mouth. It reminded Harris of the expression the vicar had whenever he questioned the validity of the miracles.

'Sir Percival, the new Sioux Republic goes live on Thursday. You can rest assured that we *are* prepared militarily. We already have a significant cache of arms, and the Japanese' – he nodded to Sakamoto – 'have promised us more assistance. But also, it's not really about hardware. It's about diplomacy. We already have the necessary paperwork ready to submit to the League of Nations *and* we have international recognition agreed in principle with four sovereign states around the world, including the Empire of Japan –' Sakamoto nodded grimly – 'and Mexico. And here's the thing, my friend, *you* are going to be the founding chronicler of this new republic.'

'Chronicler?' Harris broke into derisive laughter. 'Like the Venerable bloody Bede or something?'

Speaks With Fists cleared his throat. 'You will be the neutral observer of the rebirth of our nation, Sir Percival. It is a great privilege.'

Harris's temper broke.

'No, I *fucking* won't. It's not a privilege I want.'

Grant cleared this throat and addressed Speaks With Fists. 'I think Sir Percival doesn't realise that he has no choice in the matter.'

Sitting at a table in a half-empty railway café, Drabble put aside the day-old copy of the *St Paul Sunday Dispatch*. As could be expected, there was no fresh news about Harris, or indeed of the manhunt taking place for himself – at this geographical distance they only merited a short mention on page five. It was before seven in the morning. Drabble looked over at Charlotte and realised that he was feeling almost sick from tiredness. They had spent a long night on the train from Chicago, sleeping little, contributing to a general sense of exhaustion that was fast becoming a routine feature of life in the New World. He cast his eyes again over at the long counter, behind which cooks toiled. Their breakfast could not be long now. Charlotte was still reading *Moby Dick*. She looked pale.

He could not live with himself if anything happened to her. He watched her look up and out into the busy café – unaware of his attention. She was beautiful, and this caused him to smile, momentarily forgetting everything else. He reached forward and pressed his hand to hers. As he did this a cloud passed over him; she was so vulnerable. He suddenly felt an urge to tell her something important ... But she spoke before he could the words out.

'What is it?'

'Nothing.' He forced a smile but levity failed him. 'There's no more news about Harris,' he continued, changing the subject. He nodded towards the newspaper.

She replied with a nod of her own, and a comforting smile.

'Excuse me, ma'am –' They looked up to see an overweight, middle-aged man, dressed in a trilby and heavy black overcoat, address Charlotte. 'Do you have the time?'

Before Drabble could say a word she had pinched forward her glove, turned her wrist and crisply enunciated the hour. The man, tipped his hat, and walked straight for the door. Through the window, Drabble saw him cross the vast concourse of the station, right under a huge clock. Drabble leaned forward and took Charlotte's hand.

'We have to go.'

They left the café through the side entrance and hand-in-hand half ran towards the nearest exit from the station. Outside Drabble hailed a waiting taxicab and barked the words, 'City Hall' at the driver, as they climbed in.

The taxi set off and Drabble looked back – seeing the man in the overcoat spill out on to the pavement after them. He was cursing and looking around for another taxicab – but there was none. Drabble then saw a second man arrive at his side, dressed similarly in a uniform of civic respectability.

Their taxi turned a bend and the pursuers vanished from sight. Drabble settled back in the seat and they drove on in silence for thirty seconds or so. Then their eyes met: Charlotte's expectant. Drabble nodded.

'I'm afraid that was definitely the right decision.'

Charlotte sighed. 'Wonderful.'

She checked her watch.

'Our train leaves in twenty-five minutes.'

'And we've still not had breakfast –'

In that moment Drabble saw a café down a side road. It looked promising. He took a glance over his shoulder – there was no traffic in sight – and tapped the driver on the shoulder.

Inside the café, they sat at the back of the premises, where no one would see them, and ordered the fastest food available. Charlotte inspected the menu, half hiding behind it.

'What do we do now?'

Drabble accepted a cup of coffee from the waiter and looked over towards the counter where various staff worked in the open kitchen. He called the waiter back and asked to speak to the owner.

They left the café ten minutes before their train was due to leave, taking the street that ran parallel to the main road that they had driven along from the station. Charlotte had changed her hat for a brown headscarf.

Arms interlinked, they hurried along the street. Shops were starting to open their shutters and set up for the day. Fragments of litter swirled in the road.

Drabble explained his plan. 'At the station I want you to go straight to the platform and present your ticket without any fuss. At the same time I'm going to walk through the station from a different entrance and distract anybody watching out for us. Just act normally.'

'Like I'm in Victoria station?' she replied archly.

'Just like you're in Victoria station.'

He smiled at her doubtful expression and drew her aside. Shifting the bundle under his arm, they kissed and then held each other. They broke apart.

'It's a flawless plan,' he resumed. 'Nothing will happen in broad daylight in the station. I'll find you in the buffet car.'

She looked over at the façade of the station, steeling herself.

'It's Victoria station,' he said. 'Paddington at worst. Go to platform seven and get on the train. You'll be in Eastbourne before you know it. And I'll be right with you.'

He kissed her one last time, and then watched as she set off, his heart in his throat. He saw her enter the station and then broke into a run. Seconds later, he reached the end of the street and peered around the corner, seeing the entrance that they had left by twenty minutes before. The way was clear.

This was it.

Drabble strolled out into the station walking in a business-like fashion. He now wore a charcoal woollen overcoat, its collar raised, and a grey derby, tilted forward like he meant it. He saw Charlotte, head bowed rather, approaching the plat-form. In a second or two she would present her ticket to the inspector and be safely beyond the barrier. The station clock said one minute to the hour. He was leaving it tight.

His heart beat fast. He stared straight ahead at the ticket inspector by the barrier – looking neither left nor right and fighting the compulsion simply to run. He was three or four yards from the barrier now. The inspector acknowledged his approach with smile.

Suddenly the man's expression changed. His eyes widened in fear . . .

The train's whistle sounded – a shrill cry slicing the air. The ticket inspector reached out in alarm. He looked straight through Drabble and began to retreat, shouting. Drabble broke into a sprint.

Gunshots rang out, bullets zipping past him. The ticket inspector's chest erupted in puffs of blood. A second shrill whis-tle sounded – and there was another burst of fire. Drabble plunged into the swirling masses of steam and smoke on the platform, dodging around a statuesque porter. The man col-lapsed, clutching his chest. The train was already moving, slowly building up speed. Drabble let his bundle go and charged.

Sustained machine-gun fire raked the platform. Drabble threw himself at the door of the rearmost carriage, wildly snatching at the handle. His foot slipped – but his grip held firm and he hauled himself up onto the footplate, breathing hard.

Slamming the door shut behind him, he made straight for the buffet car. It was five carriages along – a long five carriages, it turned out, with the gunfire still ringing in Drabble's ears. He reached the buffet car – and he hurried in, pushing past a waiter, checking each table. Charlotte was nowhere to be seen. He felt his throat close up and a tightening in the chest – *where was she?* – and his pace quickened. He reached the bar – and saw the end of the carriage not far off, but could still not make out the brown headscarf or her dark blond hair. Tears pricked at his eyes as panic began to take hold ...

Then he saw her; sat at a small table, *Moby Dick* open before her by a large viewing widow. But she was not looking out of the window or at the book. Instead she focused directly ahead at the seated figure opposite. But who that was, was obscured by the headrest and a pillar. Then Drabble caught side of a crease in the top of a grey homburg, the collar of a frock coat, and a black beard flecked with white.

It was Wheelock.

'Good morning, Professor.' The American rose and grasped Drabble's hand. 'I trust our friends from Chicago didn't present you with any difficulties?'

Drabble slid into the banquette beside Charlotte, kissed her on the cheek and then took her hand.

There was a great deal that he could say to Wheelock but right now he needed answers. He took a deep breath and countered Wheelock's benign smile with a look of mild hostility.

'I think it's time you told us what's going on.'

Colonel Grant's threat had barely left his moustachioed mouth when Harris felt the collective attention of the assembled party upon him. To a man, their expressions conveyed a dispiriting implacability. He swallowed. Quite apart from the unspoken consequences of declining their offer – Grant hadn't needed to spell *that* out – it was fast occurring to Harris that being at the centre of what could potentially be the biggest news story on the face of the planet might be rather advantageous professionally. It beat being dead, too, and as far as he could ascertain, it wasn't as if he would actually be *helping* them, either, which would be bad. Of course, if he ended up providing some retrospective justification for their iniquitous endeavour that wouldn't look good; Harrises were many things but they were not collaborators. But their scheme was categorically doomed to failure as far as he could tell, so it shouldn't come to that. Moreover, whatever happened to their scheme he also knew that Lord Axminster, his proprietor, would be pleased, so long as Harris got the final word on it. He reached for a cigarette and Ferguson leaned in with a flaming lighter.

'All right –' said Harris, as he confronted the four pairs of eyes weighing him up. 'I'll do it. I'll be your Venerable *bloody* Bede.'

Chapter Twenty-four

Wheelock talked quietly, barely above the level of a whisper.

He now appeared to be a very different man from the individual whose acquaintance Drabble had made aboard the *Empress of the Atlantic*. He was somehow a bigger figure, and, peculiarly, more trustworthy – which bothered Drabble a little, because there was not a scintilla of evidence to support it. In fact, to the contrary, there was the rough questioning of Harris that remained an outstanding topic between them. But the simple fact was that Wheelock wasn't trying to kill them, not yet anyway. And that was a start. He might even be able to help, though that remained to be seen.

'What we do know is that the Japanese diplomat, Major Sakamoto, is travelling with Colonel Grant's party, which confirms what we suspected about a degree of cooperation with Japan that, likely as not, stretches to the provision of arms.' Wheelock sighed irascibly. He looked short of sleep too; heavy bags sagged under his eyes and the light from the tall window emphasised the white touches in his black whiskers and beard.

Drabble had not said it, but he regarded the prospect of the Sioux having successfully obtained the military support of the Empire of Japan as one so distant that it really could be discounted without serious consideration. Yet on listening to Wheelock, he had to confront the awkward truth that the speaker was by no means a fool and yet clearly took the polar opposite view. He could discount the idea of Japanese involvement no longer.

'Is there any news of Harris?'

Wheelock shook his head.

'I'm sorry.'

Drabble nodded, he hadn't expected any. 'What can you tell us about our "friends from Chicago"?'

Wheelock offered a cagey smile that indicated that his response would be complicated and perhaps cause his listeners more discomfort. He exhaled. 'Suffice it to say, there is more going on here.'

'You *did* mean the Mob, then?'

'Precisely.' He nodded distastefully. 'But not *just* the Mob.' Wheelock looked over his shoulder. 'There's another man I need to tell you about. His name is General James Bostonthorpe. He's the governor of South Dakota and, as you can tell, he's ex-military. He's also *extremely* ambitious.'

'How *extremely*?'

'Let's say he's certainly not satisfied with being a state governor.'

'And what's this got to do with the Sioux?'

'Well, there's a question.' He cast his gaze towards the window, thinking. 'What we do know is that he doesn't like them very much. In fact he doesn't like anyone very much – not Hispanics, Blacks, Jews, Poles – but especially not Indians. If you aren't a white American who can trace your family back at least three generations then you're not in his team. Now,' Wheelock took out his pale bone pipe and began to fill it – 'let's look at what we think we know but have no proof of. We suspect that Bostonthorpe *is* involved somehow, a suspicion corroborated albeit circumstantially by this morning's pyrotechnics at the station. How so? Well, he's flavour of the month in Chicago because he is committed one hundred per cent to the reintroduction of Prohibition, something that the Mob would welcome with open arms.'

Wheelock sighed. 'The next US presidential election is in three years and Bostonthorpe's already working to be either on the Republican ticket or to stand as an independent.' Wheelock let that settle then drew heavily on his pipe, his alert eyes adverting another disclosure. 'There is something else . . .' A fog erupted from his mouth. 'Indians from Sioux reservations across South Dakota, Wyoming, and elsewhere have been converging on Grant's ranch at Rochford outside Rapid City in the past week or two. We don't have precise figures, but it's in the thousands. We also have information that there is a new ghost dance and it is generating considerable excitement. Apparently the Indians are preparing for the return of their messiah. My sources tell me it's being called the Long Hair Dance.'

Drabble nodded, '*Phehi haska.*'

Wheelock studied him gravely. 'Exactly. It is said that the ghost of Sitting Bull is going to rise up and lead the Sioux once again to the promised land. And we've got to get there and stop that from happening.'

The train carrying Colonel Grant's Wild West Show drew in to Rapid City station like an Arabian prince floating on a magic carpet of steam. The length of the entire platform was lined by an honour guard of soldiers in dress uniform with a military band. Beyond was a vast crowd of enthusiastic onlookers, press photographers and reporters. At the centre of the martial arrangement was a cavalry officer on horseback in full dress uniform – medals on the chest of his buckskin coat sparkling and white plumage sprouting from his gold-fringed, navy cavalry Stetson. The face was podgy, bespectacled, and a small golden moustache squatted over a luscious goatee.

Harris followed Grant's party down the step onto the red carpet, as the band struck up a jaunty tune that would usually have had soldiers kicking up dust in sprightly fashion around a parade ground. The crowd cheered, and Grant and his immediate circle – which now included Fanny Howell – relished the attention.

The equestrian officer urged his horse forward and swept off his hat. The onlookers fell to a respectful hush.

'It's my great pleasure and privilege,' he bellowed, 'to welcome back these home-grown heroes – after an astonishing worldwide tour lasting more than two years. From Boston to Berlin, from Tallahassee to Tokyo, from Philadelphia to Paris, Colonel Grant's Wild West Show has dazzled the world –' Fresh cheering erupted. 'It's great to see you all home, safe and sound.' He raised his Stetson. 'Let's hear it for Colonel Grant and his Wild Westers!'

A deafening roar broke out and the soldiers – to a man – raised their caps and cheered. The civilians waved American flags and banners. Harris nudged Ferguson's elbow and nodded towards the officer on horseback:

'Who's that Johnny?'

'General Bostonthorpe, the state governor.'

'Fancies himself as a bit of a Teddy Roosevelt, does he?'

Ferguson shook his head.

'The man's a national hero ... Check out his war record.'

When the cheering faded, it was Grant's turn to respond, which he did with a speech that was remarkable in its brevity. He doffed his hat at Bostonthorpe. 'It's good to be home, folks. The boys and gals have missed the old country and I'm pleased to say we aren't going no place else now.'

The band now indulged in another military tune – all brass, beats and whistles – and the doors of the train's wagons opened and gaily decorated riders and their mounts leaped down onto platform. They began processing out behind Colonel Grant, riding abreast with General Bostonthorpe – both waving their hats to the adoration of the crowds.

Wild Westers gone, the soldiers were barked into a neat

208

column and marched out. As the cheering faded, a convoy of cars and vans drew up by the train. 'This is us –' Ferguson pulled open the rear passenger door of a weighty, chrome-grilled Cadillac. 'We're heading straight for the ranch.'

They drove in convoy through the city, sweeping along broad boulevards lined by low buildings housing shops, laundries and diners. In some ways it felt half–finished, or near deserted, but Harris realised it was simply an illusion created by the sheer surfeit of space. Here and there rocky hills, some dotted with houses, others thick with forestry, erupted from the otherwise flat landscape. They passed a sign for a Dinosaur Park – Harris made no comment – and quickly reached scruffy suburbs dotted with factory buildings. Soon they were driving along a metalled road winding through fields and farmsteads, a landscape of hills, granite escarpments, and rocky outcrops. Everywhere he looked tall trees that could have been a variety of larch or pine prospered in an environment heaving with abundance. Surely this was a handsome country, and one worth fighting for.

Evening was upon them, and every now and then, when the view opened up again, Harris glimpsed a broad horizon drenched in the red glow of a glorious sunset. It was rather magnificent.

They left the main metalled road and followed a rutted lane for a dozen miles or more. Despite the roughness of the surface and the majesty of the views, Harris found himself drifting off in the heat of the car.

He was woken in darkness by Ferguson.

'We're here,' he said, shaking him.

Harris was shown to a bedroom, his suitcase brought in shortly after, and told that dinner would be served in an hour. There was a decanter of bourbon located thoughtfully on the sideboard, so Harris took a sailor's ration and had a quick bath. He always, without fail, thought best in the bath.

Whichever way you looked at it, he was in a fix. The plan to forge a new Sioux Republic was utterly doomed. *Utterly*. The Americans would annihilate them rather than let them carve out a major chunk of the Midwest. How could it be otherwise? And then there was every chance that Sir Percival Harris would be caught in the crossfire, he thought bitterly, not to mention thousands of other poor sods. But the poor sod Harris cared about the most was himself. He needed to get out, fast.

Harris pecked at his tumbler, a resolution forming in his mind. He had to escape. Then he had to raise the alarm – something he must accomplish comfortably in time before the shooting started. Today was Monday; Grant said they were 'going live' on Thursday, meaning the whole caboodle was likely to kick off on Wednesday night.

That gave Harris time, time to work out an escape route and time to work out quite who to escape to. He had already had one idea on that score: General Bostonthorpe looked like a fairly useful individual. He had soldiers, too. And they might come in handy. If all else failed, there was also time for Drabble and potentially Walberswick to arrive on the scene and help intervene and stop the madness.

But first, dinner. He joined the other guests in the vast dining room – effectively the main hall of Grant's house – overlooked by the antlers and the preserved snouts, heads, and horns of several dozen creatures that had been unlucky enough to stray into the sights of the host's Winchester.

'Ah, it's our new recruit - the venerable Sir Percival!' Grant drawled lazily, like he'd already been too long at the bar. Harris hadn't worked out if it was the booze or a palsy of some kind, or perhaps a national characteristic that caused a partial paralysis of the verbal facets of the tongue. 'Sir Percival,' he beamed, a touch red in the cheeks. His hand swept towards the party – to Fanny, who nodded and smiled at Harris; then Sakamoto – always a man for a tight head-nod, and he didn't let Harris down this time; then Ferguson, who looked like he'd just ridden a horse to death; and then finally another whom Harris recognised immediately – the Prussian Von-what's-his-name with the swastika badge and the rather striking wife, from the ship. Von Ganshof! She sadly was absent.

Herr Von Ganshof offered a taut bob of his head and snapped his heels with ballistic force. 'Very good to meet you again, Sir Percival,' he snarled.

Christ alive, thought Harris, as he gratefully received a drink from Grant.

'Black Cloud and Speaks With Fists are with their own kind tonight, which is our loss, but I don't doubt that you will entertain us.' Grant smiled. 'Cheers, here's to Operation Laramie!'

The assembled party raised their glasses and raised their voices in chorus.

'Operation Laramie!'

Gazing across the room, Harris suddenly noticed the backdrop of the broad windows at the far end. There were lights in the distance, he realised, and some appeared to be moving. Harris stepped towards the glass, taking it in.

By God. The lights were campfires, hundreds of them, stretched out across the fields and hillside beyond as far as the eye could see. Their flames licked skyward, sending sparks flying to the heavens and illuminating the triangular outlines of countless tepees. All around then were dancing shadows. But then Harris realised, it wasn't the shadows that were dancing. It was people, hundreds upon hundreds of them, and then he heard the chanting . . .

He turned to Grant.

'What are they doing?'

Grant chuckled, though not callously, rather with a sense of mystified admiration.

'God knows,' he said. 'They're dancing to their ancestors, Sir Percival, to the Great Father and to Sitting Bull, to deliver

211

victory. And if it works for them, it works for me.' He clapped Harris on the shoulder. 'Come on, let's eat!'

If there was a new ghost dance, Harris reasoned, then there had to be a messiah. That was to say, the equivalent of Wovoka, the Johnny who had led the dance of doom in 1890. And if there was a new messiah, then he – or she – was likely out there in Grant's field somewhere and there was the faintest possibility of speaking to them and then reasoning with them. Indeed, if they weren't categorically beyond the reach of logical argument then Harris stood a very good chance of convincing them that this whole shooting match with Grant and his cronies was a bananas suicide mission so flawed that it made breakfasting on hemlock seem like a sensible alternative.

As the torture of dinner sandwiched between Sakamoto and Ferguson drew to a conclusion, Harris resolved to act. As the guests left the table he searched out Grant and thanked him for supper, before excusing himself and announcing that he wanted to get some air for a few moments. 'I also very much want to take a closer look at the Indians,' he declared in a pompous tone that he calculated to be somewhat anthropological.

Grant barely raised an eyebrow, perhaps because he understood far better than Harris could possibly have guessed the sheer implausibility of the Englishman attempting to escape the ranch on foot at night. Which was true enough. And Harris was under no illusions about that: he had no idea where he was, and after a hearty evening's hospitality, he was about ready for his bed, not staging an audacious escape plan.

But searching out the Indians' messiah, that was different. And as far as he could tell it didn't involve any acts of bravery. Harris had learnt his lesson. He might even get an interview ...

He sauntered from the party, and headed towards the field of the thousand braves, as he had already mentally labelled it. His

212

feet crunched on the gravel but already the metronomic thrum of the dance and chorus of strange voices was inescapable. As he approached, the tepees grew larger and more substantial, the hides swathing their tall sides dancing with the shadows of countless fires. The soot and smell of sweet woodsmoke filled the air, and dogs cantered back and forth searching for scraps. Harris passed into the realm of the tepees: here and there, a solitary figure sat before a low fire swathed in blankets, the flames dancing on their faces. He heard a baby crying. If the sight of a tiddled Englishman striding amidst this aboriginal conurbation prompted interest, he could think again – Harris was of no interest. He wasn't invisible, but his passing was unremarkable.

The sound of chanting was now much louder.

Whether you called it chanting or singing, Harris could not fathom. It wasn't like 'Onward Christian Soldiers' or 'Jerusalem'. It was guttural and perhaps tuneless, yet he could discern the rising and falling of voices. Above all, the chanting communicated a sense of intoxicating urgency. After perhaps quarter of an hour passing through the tepees, Harris emerged on the far side. The field opened up and he saw the flickering apex of a mighty bonfire – like the sort that villagers might burn their guy on once a year. Hefty sparks danced heavenwards above the flames which themselves must have reached thirty or forty feet.

Between Harris and the fire was a shifting line of silhouetted figures – all engaged in the dance. They formed a human barrier several hundred yards long.

Women, children, the old men and braves alike were dancing: all holding hands and moving as much or as little as they were able in time to the drumbeat. It was an extraordinary sight made all the more fantastic when Harris realised that the chain of dancers before him were actually part of a vast ring which encircled the fire. Now standing right behind the line he could see the heart of the great fire at the centre of this circle between the shifting figures, and he glimpsed the faces of the dancers on the far side reflected in its light. Many wore breechcloths, bone breastplates, and their skin was slicked with paint. Harris saw musicians beating their drums; he saw heads decorated with feathers tossing back and forth. The words of the chant kept coming back, again and again and all the time he recognised the sounds, '*phehi haska . . .*'

'*Phehi haska!*'

'*Phehi haska!*'

'*Phehi haska!*'

Just then Harris saw him, the man who must be the messiah.

Standing alone before the fire, his back was turned. His hands were raised, palms uplifted, and his bare head almost bowed, as if he was in a trance. He moved slowly and seemed to be dancing to a different beat. Threads hung from his arms and knees, and in the light of the powerful fire Harris saw the spread wings of the raven and bull's motif on his back. It was the war shirt that Black Cloud had worn on the night they had seen the show at Earl's Court – but as the solitary figure turned, Harris knew now that it was also the shirt of Sitting Bull.

It had to be. Black Cloud's eyes were shut and his mouth moved quickly in time to the beating drums. A few yards from him Harris now noticed an inner circle of dancers, amongst whose number was Speaks With Fists. Like many of the others he was dressed in a breechcloth, leggings, and a brightly decorated war shirt. In his hand he brandished a rifle, one of the Type-99s Harris had seen on the ship. So did many of the other men in the wider circle, Harris now realised.

His gaze started to dot around the landscape of moving figures. He saw faces lost in trances; he saw rifles, bows, and hatchets; he saw strange and forbidding headdresses forged of bison, porcupines, and rodents; he saw masks of unknown deities carved in timber or woven with grasses. And underlying it was that fast repeated beat of the drums and relentless cries of '*Phehi haska . . . phehi haska . . .*'

Harris staggered backwards, gulping for air, feeling dizzy. He had to get away. The noise, the chanting, the heat of the fire . . . it was just too much.

He turned and ran.

Chapter Twenty-five

The next morning Harris rode out for a tour of the ranch with Grant. His equanimity had returned with the daylight, he was glad to discover, but he couldn't have known it. On riding out he also discovered that the house was absolutely surrounded by tepees – 'lodges' was what Grant called them. They didn't just occupy the field he had crossed. He stopped counting the tepees when he reached a hundred. Everywhere Indian women were concluding the business of breakfast and barefooted children ran around. No menfolk were to be seen. Harris was taking notes.

'Who are these people?'

'Mostly Sioux of one type or other,' drawled Grant, leaning back lazily in his saddle. He had a pistol with an ivory grip in a holster on his hip, and his Winchester slotted into the folds of the saddle. 'There are seven main tribes within the Great Sioux Nation, as was – and there's quite a few of them here. But there's a smattering of Cheyenne too. Believe me –' Grant turned to Harris, 'there's no shortage of volunteers to take a pot-shot at Uncle Sam for what he's put these poor bastards through over the last two hundred years.'

They passed through a narrowing of the trees and emerged into a vast grassy field, sheltered in the east by rising hilltops covered in trees. It was a handsome landscape, no doubt about it. But turning the corner Harris forgot the topography: a hundred or so Indian men lay in a line, pointing rifles at distant targets. Harris saw them fiddling and adjusting their weapons – moving the bolts back and forth and so on. Grant glanced at his watch, and barked at the superintending officer.

A staggered volley of fire came from the prone line of riflemen, puffs of smoke erupted from the muzzles – with dust and earth being thrown up at the butts at the far end of the range. Grant lowered his binoculars – 'Not bad,' and passed them to Harris. 'Another thousand rifles arrived overland from San Francisco yesterday – ahead of schedule. And we've got more than enough volunteers to use them.'

They rode on as a second volley of fire came from the riflemen, steadying their mounts – and then a new crowd of men caught Harris's attention. This time several hundred Indians were being drilled under the close inspection of Ferguson, whom Harris saw on horseback. 'They look pretty sharp, don't they?' declared Grant, taking a swig from a hip-flask. 'Ferguson's a good man. He was a Rough Rider, you know.'

They trotted on, passing into another wooded section, and then out into another vast field.

Before them were a dozen pieces of artillery – wheeled field guns, with tenders and teams of horses standing by. They were similar to the sort of thing Harris had seen the Royal Horse Artillery firing off in Hyde Park to mark royal birthdays.

This was getting more serious.

Harris swore under his breath, and drew level with Grant, 'Where in God's name did you get these from?'

'The Germans – Herr von Ganshof in particular.' Grant chucked. 'Turns out it's a lot easier to get hold of this stuff than you might imagine. Especially if they want you to have it.'

'But what are they for?'

'You said yourself that rifles wouldn't be enough. If Operation Laramie turns nasty, having some proper hardware won't hurt. I'd rather not use them, sure. But artillery will make

Uncle Sam think twice before hitting us – and that'll buy us time for the diplomatic effort to play out.'

They stayed a while, watching the gun crews perform drills – loading, sighting, firing and unloading. Grant smoked a cigarillo and Harris had a pipe. The artillerymen looked competent enough.

'Tell me,' asked Harris. 'Why are *you* doing this?'

Grant thought a moment before replying and when he did there was a sort of inscrutable, amused look on his face. 'I decided it was time to even things up a bit for the Sioux. The way they've been treated has never stood right with me. Personally, I'll do well out of it, of course – I'll get a fair bit of land for myself. But that's not it, well – not all of it. It's about justice for the Indians. Plus, since I'm involved from the get-go, I can expect to have an important say in the running of the new country. I'll be Prime Minister –' He grinned at Harris. 'I know, it's a lot to take in. Black Cloud will be the republic's spiritual leader and Speaks With Fists will make a pretty formidable Interior Minister. Don't you think?'

'And who'll be President?' asked Harris flippantly.

Grant leaned over, 'Bostonthorpe.' He flicked his heels and trotted away. 'Come on, *Bede*.' He glanced back and grinned, 'There's more to show you.'

The tour of Grant's ranch and the military preparations concluded shortly before noon, but not before Harris was more convinced than ever that it was an utterly doomed enterprise. Yes, the military preparedness was rather more impressive than he had thought likely, but its scale was negligible. And for all of the talk of a diplomatic solution, the fact was that the wheels of diplomacy had a habit of turning a damned sight more slowly than those of war. By the time the diplomatic solution kicked in, thousands of Sioux warriors would be lying dead – crushed under the heel of the United States military. And that was before one considered what might happen to their loved ones. The world had moved on a great deal since 1890, but scratch at the surface and the old colours might well show through.

So Harris knew what had to be done: namely, what he had failed to accomplish the night before. He needed to go to the messiah at the heart of the new ghost dance, Black Cloud, and do his utmost to convince him of the disaster awaiting him and his people. He had to abort this disastrous course of action. Quite how such attempts at reasoning squared with the trance-like state that he had seen Black Cloud in the night before remained to be seen. What was likely was that the old chief, and those around him, would not take kindly to any of it.

That did not negate the necessity of Harris trying, though. Excusing himself from Grant's company, he asked for directions to Black Cloud's lodge. 'The chronicler really ought to hear from the spiritual leader before the great hurrah, what?'

'I'll take you.' Grant remounted and led them away.

The experience of the Indian encampment in daylight, as well as from horseback, was different from the night before. With the menfolk absent in military training, women, children, and elders were gathered in groups sitting on rugs before their tepees or around fires with cooking pots in anticipation of lunch. Others looked out from tepees, gazing at the flames and keeping warm, skinny-looking dogs curled up beside them.

'In all my days,' declared Grant, 'I've never seen so many lodges in one place. It's extraordinary.' Harris heard him chuckle and saw him shake his head in amazement. Looking over, he took in the sight of the broad sloping meadow peppered with tepees.

This was presumably what remained of the National Hoop, thought Harris, recalling Black Cloud's chosen expression during their last conversation aboard the *Empress of the Atlantic*. It was the sum total of the humanity of the Great Sioux Nation

219

left behind after more than a century of white incursion, oppression, and neglect.

'He's over here.' Grant drew his reins aside and walked his horse between two lodges into what Harris realised was an opening of sorts, at the centre of which stood a tepee. It was no different from the others: its tall frame was swathed in a layer of stitched skins stretched over a conical frame of timbers which protruded from the apex. Just beneath that a flap in the skins acted as a chimney and wisps of smoke tumbled from it in the breeze.

Several Indians sat outside its entrance cross-legged on rugs, smoking. Half a dozen ponies were gathered to one side, feeding, and there was a depleted heap of firewood and kindling. Grant nodded towards the tepee and lit a cigarillo. 'I'll wait out here.'

Harris bent down and entered. The tepee smelled strongly of woodsmoke and something else – animal fat, from some beef being roasted over the open fire in the middle. Despite it all, the air was surprisingly clear and Harris saw half a dozen Indian men sitting around the fire; immediately he noticed Black Cloud and Speaks With Fists among the number. Two women prepared food on the near side of the fire.

Black Cloud saw Harris and beckoned him over. The small seated party moved back to permit him access to their circle. Wordlessly Harris sat down next to Black Cloud, who was keeping warm under a red blanket and smoking. He took out a packet of Player's Navy Cut cigarettes from the folds of the blanket and offered it to Harris.

'I hope you haven't come here to try to talk me out of this ...'

Harris prized out a cigarette and leaned towards a flaming stick being held up by the watchful man on the other side of Black Cloud.

'What makes you say that?' Harris said after a pause.

'I can see it in your face, Englishman.'

Harris nodded, not strictly speaking in a gesture intended to convey agreement but rather of understanding.

'I gather that you are the new messiah?'

'No.' Black Cloud frowned and shook his head. 'I am the old messiah . . . old enough to know better. But, yes, young enough to be a messenger for the Great Spirit.' He glanced upwards as he said this, and Harris realised that Black Cloud at last looked like he belonged. Harris had not been aware of his not belonging before, but now that he saw it, its former absence, albeit latent, could not be unperceived. Harris drew on the cigarette – it was coarse but entirely satisfactory. The rich smoke billowed from his mouth, encircling Black Cloud, and he summoned his question, the only question he could really ask, under the circumstances.

'What happened?'

Black Cloud inspected him momentarily and then slowly looked left and then right, sharing glances with the group sitting with him. He nodded sombrely to Harris and began.

'Seventeen years ago, when I turned sixty, I experienced a powerful vision. It look me many years to understand it . . . which was stupid of me, but I blame the show for blinding me to its import as indeed the years overseas blinded me to so much. Of course, it was through the Wild West Show that we gained influence and important allies so it was not without value, but at the start, when I first began to comprehend the significance of the vision, I did not see that.'

Harris had taken out his notebook and begun to write. He nodded for Black Cloud to continue.

'Tell me about this vision.'

'I was an old man, as I am now. I found myself standing on a rocky clifftop overlooking the Black Hills, separated from them by a great valley. It was day but darkness filled the sky and a storm raged from the four directions causing a great swirling

221

cloud above. I knew I had to take shelter, but my feet were planted to the ground and I could not move. As I became increasingly concerned a horseman arrived and I saw he was my father's father. I was overjoyed to see him . . . I had not seen him since I was a boy – he died at Greasy Grass – and I wept. "Go home," he said to me in a voice that was not his. "Go home to your people."

'My grandfather then galloped straight at me – and his horse jumped and he flew into the air and was sucked up into the eye of the storm above me. I cried out – and then I saw hundreds of horsemen coming from the sky. They galloped down from the blackness of the clouds in a long wheeling arc until they reached the far side of the great valley before me, and then they sped towards me, advancing in a broad line that filled the horizon. Just then it began to rain hard. And I saw that in the middle of this line, at the front, were Sitting Bull and Crazy Horse, either side of my grandfather. They had both been dead these many years by the time I had this vision, you understand, and in my vision I knew all this. They were ghosts sent by the Great Spirit.

'Just then a rainbow sprang up from the river deep below and Sitting Bull and Crazy Horse led the army of warriors up it. Rising up they reached the bold stony pinnacle upon which I stood – and then this army floated in the air before me. I heard drums and an eagle flew overhead, and Sitting Bull shouted my name in command. He had on the war shirt that he wore at Greasy Grass and he pointed at me and raised his lance. Only then did I see that its point was piercing the head of Long Hair Custer. Sitting Bull then raised his other hand, showing me his sacred pipe – his *chanunpas*, as we call it. It was the very one we found in the British Museum. He took a smoke and then handed it to my grandfather, who smoked and then passed it to Crazy Horse.

'Crazy Horse gave the pipe back to Sitting Bull, who then

shot up into the sky and galloped into the eye of the storm. Crazy Horse and my grandfather followed and so did the rest of their force. Scores of Sioux warriors I saw, dressed for combat, spiralling up into the heavens after them. And then as the very last horseman vanished into the swirling clouds the rains ceased, and the Bluecoats rained down, falling like arrows.

'After that the rains resumed and I was flying through the air with my grandfather. We saw a field filled with bison and then another. Then I saw the mountains and fields erupt with trees as once there had been; the game was bountiful. Next we flew over the homes of *wasichus*, their farmsteads, towns, and cities. Here the air was filled with smoke and I saw their buildings burning and their corpses lying for the scavengers. There came strong thunder and we galloped in the sky high above a mighty mountain in the Black Hills that we know as the Six Grandfathers. It is the one that is being grossly disfigured with the faces of *wasichus'* leaders. The rains grew stronger and quickly washed away the faces of the *wasichus*, and when I looked back I saw the Six Grandfathers returning to the way they were before. I was content and looked up to find my grandfather but he had vanished into the swirling, dark heavens.'

The elderly chief took a long drag on his cigarette and then tossed it into the fire. He addressed the flames. 'I remember in my vision thinking that I had seen those dark heavens before. Somehow I recognised them. And then I remembered that as a boy, I had seen them. And now I understood and remembered. I also knew what we had to do. I had to rescue my people before I was too old. Sitting Bull and Crazy Horse had showed me the way. But it took me many years to come to all of this and to follow in the path of Wovoka.'

Harris finished scribbling the quotes down and then met Black Cloud's gaze.

'How did this vision inspire the new ghost dance?'

Black Cloud tilted his head. 'We have our ways, Sir Percival.

223

The dance is important to us for reasons that the *wasichus* cannot understand. Knowing what the vision meant, which I now did, helped me to understand the steps we needed to take. Follow the path directed by Sitting Bull, observe the ritual, and in time the Bluecoats will fall. It is simple ... and as you can see it is coming to pass. The dance has delivered us weapons and powerful allies; it has revived the hitherto shattered spirit of my people who are now prepared to fight once again. I truly believe that we are about to accomplish that which Sitting Bull and Crazy Horse failed to accomplish – but with their help, we will. The lands of the Great Sioux Nation are about to be reclaimed. The Great Spirit wills it. Sitting Bull is with us.'

Black Cloud threw back his blanket and lifted up a long pipe hewn from reddish stone; twelve feathers hung from it, representing each of the dozen moons of the year, and Harris saw the motif of a bull's horns carved into it, beside a setting sun. Sitting Bull's sacred pipe. Black Cloud raised it high above his head and muttered words of prayer, before turning and passing it with great care to Speaks With Fists.

'Now,' Black Cloud turned back to face Harris, 'I must rest ...' The elderly chief began to rise and shook his head as Harris began to remonstrate. He pressed his leathery hand to Harris's heart and the Englishman fell silent. 'You are not a bad man for a *wasichu*, Sir Percival. Go not against your nature. Obey your nature as I obey mine. It is all we should do.'

With that Black Cloud withdrew his hand and went to lie down, taking one of the mattresses in the dark edge of the tepee. Harris watched him pull several blankets over himself and turn away.

The interview was over.

Drabble, Charlotte, and Wheelock took a pair of rooms on the second floor of the Rapid City Station Hotel, overlooking the main street. It was dusk and the broad thoroughfare was coming alive with flickering and coloured lights, promoting diners, a theatre, a cinema and saloons. Motorised and horse-drawn traffic trickled back and forth. The centre of the world, this was not. They ate in the room to keep out of sight and discussed the arrangements for the night ahead over dinner. Wheelock and Drabble were going to reconnoitre Grant's ranch and see what they could learn. Charlotte was to remain at the hotel and raise the alarm if anything untoward occurred. After coffee Wheelock smoked a pipe and produced an immigration stamp with which he carefully inked Drabble's passport – even appending the appropriate documents and signing it off.

'Congratulations, you're now legal,' he had told him, handing it over. 'You should know that I'm also having this sad business with poor Captain Walberswick dealt with.'

Drabble had watched Wheelock wielding the stamp: he looked like he'd done it before, and not just once. But Drabble did not comment. Instead he simply thanked him. 'I never realised that the influence of the Bureau of Indian Affairs stretched so far,' he said.

Wheelock replied with a smile, and fetched up his pipe.

'Have we agreed our plan of action?'

'We have –' assented Drabble. He turned to Charlotte, who looked up from Melville and frowned at him.

The men shared a glance, and Wheelock eased himself from his chair, collected his hat, and addressed Drabble. 'I'll see you outside.'

When the door shut, Charlotte laid down *Moby Dick*.

Drabble went to her and took her hand.

'Someone has to stay here to pass on the word if we don't come back . . .'

'That's what I'm worried about.'

He put his arms around her waist and kissed her. She pulled away and stepped towards the bed. 'Ernest, I mean it. What if you don't come back?'

'It'll be all right –'

'You're fond of that expression, aren't you?' She looked at him over her shoulder. 'You can't know that.'

Drabble stared her at her back – noticing the way her dark blond hair fell across her neck and splayed across her shoulders. There wasn't time . . . Charlotte was right, of course. But they had no choice. He gently took her hands in his and guided her to the bed where he sat, and she perched on his lap.

She was about to say something when she got up and went to the window, and looked out.

'Just make sure you come back in one piece,' she said, her voice faltering. 'And find that idiot friend of yours –' Charlotte turned to him, tears in her eyes. 'I know he's like a brother to you.'

'Unfortunately he's the only brother I've got.'

They kissed and then held each other.

After a while, there was a knock at the door. It was Wheelock. It was time to go. Drabble lingered at the door.

'Don't let anyone in,' he said. 'And if we're not back by morning, then you call Colonel Fitzgerald in Fort Defiance. Tell him everything.'

'Go on –' Charlotte looked away and picked up Melville. 'Wheelock's given me the details of Grant's ranch . . . and the telephone number for Fort Defiance – it's all written down in here.' She patted her copy of *Moby Dick*.

Wheelock drove the small Ford through the city and its outskirts, passing factories, then farmsteads, before passing a National Guard base, and then reaching broad woodlands and hills. In the distance the Black Hills loomed over the horizon in the fast vanishing light. Soon the headlights were boring a yellow hole in the encroaching oblivion as they drove in silence, talking only to confirm directions.

The ranch was about twenty miles further along the highway and then about half that again on the side road. 'We should

226

be there by eleven,' announced Drabble, as he folded the map away. 'Then we've got to get in . . .'

Wheelock glanced over from the steering wheel. 'I've some options . . .'

At Grant's ranch the party had gathered for pre-dinner drinks. This time the crowd included Sakamoto, Ferguson, von Ganshof, his wife, and Fanny Howell. They were also joined by Speaks With Fists, as well as a dozen other Indian chiefs of importance from the gathered bands. In addition there were several guests from neighbouring estates and the Wild West Show. Harris was making for Grant when a servant got there first. After a word in his ear the colonel hurried from the room, leaving Harris casting about for an alternative.

'What-ho, Fanny –' Harris sidled over to her, smiling winningly and rallying at the sight of several sensational inches of compressed cleavage. 'Looking forward to being the Second Lady of the forthcoming Sioux Republic?'

She replied with a weary eye roll.

'Is the capital going to be Rapid City?'

'It is, as a matter of fact.'

'Well that should put it on the map, rather.' They clinked their glasses.

'Cheers to that.'

'Good health – and I can't help thinking that the Colonel's chiselled features would look rather spiffing engraved into the side of Mount Rushmore, don't you?'

Miss Howell smirked at him conspiratorially – she did not miss Harris's mild sarcasm – and then surveyed the rest of the party with a hostess's eye.

'Which reminds me –' Harris shot her another winning smile. 'Would it be possible to make an excursion into Rapid City? I'd very much like to see it as it *was* before the new republic is announced, for comparison purposes . . .'

'Uh-uh –' she wagged her finger at him. 'Everyone knows, Harris, there's no leaving the ranch until it all begins.'

'Oh yes, that!' He cleared his throat, and spotted Grant striding towards them, his expression one of concentrated seriousness. He handed Fanny a small note – a telegram, and then addressed the room.

'Gentlemen – good news. We are bringing forward our plans: Operation Laramie begins tonight!'

A cheer went up from the gathering.

'We take Rapid City at dawn!'

They had been going for about thirty minutes when Drabble decided he couldn't wait any longer. He turned to Wheelock, looking at his profile in the darkness, and broke the silence.

'Why did you beat up Harris?'

Wheelock didn't take his eyes off the road. Drabble could not see his expression but watched him nonetheless.

'It was a bit heavy-handed,' Wheelock said at last, in a tone that conveyed contrition. 'In all honesty, we didn't know whose side you were on then.'

'It was a hell of a way to find out.'

The American looked over and smiled. 'No serious harm done.'

'That's not the point.'

Wheelock changed gear and drove on in silence. Drabble threw another question into the interior of the Ford.

'And where is your Neanderthal colleague now, out of interest?'

'Agent Pollard, you mean?' Wheelock looked over. 'Why, he's still in St Paul. His job was to prevent the mob from boarding the train – and to help you both board it. Fortunately for us,' Wheelock cleared his throat in such a way to emphasise the following statement – 'he *succeeded* in that objective. Unfortunately for him . . .'

Wheelock left his statement unfinished and Drabble realised what he was saying – or rather wasn't. He also experienced a fleeting glimpse of recognition.

'Was he the porter on the platform?'

Wheelock glanced over and nodded.

They drove on for a mile or so. Drabble stared out at the dark clouds, their arches and swirls picked out by the moonlight, that towered over the high landscape of inky black hills. He suddenly felt rather foolish.

'You don't work for the Bureau of Indian Affairs, do you?'

Wheelock glanced over.

'I'm afraid I wasn't quite straight with you there.'

And not for the last time, either. Drabble looked out and saw a farmhouse in the distance, a lonely light shone in its window.

'So *who* do you work for then?'

Wheelock clicked his tongue – and then let out a long sigh. It sounded like the result of someone wrestling over whether or not to tell the truth.

'All right –' He spoke the words slowly as if coming to a resolution. 'I'm with US Army Intelligence.'

That made sense, more sense than the Bureau of Indian Affairs, but Drabble wasn't going to let him off so lightly. 'And how do I know you're telling the truth this time?'

Wheelock cracked a smile which Drabble caught in the gloom.

'I'm afraid you're probably just going to have to trust me.'

'I'll agree to do that on one condition.'

Wheelock grinned. 'Name it.'

'You tell me everything you know about *wampum* belts.'

The American glanced over. 'Oh yeah?'

'Yeah,' replied Drabble. '*And* Pocahontas.'

229

Chapter Twenty-six

Wheelock stopped the car and Drabble inspected the map under the light of a torch. It was pitch black outside, and they were lost – or putting it in the best possible light, they were yet to locate Colonel Grant's ranch.

'A map without a compass is worthless,' Drabble repeated word-for-word the exhortation of a master of his from school twenty years before. Wheelock slipped the Ford into first gear.

'Come on, I think it's up here. Let's keep going.'

'Well there's nothing lost in trying.'

They moved off, the small Ford dipping and jerking in the uneven road. After a hundred yards or so the road swept around to the left and they passed through dense woodland. Then they saw it on their left; a high fence adorned with loops of barbed wire visible through the trees. In the distance a lighted area showed tall gates and a couple of sentries.

'Shit –'

Wheelock killed the headlights and yanked the wheel round, mounting the grassy bank and narrowly missing a tree. They bumped down onto the road and Wheelock stamped his foot down, speeding the Ford away. Through the back window Drabble saw the sentries dart out into the road and powerful torchlights flash towards them.

The moon emerged from the cloud cover giving just

enough light to see the road by. Wheelock leaned forward over the wheel.

'Over there –' Drabble pointed towards a grassy track leading off right into the trees. Wheelock braked and the Ford veered across the road into the deep cover.

He switched off the engine and they sat in the darkness, their eyes becoming accustomed to the night. 'Let's go,' announced Wheelock. He got out and went to the boot. 'Here –' He placed a dense metal object into Drabble's hand, an object he knew immediately to be a handgun. 'It's loaded.'

They walked through the trees until they reached the perimeter fence. Drabble felt the heavy weight of the gun in his hand . . . it weighed him down, for want of a better expression. It told him what he knew already, that this was now a very serious matter indeed. He had, he realised, somehow half hoped all along, that notwithstanding the fireworks at St Paul, that he might settle all this with Grant and whoever else was involved with some reasonable discussion – perhaps a little subterfuge or sleight of hand, but at worst the throwing of a punch or two. But striding in the shadows alongside Wheelock, with both of them sporting Smith and Wessons . . . well, that was rather a different kettle of fish. They reached the fence, finding that it was not just substantially constructed but also annoyingly high. Drabble immediately began climbing a tree closest to it.

'Drabble,' Wheelock whispered. 'I've got bolt cutters.'

He sliced a hole for them and they made their way through the trees on the far side. The night was dark again, the moon having slid behind the high cloud once more. Out of the tree cover, they ascended a gently sloping grassy meadow, the ground spongy underfoot. There was the tang of woodsmoke in the air as well as the distant sound of horses and mechanised vehicles. As they approached the brow of the hill the noise grew louder. They could hear horses, the engines of cars and miscellaneous shouts of orders. There was clearly a great deal of activity going on. But to what end?

They pressed on.

Nearing the top of the hill, they saw a large house with broad, lighted windows and barns and outhouses all lit up. After half a dozen more paces they crested and the landscape opened up beneath to reveal the foreground. They immediately saw a vast field of tepees, with countless fires and figures moving around them. Wheelock halted in his tracks.

'Good God.'

Drabble's gaze tracked to the mechanised noise he could still hear; seeing headlights on what must have been a private road leading to the main gates.

'They've got trucks.'

'And cavalry,' said Wheelock, peering through a small pair of binoculars.

'A lot of cavalry.'

And the mass was on the move. Headlights from lorries and cars picked out details of the convoy here and there. Drabble saw the long barrels of artillery, he saw wagons and horsemen with slung rifles going two by two. The feathers in the head-dresses of the Native American warriors and the Stetsons of the cowboys were picked out in flaming torches. The convoy stretched from the house all the way to the gates, and more were coming.

Wheelock cursed, 'They've got artillery.'

They were too late. It dawned on Drabble first and he turned, starting for the fence.

'Come on.' He looked back at the army. 'All we can do now is call Fitzgerald.'

But Wheelock did not move.

'Wheelock —'

'Drabble ... *look*!'

Wheelock was pointing towards the floodlit gatehouse, and

held out his binoculars. There, bathed in light, Drabble saw him: Black Cloud, dressed in his war-bonnet of eagle feathers, erect on horseback. The lights caught his cotton war shirt – doubtlessly that of Sitting Bull – and the red warpaint of the braves accompanying him. Behind him more chiefs were following.

Then in the group of horsemen after them, one equestrian figure leaped out immediately. It was Harris. *Christ.* Drabble's heart sank, and a feeling of panic struck him: the stupid sod had done it again . . .

'Shit –' Wheelock gripped Drabble by the shoulder, the small lenses of his spectacles glinting in the moonlight. 'We've got to get to the car before the road gets clogged up. *Shit.* We've got to warn Fitzgerald.'

They broke into a run, making for the fence as fast as they could. But their pace was limited by the uncertainty of the ground, as each footstep landed blind in the darkness.

The night played tricks on them too: it seemingly brought them much closer to the trees shielding the fence than they really were. But it couldn't be that far now, thought Drabble. He glanced over, Wheelock breathed heavily at his shoulder, but he was keeping up. For an older man, he was still pretty quick.

Then the world went white – cold, bold, blinding white, so white it burned the backs of the eyes, and left them staggering. Drabble's foot sank into a soft hole; he stumbled, and went down. Wheelock – framed in light from powerful torches – pulled his revolver and fired. His barrel erupted in flame. A light vanished. Drabble scampered to his feet. Wheelock, now advancing, fired again.

'Run,' he shouted. '*Run!*'

Suddenly, half a dozen bursts of flaming yellow light appeared before them – the ear-splitting sound followed.

Drabble threw himself to the ground, shots racing over his head. But Wheelock wasn't so lucky. He appeared to stall

233

mid-stride and the gun fell from his hand – as the yellow flashes persisted. And then his body was collapsing, spinning to the ground. It landed with a forceful thud just near Drabble, bringing him back to his senses.

He rolled into darkness and began to crawl fast, before breaking to his feet and sprinting towards the wooded cover. He heard shouts of 'over there!' and readied himself to dive – and be blinded by light.

Drabble reached the trees. Somehow the lights had not found him and he sank down, catching his breath behind the tree. He looked out: six torches now strayed across the field searching for him. He had to keep moving, he told himself. The hole in the perimeter fence was just a little further on, past the corner. If his pursuers thought about it they could cut him off, but if they hadn't found the opening . . . then he had half a chance. Then if he could get to the car in time . . .

Drabble stopped, and looked out; the six lights were separating into pairs, and one of them was heading off in the direction of the gate-house, effectively cutting off his potential line of rearwards retreat. The other two pairs of hunters were now sweeping towards him.

He advanced and broke into a run. By following the treeline he could still make it to the hole in the fence at this rate. Plus he still had the revolver and he would use it if he had to. After a thirty second burst, he halted again behind a tree, and surveyed the scene. *Damn it.* Two of the guards were now coming his way along the perimeter woodland. They were cutting him off. And they were approaching fast. The lights of their torches licked the trunks of the trees just ahead of him, casting shadows over him. He looked up – and then to the left where lights were now showing in the road from the lorries and the burning torches of the cavalry.

Beams of light now cut through the trees around him; the guards were upon him.

He shinned up the tree before him, reaching the third main sprouting of branches before he even paused. If the guards realised he was here then he would be seeing Wheelock again a whole lot sooner than he would like. But so far they had not been shining their torches aloft . . .

Drabble remained perfectly still, holding his breath, and watched as the guards and their torches approached. He was highly conscious of every sound he was making, but he knew that the noise of the lorries and the horses would mask it all and more.

He saw the torches begin to pass underneath. He exhaled with relief.

Suddenly he was bathed in light.

'Hey – *you*!'

A shot boomed out, splintering the bough next to him. Drabble hurled himself from the tree – right towards the light that glared at him. He landed hard, knocking the guard for six, but at a price. Drabble cried out in pain, gripping his ankle.

A light fell on him.

'Don't move.'

Charlotte put *Moby Dick* down and looked again at the clock. It was five minutes since the last time she had checked, and just after one o'clock in the morning. It was still too soon for Ernest and Wheelock to be back. She picked up the book and found her place – her eye settling on the passage she had just abandoned. But it was no good. Focusing was impossible. Charlotte found herself contemplating fetching a glass of water from the jug before she even realised her mouth was dry. It was no good. She shut the book.

Then she opened it again and turned to the inside back cover, where Grant's address was inscribed on Wheelock's insistence along with a telephone number for Colonel Fitzgerald at Fort Defiance. She had been told to stay put and raise the alarm in the morning. Well, she thought. There was more than one way of skinning a cat. Charlotte had other ideas. She got her coat and gloves.

Was she being foolhardy? Quite possibly. Wasn't she better off doing as Wheelock had so fervently impressed upon her?

Not on her life. And certainly not on Ernest's either.

At the front desk of the Rapid City Station Hotel, Charlotte asked the night porter to telephone for a cab for her.

'Where did you say you were going?'

She showed him the page of the book.

'At this hour?'

The cab took Charlotte through empty, darkened streets. The only pedestrians she saw were ones that were asleep – slumped in the doorways of inauspicious premises or on benches in grotty asides. After the commercial centre, the planked houses gave way to scrub and trees and light industry – before the shadows of any structures vanished from sight and it was all just blackened fields and spooky woodland casting spidery webs in the night sky.

That was when the doubts began to creep in. She *was* being foolhardy. She was undoubtedly putting herself in danger and that might put Ernest in danger too – if he felt compelled to assist her. Charlotte hadn't considered that before. Her father always said she was impetuous. And she should have left a note behind just in case Ernest arrived back early while she was absent. He would be beside himself with worry. She contemplated telling the driver to turn around as they passed a dark-looking factory.

Then something unexpected happened. Charlotte heard the driver mutter irritably, and she looked up to see lanterns swinging in the road ahead. There were soldiers with wooden barriers blocking the way. The driver stopped the taxi and rolled down the window.

'The highway's closed sir,' a soldier announced, as cold air swept in. He turned to Charlotte and touched the brim of his helmet, 'Ma'am.'

'Hang on –' It was the driver, he was angry. 'I got an English lady here that I gotta get to Rochford.'

'Not tonight you're aren't, sir.'

'Oh, for God's sake. What's the National Guard doing out anyway?'

'Can't say that I know, sir – but what I do know, is that no one is coming through.'

Chapter Twenty-seven

Drabble lay on a bed staring at the wooden panelled ceiling. He had received a nice graze above his left eye during his capture – administered by one of the guards – but his ankle had settled down. He had been locked in the room for about forty minutes, since being brought to the house at gunpoint. This meant that Wheelock had been dead now for about an hour, following an act of undoubted bravery that had almost certainly saved Drabble's life. Not for the first time during this moment of captivity did Drabble wonder why men who had so readily gunned down Wheelock decided to spare him. The only conclusion he could fathom was they thought he might serve their purposes as a hostage, if it came to it. Although two hostages would surely have been better than one, thought Drabble bitterly.

Grant's ranch was an ostentatious, sprawling homestead with boulders for doorposts and was seemingly deserted, except for his jailers, who numbered about six in all. From the window he could see a vast field of tepees, mostly in darkness. Only the main gates were still lit up and manned by guards.

Looking down at the ground from the window, it wasn't too far away, and Drabble knew that if he hung from the ledge, he probably had an even chance of walking away from it. But as he had already hurt his ankle leaping from the tree, the odds of that were now against him. But he could potentially suspend himself with something and thereby reduce that risk sharply.

The first challenge was the window, which was locked and had small panes. Conceivably the frame could be broken and there was a chair in the room that was possibly up to the job. Once breached, however, he would then have to take his chances crossing the courtyard and the tepee field. But after that, once under the cover of darkness, he had every chance.

Drabble stripped the bed and twisted the sheets into tight cords, tying one end of the completed rope to the bedstead. He then took up the heavy wooden chair – weighting it in his hands – and swung at the window. The panes shattered but the central wooden pillar of the window frame held solid. Drabble brought it back again and swung harder ...

A splintering sound rent the air and this time the chair followed the timber mullion out of the window. Drabble smashed out the remaining shards of glass, wrapped the sheet cord around his waist and climbed from the window. He backed out while simultaneously taking up the tension on the line.

Just then he heard shouts from inside and the bedroom door sprang open – only for it to slam into the chest of drawers that he had jammed in front of it.

Drabble chuckled as he pushed off from the window, teasing out the sheet and jumping off with his toes. Bounce, bounce, bounce ... He reached the end of the bedsheet rope and dropped the last few yards, landing with most of his weight on his stronger ankle and finishing with a roll. He got to his feet just in time to see two men with torches running along the driveway towards him. They must have come from the gatehouse. He cursed under his breath. They were quick off the mark – mind you, that chair through the window was hardly subtle. He turned towards the field and saw more torches in the distance bobbing towards him. Damn it.

Behind him he heard a shout.

There was nothing else for it. He sprinted into the field of tepees, lurching into the darkness, and then made a direct line for the floodlit gatehouse. His route would cut between the two sets of guards. Plunging into the night, the lodges shielded him from the searching beams of his pursuers' torches.

Drabble stumbled over a burnt-out fire, smashing through a wooden cooking frame, and felt the hot ashes scorch the soles of his shoes. A dog yelped and scrambled out of his path. He passed the black outline of the next tepee and checked left, seeing that the two guards coming down the drive had crossed into the field to cut him off. *Of course they had*. Blast it. His only hope was to outpace them ...

Focusing ahead, his eyes were adjusting and he hurdled the next smouldering fire – a test his weaker ankle passed on landing. Looking right, he saw that the guards coming in from the field were making slower progress – but the cover of tepees was now gone and he was entering dead ground between here and the gatehouse. He glanced left; he *was* outrunning the duo from the drive. So far, so good ...

Suddenly a gunshot rang out. He saw the flash of the muzzle and ducked – just as a loud crack crashed his eardrums as the bullet streaked past. Drabble veered right. The shot had come from directly ahead – outside the gatehouse. *So there were more goons in the gatehouse*. Of course there were more goons in the gatehouse. *Damn it*.

He put his head down and charged for fence.

The treeline before it was just twenty yards or so away now. He could be there in under ten seconds.

There was a shot; this time it boomed over his shoulder. Drabble flinched but didn't break his pace. Keep running, he told himself. *Just keep running*. Just a couple more seconds ...

Drabble sped into the trees just as a powerful torch cast a shadow through his legs.

He dodged right, deeper into the wooded margin and started up the first tree he could find. In the distance – and getting closer – he heard shouts. Pulling himself up, he rose quickly from branch to branch and was soon at the same height as the barbed wire atop the fence. He tore off his jacket, flung it over the wire – and hurled himself after it. The barbs clawed at him through the tweed but it saved him a massacre, and he rolled himself over the top, sliding down the outside far quicker than he would have liked. He landed hard, but was still mobile, and more importantly: he was outside.

'Freeze!'

Drabble raised his hands and turned in the direction of the voice, his eyes squinting into the glare of a torch. As his eyes adjusted he saw a gun trained on him.

Suddenly he heard the growl of tyres on gravel – and a taxi hurtled towards him. The guard fired then dived for cover as the taxi swerved towards him and then roared past, squealing to a halt by Drabble. The passenger door was flung open.

'Get in!' bellowed the driver. Drabble threw himself inside, as the cab's wheels began spinning. The car charged away.

Drabble looked up and saw Charlotte. 'I don't remember ordering a taxi . . .'

The driver cackled before she could reply. 'Jesus H Christ!' he bellowed. 'I haven't had that much fun since 1918 – where to now, folks?'

Colonel Grant's army was approaching the outskirts of Rapid City. Harris was with Ferguson towards the rear of Black Cloud's party of chiefs – gratefully a ceremonial unit, as far as he could tell from the average age of its members. For now they headed the column but Harris hoped that when it came to the fighting – if there was any – that they would step back and let the braves armed with their Japanese Type-99 rifles – and sharpened bayonets – do the heavy lifting. Not far behind them, Colonel Grant rode in one of the three armoured cars, accompanied by Fanny.

But there wouldn't be any fighting, would there? After all,

who knew they were coming, and who would there be to fight them anyway? That's what he kept telling himself. Much more likely the fighting would come *after* they had seized the city, in the days or weeks to come, once the US government got their measure and decided to bear down upon Grant and his absurd cronies.

Up ahead Black Cloud raised his hand and halted the column. A horseman cantered forward and conferred with the chief. Harris saw anxious glances. He looked over at Ferguson and saw that the former Rough Rider was not happy. The messenger galloped past them back down the line. Ferguson spurred his horse and hurried forwards.

Harris heard him curse, then saw what the fuss was.

The way ahead, perhaps two hundred yards or more hence, was blocked.

By soldiers.

Tons of them.

Harris's heart leaped with glee – but his joy was short-lived.

The line of soldiers stretched before them, filling the entire expanse of ground ahead. Slowly they began lighting torches – showing the extent of their number. There were darker, angular shaped structures among them. Ferguson, returning to Harris's side, cursed.

'Have they got tanks? *Shit* –' His horse shied. 'That's not fair.'

Tanks? Harris swallowed. *Cripes*. Tanks did not sound good. Christ. His mercury started to go into free fall. He looked at the trees to the right and considered making a dash for it . . . he was only the chronicler, after all. And if he died in the opening salvos he couldn't very well tell the story, could he?

As this played out in Harris's mind he heard the sound of a labouring engine – and Colonel Grant's armoured car accelerated past them. It jerked to a halt beside Black Cloud. Harris saw Grant get out and begin conferring with the chief.

Ferguson rushed forward and Harris heard him exclaim, 'We can go round them', before Grant finally erupted, 'Get into position!'

Ferguson was the first to obey; he bounded past Harris, shouting for the bugler.

A note chirped out and the great column began to fragment and then reconfigure itself on the perpendicular to confront the line of solders blocking their progress. Grant's car powered back to the rear and Harris pulled alongside Ferguson.

'What's going on? Didn't you just say, they've got tanks!'

'Don't worry,' he chuckled, 'they're National Guardsmen. They've probably never used them before.'

That wasn't much consolation: they obviously knew enough to get them here and at this range, the issue of expertise scarcely came into it. Harris looked over at Black Cloud, his ramrod back straight as ever, and his lance fluttering with feathers and charms. He'd ruddy well need more than Sitting Bull's war shirt to protect him from that lot. A shiver ran down Harris's spine. Then the National Guard turned on the floodlights.

Massive beams strafed through their position, turning the scene white and casting everything in shadow. A voice assailed them over a loudspeaker which emitted ear-splitting squeals and hisses.

'You have seven minutes to disperse before we commence firing.'

Harris recognised the voice immediately. It was the very Johnny he had seen at the station – General Bostonthorpe.

'If you disperse now, you will be treated fairly.' The hissing and squealing of the megaphone ceased and the lights went down, plunging them into an intense darkness.

But if Bostonthorpe was sitting over there with that lot – *what was going on*? After all, he was meant to be the bloody ringleader of Grant's whole show. Wasn't he? He was going to be *el presidente* . . .

Harris saw Black Cloud turning back in his saddle, his white and brown pinto horse turning too, presumably to see the state of play. The announcement did not appear to be slowing the deployment of Grant's army, mind you, but a murmur had begun.

Black Cloud raised his lance and a hush fell across the army.

'We attack as planned,' the chief declared, his voice powerful. 'We have everything to gain. The spirit of Sitting Bull is with us.'

A roar went up from the Sioux warriors – and the cowboys cheered. Harris – now looking left and right – saw that their line had been formed. Warriors, Wild Westers, and estate hands stood shoulder to shoulder, bayonets fixed on their Japanese rifles. In the rear Harris heard the crack of whips and the teams of horses drawing up the artillery. Holy smokes! He saw the German guns being wheeled out at the double. Tanks or no tanks, that lot would make a nasty hole in the National Guard. Christ alive. Grant was now back there barking orders at them. He was going to go down fighting – and that meant the rest of them were too.

Harris crossed himself, his eyes flitting about for an escape route. This was all about to get seriously messy. No ruddy joke. They were about to be annihilated. Panic surged through him, tightening his spine and sending a spasm through his legs to his toes. His horse felt it, and shied.

Colonel Grant's men cocked their rifles. The sound was terrifying: a thousand rifle bolts being locked into place. Tears came to Harris's eyes, blurring his vision which flared with a hundred or more flaming torches on both sides. He wrestled to control his horse . . . They outnumbered the National Guardsmen but, *but* the National Guardsmen – whether they'd use them or not – had tanks. Tanks. TANKS! His brain kept shouting the word inside his mind. For God's sake, this was madness.

Suddenly there came a shout. 'Horseman!'

Harris looked over, and caught sight of a figure galloping into view between the two armies. Good God, it was . . .

Drabble, a white flag flying from his makeshift lance, dug in his heels, pressing his stolen mount to go faster. His target was Black Cloud, whom he could see in the middle of the Indian force. As he approached the Sioux leader saw him and raised his arm – and the braves before him parted to let him through.

The chief regarded Drabble silently for a moment; in his war bonnet, and war shirt, and with the ribbons and strings attached to his arms, Black Cloud looked every elderly inch a man ready to fight if he had to. Drabble met his gaze.

'Command your men to lay down their arms. Do it now –' he felt his voice rising to be heard by the warriors around them – 'and you all may live and return to your families and homes. Delay and you will die, and so most likely will your women and children in the reprisals.'

Black Cloud's face was impassive and Drabble felt his temper break.

'Damn it, Chief,' he growled. 'You're running out of time. Those men will spare no one. You of all people know that – you've seen it happen before.'

Black Cloud looked back, he had heard something perhaps – and Drabble saw Grant approaching. They didn't have long. Drabble trotted towards the chief: 'This is an attempt to wipe out the Sioux for good, Black Cloud. Bostonthorpe has double-crossed you. It's a trap.'

Grant arrived, furious, pistol in hand. 'That's bullshit. This is Bostonthorpe's way of eliminating the Guardsmen – he's on our side! Ferguson, Black Cloud – we out-number them; tell your men to start firing now! *We must attack!*'

His voice was drowned out by the powerful hiss of a megaphone.

'Hostiles, you have sixty seconds to lay down your arms and

245

surrender – or we will open fire. I repeat, we will fire upon you.'

Drabble reined his horse, spinning it around. 'Lay down your weapons,' he shouted back towards Black Cloud's braves. 'It's your only hope. They will not fire on unarmed men!'

Black Cloud's hands went to his war bonnet and he slowly raised it in a gesture of defeat that made Harris think of a chess grand master tipping over his king. Immediately the Sioux section of the line began to fragment. It was miraculous.

Grant cursed – and rage erupted within him. He raised his revolver . . .

'Drabble!'

He fired just as Drabble spurred his horse.

This massacre had to be stopped – and if it couldn't be, then Drabble didn't see any reason why he should fall alongside Grant and his men without damned well trying first. He sped into no-man's-land – his white flag of truce held high – and charged for the National Guard's line, just as the voice returned over the hissing megaphone.

'*National Guardsmen, open fire!*'

A streak of golden sunlight broke through the low cloud in the east, lighting Drabble's way and blinding the Guardsman. In that moment the world became silent and all Drabble was aware of was his own breathing and the powerful strides of the galloping horse beneath him. If he was afraid he didn't know it.

A bugle sounded.

Two hundred yards away Harris heard the bugle and turned back. *What was that?* He spurred his horse and started in the direction of the front line.

Good God.

Dozens of uniformed cavalrymen were pouring into the field, blocking off the National Guardsmen. More mounted troopers now swept around him and another detachment

246

flooded around Grant and swamped the artillery. There were shouts and then all along the line he saw the Wild Westers and Indians begin to throw down their weapons and raise their hands in surrender as the whole ground swarmed with troopers. It was all over.

Harris chuckled gleefully and suddenly spotted Sakamoto among those being rounded up by the cavalry. Now that would take some explaining!

Then he remembered Drabble ... Where was he? Harris looked over towards the phalanx of National Guardsmen, his horror mounting. Ernest ...

Drabble's horse reared as he reached the National Guard's line. To his astonishment the men were lowering their rifles, and curiously seemed to be looking right through him – as though he were a ghost. Suddenly they began cheering.

'It's the cavalry from Fort Defiance!' one of them shouted. 'It's Colonel Fitzgerald.'

Drabble looked back and saw mounted troopers overwhelming Black Cloud's force. Behind him the cheers rolled into a hearty roar of celebration and Drabble found himself breaking into a pained laugh. Charlotte had ignored Wheelock's instruction to wait till the morning and decided call in the cavalry hours sooner. Thank God ...

Chapter Twenty-eight

Over the next week every single newspaper in America and around the world published an account of the heroic suppression of the rebellion that had erupted among the Lakota Sioux. The closer to the action the newspaper was, the more vitriolic its reporting. Of the various figures involved one in particular was lionised. General James Bostonthorpe's star had never risen so high, and now he was universally recognised as the victor of the Battle of Rapid City and the saviour of South Dakota – not to mention significant portions of Wyoming, Montana, and North Dakota. Not only had he faced down a hostile force with his scratch National Guard unit, but the Indians concerned were in a trance-driven frenzy of millenarian religious fervour. So reported the papers. At a stroke all the sympathy which had built up for the Indian cause over the near half-century since Wounded Knee had been eviscerated.

And then, the day before, the story had received a new lease of life, when the principal newspaper in Pierre, the state capital of South Dakota, announced the following on its front page:

Bostonthorpe _WILL_ run for President!
Hero of Rapid City to stand in 1940

Beneath it was a heroic photograph of the South Dakota governor in military fatigues, taken at the battle where he was credited, as the commanding officer of the National Guard unit, of a great victory. The fact of the US Cavalry's appearance and interruption of the conflagration appeared to be lost in the telling. As a piece of propaganda Mussolini would struggle to better it, and he edited eight newspapers a day.

In the aftermath of the standoff, Grant and Ferguson had been arrested and were being held in solitary confinement in a military prison, beyond the reach of reporters or indeed of civilian legal protection. The same was true of Black Cloud and Speaks With Fists, who were counted among the prime ringleaders. The other Indians involved had been rounded up and sent back to their reservations and no further action had been determined against them – yet. Sakamoto had been officially deported from the US. Investigations at the ranch had uncovered startling evidence – maps and documents – revealing the scope of the conspiracy. Brave Wheelock's body had been located – and added to the dizzying list of charges facing Grant. The papers had had a field day. Along the way United States senators and members of the House of Representatives had begun falling over themselves to call for the death penalty to be imposed on Black Cloud and Speaks With Fists, as well as Grant and his co-conspirators, with vote-winning venom.

Then came the Governor's well-timed announcement of his future Presidential bid, with its signature polices of conscription, the reintroduction of Prohibition, a hardline, closed-door immigration policy on non-whites, and an absolute insistence on neutrality in any future European conflict.

Harris laid the newspaper to one side. His mouth was dry and the base of his stomach felt like someone was tap-dancing on it. He was nervous. He told himself again that it was ridiculous that at the age of thirty-four, when he had interviewed countless princes and prelates, that an interview such as this might cause him anxiety. But it did. That was the simple fact.

Because this interview was going to be unlike any other he had done in his life.

He looked down the long neo-classical corridor for signs of a 'restroom', and heard the door crack open.

'Sir Percival —' the voice was the placid tenor of an assistant. 'Governor Bostonthorpe will see you now.'

Harris exchanged a glance with Drabble, who picked up his borrowed camera.

The Governor sat behind a broad kneehole desk in a leather chair of throne-like proportions, smoking a cigar. Behind him were the flags of the USA and South Dakota. There was also a reproduction of Charles Wilson Peale's portrait, *George Washington at the Battle of Princeton*, which Drabble recognised instantly. For a politician who relished his rank of general as much as his political ambitions, it seemed unlikely that the artistic selection was coincidental. In a stuffed gilt armchair beside the desk sat an earnest-looking political adviser, who was introduced as Erskine.

The secretary departed through a side door and Boston-thorpe, flourishing his hand towards the chair, invited Harris to take a seat, adding that time was short. The governor did not acknowledge the presence of Drabble, who immediately bus-ied himself with his camera.

Harris remained standing, prompting Bostonthorpe's heavy eyebrows to lift. But if he was taken aback he hadn't smelled a rat. Not yet. Harris began.

'Governor, I gather that before you announced your presi-dential ambitions, you had your eye on a very different presidency ...'

'What?' Bostonthorpe chuckled — bemused no more — and glanced sideways at Erskine, who cackled obsequiously. His shrewd eyes examined Harris for evidence of premature senility.

'Governor, I have evidence that you conspired with Colonel Grant to become president of the putative Sioux Republic —'

Bostonthorpe broke into a throaty laugh. 'What is this?'

'On the eve of the so-called "Battle of Rapid City" —' Harris permitted his tone to rise accusingly as he had seen barristers do most effectively in court, 'Colonel Grant told me himself that you were going to be the president of the new republic. Do you deny this?'

'Everything that man says is *a lie* —' Bostonthorpe took a scornful puff at his cigar. 'He's determined to drag everyone down with him. And of course he accuses me of being involved *precisely* because I am the one who stopped his pernicious plot.' Bostonthorpe rose from his chair, 'Now I thought this was meant to be a proper interview, but if you've only come here to throw around bogus accusations you should go.'

Harris stood his ground.

'How did you know the attack was coming in the first place?'

'I have explained: I was tipped off —'

A bulb flashed — '*Woomph!*' — whitening Bostonthorpe's features, mid-protest. The camera clicked. Drabble started changing the flash-bulb.

'Who tipped you off, Governor?' Bostonthorpe gritted his teeth at Harris, who pressed on. 'And why were you in Rapid City when you would normally be two hundred miles away here in the state capital, Pierre?'

Bostonthorpe turned to Erskine. 'Get these losers out of here.'

Harris raised his voice as Erskine bolted from the room.

'Do you deny being part of the conspiracy, indeed do you deny being its ring-leader?'

'This is ridiculous!' The podgy face glowed red with anger — the wet lips narrowing so that the short moustache and goatee met in indignation. 'GET OUT!

Woomph!

He glared at Drabble: 'And STOP taking photographs of me. ERSKINE!'

Harris stepped towards Bostonthorpe.

'Tomorrow, my newspaper, the *London Evening Express*, will report the facts as I have best established them – namely that you, General James Bostonthorpe, *were* a co-conspirator, and, not only that, but that you *were* to be announced as president of the new Sioux Republic. Furthermore, we *will* report that you instead decided to betray your co-conspirators at the so-called Battle of Rapid City in order to support your US presidential ambitions. Finally, we will report that you would have overseen a bloodbath of the Indians if the US cavalry hadn't arrived first.'

'This is absurd ...' Bostonthorpe's eyes glistened with rage, his chest inflating. He glanced at the door – just as it opened and Erskine arrived with armed policemen.

'Seize them!' he barked.

Woomph!

The bulb exploded, dazzling the policemen.

'The story is filed already –' exclaimed Harris as the policemen got hold of him. 'By this time tomorrow everyone in the English-speaking world will know that you are guilty of treason and a false patriot.'

Bostonthorpe bridled.

'Print and be damned. I'll sue every newspaper in every jurisdiction that prints your lies and by the time I'm through I'll be richer than Midas. You on the other hand will be ruined – financially, professionally, and reputationally!'

'And so –' Harris tore his arm free, 'will your hopes for the presidency in 1940.'

Woomph!

'There's no smoke without fire – who's going to touch a nationalist who conspires against his own kind?'

Bostonthorpe showed his teeth, 'The Indians aren't our kind ... damn you. *You know that.* Nor are the blacks or the Jews or the filthy Mexicans. They all need to be purged if we're going to fulfil America's national potential – and, *yes*, we could have made a good start at Rapid City. But have no fear, my presidency will deliver the shock that America needs!'

Bostonthorpe was breathing hard. 'Print your newspaper lies if you must! Now, Captain, get these losers out of here!'

Epilogue

The horn of the SS *Empress of the Atlantic* gave a prolonged blast and the dockers heaved its mighty mooring lines off the Samson posts, releasing the ship. Drabble, Harris, and Charlotte stood among the crowds waving farewell to the New World.

'I don't think I'll miss it,' declared Harris. 'The buildings are too tall, the country is too wide – and the people are frankly too unpredictable.'

'And there was me thinking what a shame it was that we didn't get to see more of it.' Drabble put an arm around Charlotte's waist and drew her closer.

'We'll get to Virginia next time,' she said, smiling at him. 'The *wampum* belts will wait.'

Drabble leaned in and kissed her. Harris harrumphed.

'Oh, *per*-lease! Let's get to the foredeck bar; we'll be able to have drink and enjoy a view of the Statue of Liberty – I missed her last time, so I'm damned if I'm going to make that mistake again.' He stalked off leaving Drabble and Charlotte to follow.

After their audience with General Bostonthorpe nothing had happened immediately. The day following the publication of Harris's story in London, the *New York Times* ran its own version of the facts, leaving some out. The following day it was across the entire country – along with Bostonthorpe's thumping denial, of course. Not that it did him much good, because two days later Fanny Howell was discovered performing shooting tricks in a saloon for loggers in Squamish in British Columbia, over the border in Canada. She told reporters from the *Vancouver Sun* that the South Dakota Governor had been involved in the conspiracy from the start. That was good fodder, but the killing blow was the telegram she had in her possession from Bostonthorpe – the one that Harris had seen Grant pass her on the night of the attack. It was just four words, but they were explosive:

'PROCEED AT MIDNIGHT – BOSTONTHORPE'

And having arrived at a confessional moment in her career, Howell also owned up to the thefts of the Sitting Bull artefacts from the British Museum. This was done for the furtherance of the conspiracy and at the behest of Black Cloud and Speaks With Fists, whom she blamed for the murder of Walberswick.

Once news broke of the Bostonthorpe telegram, the writing was on the wall for the governor. He resigned his office immediately and was apprehended by the Canadian Mounted Police attempting to cross illegally into Manitoba.

As for Pocahontas, Drabble was pretty certain that the person who had located her grave was the very same person who had also broken into Syon House to inspect the portrait – and that, likely as not, was Wheelock. When Drabble put this to him in the car on the way to Grant's ranch, Wheelock had declined to confirm it, but he didn't exactly make efforts to deny it either. Drabble suspected that he was acting on behalf of the US government, which rather naturally had a legitimate interest in both Pocahontas and the buried treasure. Since the man's death Drabble had learned that Lieutenant-Colonel Herbert Wheelock, PhD, as he had been in fact, had enjoyed a distinguished career in the United States Army, having being decorated for his gallantry during the First World War. Newspaper reports simply mentioned that Lt-Col Wheelock was on secondment to the

United States Federal Government and had died during a hunting trip.

Finally, it seemed highly unlikely that the fate of Dr Yorke would ever be properly understood. Certainly nothing had emerged thus far, and Drabble was even beginning to wonder if his death was actually unrelated to the Sioux conspiracy case.

Drabble, Harris, and Charlotte raised their glasses as the *Empress of the Atlantic* passed the Statue of Liberty, and offered her a toast.

'The French gave it to the Americans as a kind of sarcastic statement of one-upmanship,' declared Harris. 'Did you know that the New York Governor of the day, Grover Cleveland, refused to pay for its erection – and it was vetoed in Congress? So in the end a newspaper ran a campaign to raise the money by public subscription, which they did. Funnily enough, by the time it was finally slapped up on the pedestal, Cleveland was president so he ended up officiating over the dedication after all.'

'It's very big.'

'Well, it would be.' Harris knocked his pipe free of ash. 'The French have got an equally enormous inferiority complex.'

The great feminine figure passed from view, and Charlotte and Drabble shared a significant glance. She slipped off her glove, revealing a gold band inset with tiny sapphires on the ring finger of her left hand.

'Harris ...' Charlotte laid her left hand on his forearm. 'Ernest has something very particular he wants to tell you.'

Harris looked up from the ring slowly, his lips puckering the stem of his pipe. The colour was draining from his face.

'Good God –' He got to his feet, his eyes watering prodigiously. '*Good God!*' He embraced Charlotte and then he reached out, seizing Drabble's hand. The pals embraced.

'What news ...' Harris made a decent show of looking

256

happy, *and he was happy* – but by God he also felt absolutely miserable, to the core of his very soul.

He snatched up his champagne glass.

'Cheers!' He beamed at them both, tears streaming down his pink face. He forced another smile and turned to Drabble. 'And now I expect you want me to be your best man ...'

Author's Note

The pretext for *Ghosts of the West* came to me during a river cruise on the Thames with my family, while I was still writing *Enemy of the Raj*, my second Drabble and Harris book. We passed the Mayflower pub in Rotherhithe and I was reminded that this was close to the embarkation point of the ship of that name in 1620, which carried 102 settlers across the Atlantic. They arrived in November at what became known as Plymouth Bay in Massachusetts and formed the first permanent European settlement in North America.

Thirteen years before that, in 1607, another group of colonists had arrived from England and landed in Virginia, several hundred miles to the south. Their settlement – rather interestingly – also claims to be the first permanent one by Europeans on the continent, albeit there was brief abandonment in 1610, which presumably allows for Plymouth Colony's claim.

The Mayflower pub reminded me that not twenty miles from there, in Gravesend in Kent, were the remains of a very important person associated with the Virginian settlement.

As many readers will know, Pocahontas was the daughter of Powhatan, who was the chieftain overlord of the Tsenacommacah, a confederation of coastal tribes in Virginia. He had the dubious pleasure of having the Europeans arrive on his watch, while his daughter became rather more intimately acquainted with them and eventually married one John Rolfe. Mrs Rolfe subsequently travelled with her husband to London in 1616 and was entertained at Court, where she would have rubbed shoulders with King James I, among others. She also stayed in Brentford while living in London, and that paved the way for my invention of the portrait of her at Syon House, to this day the London home of the Duke of Northumberland.

As it states in *Ghosts of the West*, Pocahontas died aged about twenty-one, at the start of her return journey to Virginia. The ship put in at Gravesend in Kent, and she was buried at St George's Church, where this book begins. The exact location of the grave remains unknown to this day – which is where my story deviates from the truth – but Pocahontas may well be resting under the church's chancel, which is the approximate location given in this story. There is a statue commemorating her association with St George's in the churchyard and indeed, as Drabble points out, there was an unsuccessful attempt to locate her remains in 1923.

Crucial to the story of *Ghosts of the West* is what happened next: when those first colonists arrived at the turn of the seventeenth century in Virginia and Massachusetts, it is estimated that around 500,000 Native Americans inhabited the North American continent. Some estimates put it considerably higher. By 1900, just 300,000 Native Americans were left, while the European immigrant population had swelled from zero to around 100 million. Meanwhile, the indigenous population went from enjoying a free rein across the entire continent to being shepherded into several hundred reservations. (Today there are 574 federally recognised tribes in the US, occupying some 326 Indian reservations covering 15 million square acres, equivalent to around 23,000 square miles or a territory a little smaller than Latvia.) The horrific story of what happened between 1600 and 1900 is at the heart of this novel and deliberately personified in the character of Black Cloud, who is in part inspired by Red Cloud (1822-1909), the real life chief of the Oglala Lakota (a branch of one of the seven constituent tribes of the Great Sioux Nation), who in my view deserves a statue if anyone does.

As it happens Red Cloud successfully battled the United States Army for two years in the late 1860s – during the era after the American Civil War when the Plains Indians were having their lands taken amid various gold rushes. He lived to tell the tale, having crucially driven the US to the negotiating table and forced it to backtrack on its expansion into Indian territory. He then went to Washington to meet the Great Father (President Ulysses S. Grant) and that's when he discovered what the Native Americans were really up against. After that he seems to have counted his blessings and became a conciliator. In any event his hard won peace, the Treaty of Fort Laramie signed in 1868, quickly began to unravel.

In the wake of Red Cloud were leaders such as Sitting Bull (1831-1890) and Crazy Horse (c. 1840-1877). Both of these were key individuals at the Battle of Little Bighorn in 1876, the principal military engagement of the Great Sioux War of 1876, when a combined force of Lakota and Dakota Sioux, Cheyenne and Arapaho comprehensively defeated Custer and the Seventh Cavalry. That, perhaps inevitably, was the prelude to a greater defeat of the Native American cause, aspects of which are detailed by Colonel Grant in his grand reveal of the plans for the Sioux Republic.

Like Black Cloud, both Red Cloud and Sitting Bull went on to feature in and tour the world with Buffalo Bill Cody's Wild West Show, which transparently inspires many of the details of Colonel Grant's Wild West Show, just as Cody (1846–1917) does with Grant himself. The story Black Cloud tells of Cody's show performing for Queen Victoria and her remarks are inspired by *Black Elk Speaks*, John G Neihardt's first person narrative of Black Elk, an important medicine man of the

Oglala Sioux, who shared his story with the writer over a series of interviews in the early 1930s. Those who know this book will recognise how it has clearly inspired much of the vocabulary but also the cadences of Black Cloud's speech, in addition to aspects of the vision which Black Cloud reveals to Harris. Similarly, Black Cloud's life maps that of Black Elk, who also fought at the Battle of Little Bighorn as a boy (he was just thirteen), and later travelled the world in a Wild West Show. He died in 1950, aged 86, at Pine Ridge Reservation in South Dakota.

As you'll see, Black Cloud, who is not a medicine man as such, is a little older and in the dating I was inspired by a chief named Flying Hawk who fought in both Red Cloud's War and later at the Battle of Little Bighorn. Chief Flying Hawk, (who served as a translator for Black Elk and Neihardt during their interviews for *Black Elk Speaks*), also went Wild Westing with Buffalo Bill Cody and was in the show for thirty years from the late 1890s through to 1930. His and Black Elk's longevity brought home to me the possibility of Drabble and Harris meeting someone like them in London and getting a first-hand, eyewitness account of Custer's Last Stand.

For Red Cloud's exploits – but also for the thunderous march through the bloody and remorseless history of United States-Native American relations – I am indebted to Dee Brown's masterful *Bury My Heart At Wounded Knee*, which was published in 1970. Chapter by chapter she charts the western expansion of the United States' frontier and the gradual near-elimination of the inhabiting Native American tribes – the Navajo, the Crow, the Cheyenne, the Sioux, the Modoc, the Nez Perce, the Apache, the Comanche, and the Ute, and more. This goes right up to the last major engagement in the Indian Wars of the United States – at Wounded Knee in 1890, where, as this story relays, a religious leader named Wovoka inspired the ill-fated Ghost Dance, which prompted a heavy-handed military response from the US army and a bloody massacre of nearly three hundred Native American men, women, and children – the aftermath of which Black Elk was a witness to.

It is not a story that brings credit upon the United States, and part of my hope for *Ghosts of the West* is to bring it to life, perhaps for a different audience from the one that knows it all too well.

Rather more alarming still is the fact that Wounded Knee was not the end of it all. America's 'Indian Wars' continued with skirmishes and small armed conflicts breaking out right up until the 1920s, when the Apache Wars are said to have concluded in 1924. Like many I expect, I was shocked to discover how recent that past is. Moreover, in 1923 the Sioux began a legal challenge to the loss of the Black Hills in breach of the terms of the Fort Laramie Treaty of 1868. This ultimately led to the 1980 US Supreme Court ruling, in the case of *United States v. Sioux Nation of Indians*, which found in their favour and ordered substantial compensation to be paid. With interest this has now reached in excess of $1 billion but to this day the Sioux have rejected the money. They want their land back and the issue remains very much alive.

It's appropriate to mention that despite the historic context, I have obviously taken some distinct liberties with the truth during the writing of this book: there was, as far as I know, no grand plan for the Sioux tribes – with or without foreign military aide – to launch a separatist bid for freedom from the United States during the 1930s. This is all very much a flight of fancy on the part of the novelist, but I have intended to establish some justification for the cause nonetheless. Similarly, Governor Bostonthorpe is in no way based on the actual Governor of South Dakota of the time, but rather inspired by the sort of populist, fascist figures that existed in the politics of 1930s America, as well as elsewhere.

To thanks; above all I must thank my wife Ashley, to whom

this book is dedicated, for her incredible support and help – not least with our young children – throughout the course of researching and writing of this book. Without her forbearance it would not have been possible. In addition, I would like to thank my editor Greg Rees and my editor at Headline Accent, Jess Whitlum-Cooper. Finally, I should like to thank my agent Louise Greenberg for her support, insight, and encouragement.

Next I should say that while this book is dedicated to my wife Ashley, it was formed with the memory of my uncle, William Spouse, very much in my mind. William, who died in November 2019, loved a good western and one way or another I spent a fair amount of my childhood watching his VHS tapes of old John Wayne movies. As such, it is my intention that there is a bit of a good western at the heart of this third Drabble and Harris book, and I hope that William approves.

I should also mention a few friends whose names have found their way into this book. My old pal James Grant has unknowingly lent me the Colonel's surname, but that's as far as the similarities go (though he too likes a good Western). Similarly, I borrowed Charlotte's surname from the medieval historian who taught me while at Newcastle University a long time ago now and to whom I remain indebted, Professor Bob Moore. It struck me that Charlotte's august father, himself a prominent academic in the historical field, could have no finer surname. Captain Rossiter's name is inspired by my uncle, Patrick Rossiter, and while I think of it the dining location aboard the *Empress of the Atlantic* – rather unimaginatively, the Restaurant – is borrowed in fact directly from the *Titanic*, which likewise had a swimming pool and Turkish baths located deep in the bowels of the ship for the exclusive use of first-class passengers.

It is impossible to conclude this author's note without mentioning the topic of the Covid-19 pandemic, which has been a constant for most of the time that I have been writing this book. Suffice it to say that *Ghosts of the West* has given me ample excuse to travel far from the grim present and for that I am grateful. I sincerely hope that by the time this book is published, the pandemic is itself history – or heading very quickly that way. I am sure that one day it will offer historical fiction writers of the future a fertile basis for their own stories and I hope that they behave with appropriate sensitivity to the facts.

Alec Marsh
London,
February 2021

 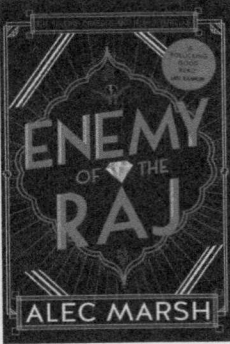 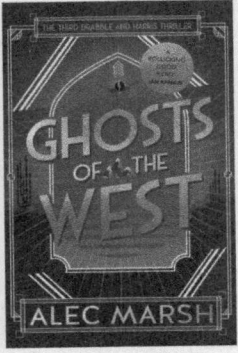